DIAMOND VAL

Bruce Harris

The Book Guild Ltd

First published in Great Britain in 2023 by
The Book Guild Ltd
Unit E2 Airfield Business Park,
Harrison Road, Market Harborough,
Leicestershire. LE16 7UL
Tel: 0116 2792299
www.bookguild.co.uk
Email: info@bookguild.co.uk
Twitter: @bookguild

Copyright © 2023 Bruce Harris

The right of Bruce Harris to be identified as the author of this
work has been asserted by them in accordance with the
Copyright, Design and Patents Act 1988.

All rights reserved. No part of this publication may be
reproduced, transmitted, or stored in a retrieval system, in any form or by any means,
without permission in writing from the publisher, nor be otherwise circulated in
any form of binding or cover other than that in which it is published and without
a similar condition being imposed on the subsequent purchaser.

This work is entirely fictitious and bears no resemblance to any persons living or dead.

Typeset in 11pt Adobe Garamond Pro

Printed and bound in the UK by TJ Books LTD, Padstow, Cornwall

ISBN 9781 915603 722

British Library Cataloguing in Publication Data.
A catalogue record for this book is available from the British Library.

Dedicated to the memory of Jacqueline Anne Babb,
née Astbury, 1950 - 2023

CONTENTS

PART ONE	The Making of the Corporation	1
PART TWO	The Battle for the Corporation	45
PART THREE	Amélie's Journey	55
PART FOUR	Austin's Journey	81
PART FIVE	Jennifer's Journey	115
PART SIX	Paul's Journey	139
PART SEVEN	Eve of Battle	159
PART EIGHT	The Board Decides	193
PART NINE	Aftermath	213

PART ONE

The Making of the Corporation

Thursday July 15th 1976

The heat was so persistent that Valerie had taken to using as much of the morning as she could for work purposes, starting as early as possible. She struggled to sleep in any case, and today was far from the first day that she found herself beginning the restaurant's preparations at seven thirty in the morning.

Her 'By the Brook' restaurant was now four years old and almost unrecognisable from the shabby old King's Arms pub she had taken over. Neatly positioned at the end of the high street, which crossed the river near to her restaurant and gave her a suitable name for the place, By the Brook was embraced by many of the local people who had tired of the 'traditional' King's Arms, traditional in the sense of being a 'drinking den' for a predominantly, in fact almost exclusively, male clientele.

Conversion hadn't been particularly difficult. The 'Arms' had been a warren of bars and snugs, and once Valerie had established that knocking a few walls down would not cause the entire building to disintegrate, she opened the space up to accommodate a decent number of covers. She demolished the outside toilets in the yard and converted a storeroom within the building to include new toilets, thereby increasing the outside parking space available. She employed a chef at rates of pay she knew she would not be able to sustain for long, and gave the place a much lighter and airier feel.

After a nightmare six months, when the regulars drifted away and some nights saw numbers of customers she could count on her fingers, people started asking about Christmas functions, and Valerie and her young chef Cal pulled out all the stops to make the bookings they got work. From then on, things first started looking up, and then accelerated almost startlingly. She added an outside space with a simple enough use of decking and a view of the river and the countryside beyond, and a year in, she was looking at spreads in the glossy county magazine and events being reported in the local papers.

And she'd done it all, as she did not tire of reminding people, as a single mum. True, her mother had been invaluable in taking care of little Austin, born in 1970 and a result of her marriage to Mr. Maurice Foster, a businessman of 'a lot of vision but not much action', as her mother had described him. Maurice's idea of being a landlord consisted of drinking with his customers and, not infrequently, gambling with them. When both her marriage and her business with Mr. Foster had fallen apart, Valerie sought and won an uncontested divorce and custody of Austin – a boy who, incredibly enough, had been named after Mr. Foster's car, Valerie later discovered after her initial suspicions. Maurice, after initially pledging to fight for custody of his son, was side-tracked by a business offer from an Australian-based cousin, and travelled there to continue his unique brand of relaxed landlording, leaving Valerie holding the baby both literally and figuratively. Austin, even at the age of six, had already drawn his own conclusions, and he reacted negatively to his father's occasional attempts at contact, which were noticeably becoming more occasional as time went on. Valerie inspected the place after last night's clearing up. Even Wednesdays could now be quite full, especially at this time of year, and as usual, one or two corners had been cut, one or two inconveniences brushed away. Apart from Cal doing his stuff in the kitchen, she had one permanent waitress in Janine and one part-time waiter in Peter; any additional labour was usually students, as and when she could get them. The garden, which had been painstakingly brought back to life after the sorry mess inherited from the King's Arms, could now be used for warm evenings and overspill on busy nights, and while limited to only another twenty-four covers, it provided a view of the brook and a peaceful rural atmosphere, if sometimes accompanied by suitably rural aromas from the Warriner farm on the road out of town.

Many of the names on today's booking list she knew, and it pleased her that the restaurant was developing a dedicated bunch of regulars, even including a few from the surrounding villages. But much as the familiar names reassured her, a few new ones were additionally welcome, because they made it increasingly likely that her business would endure.

Valerie was still only twenty-eight years old; she knew by now that she was the only woman in the town to be in sole control of her own business, and while she took pride in that fact, it also intimidated her, and she knew that it did, in some respects, make her more vulnerable. The town, peaceful as it was as a general rule, did have a few dubious characters, mostly young, directionless men who could be very difficult when they got together and decided to make a night of it. She had already, with her mouth dry and her heart pounding, ejected a group of five on a Saturday night who were becoming too noisy and boisterous for her other customers to be comfortable. Sam Deakin, a local police sergeant, had offered to help if and when she needed it, and it seemed to be an offer that came without strings attached – Sam was a happily married man.

But her marriage to Maurice had sapped her confidence to the extent that any setback could set her off on a chain reaction of anxiety. One day, she relished the idea that the town was taking her to its bosom; the next, she had suspicions, when she felt eyes watching her carefully from various tables, that she was disapproved of and suspected of something or other, though she couldn't quite tell what.

As she glanced through the bookings, she caught sight of herself in the well-polished mirror on the other side of the room. A glance of a few seconds was enough; she liked to look her best, but she was not a vain woman. Her figure was fuller than she would wish, but the weight problem she had fought against all her life was under control as a result of hard work and almost constant movement during working hours; her calm, dark eyes, not exactly black but not far off, gave her an intelligent look with a little mystery attached, and her high-boned face and short haircut added to the impression of independence. Ever since her experience with Maurice had firmly stopped her attempt at being the flirty barmaid as well as the landlady, men had treated her properly if warily and that, for the moment, was enough. She didn't want a business partner, since the profits so far provided a decent income for one but probably not for two, and she was, in any case, afraid of turning up another Maurice. Genial, easy-going men could be attractive, but would probably make bad business partners, and serious, professional businessmen might take over her business and therefore her independence. The Maurice failure had hurt her on many fronts, and she knew the rebuilding exercise still had some way to go.

There was always one name which was different and therefore interesting, and this time it was Gilard; table for four, eight o'clock. One of those names with an indefinite pronunciation, because it could be said an English way and a French way. Dodgy as it could be sometimes, she generally stuck to the English way.

True to her usual way of supporting local traders where she could, she did her shopping round during the morning, relying on her suppliers to deliver the bulk of the goods later in the day; she had no intention of staggering around the town with heavy bags.

In the nearest newsagent, now run by the Corbridge family, Tom Corbridge shone a light on the Gilard mystery. Tom was a local councillor who knew everything that was happening or was shortly going to happen in the town, and he generally had no compunction about letting people know all about it.

'Looking forward to dining at the Brook tonight, Valerie,' he said, as he handed over a couple of local papers; Valerie liked to see what the opposition was doing, as well as check over her own advert.

'Oh, good, Tom; you're very welcome, of course. I didn't see your name on the bookings list.'

'Well, we're being wined and dined, I'm happy to say. Chap called Gilard, Hugo Gilard. Aiming to take over the old Denning place.'

Denning's had been the town's menswear shop, going slowly more and more old-fashioned and vulnerable to the competition, until old man Frank Denning had given up the unequal battle and retired. His ex-shop had been empty for over a year and was making other occupants of the High Street increasingly nervous.

'Just as well, I should think, Tom. Next thing we know, we'll have squatters in it, or even a few of the local junkies.'

To be successfully amongst them you have to sound like them, Valerie thought as she reflected on the statement she'd just made. Just don't start thinking like them, girl, if you can possibly avoid it.

'Absolutely. But he seems like a sound enough chap. He obviously knows about my clout on the Planning Committee. I'm not saying I'm anyone's for a good steak and chips, but it obviously helps concentrate the mind.'

Corbridge laughed, a little nervously; he probably knows himself what some people say, Valerie thought, but remarks like that don't exactly help.

'But I doubt we could find a better place to do business than the Brook, Valerie. I'm looking forward to it.'

Faux pas followed by flattery; a familiar enough technique, Valerie thought. Maurice, firmly fixed to his bar stool, being mine host, returned yet again.

'Good. Well, we'll do our best to live up to expectations, Tom. See you later!'

As the evening approached, Valerie found herself feeling sympathetic towards Mr. Gilard even before she'd met him. She imagined a young entrepreneur, keen to make his mark but still wet behind the ears, a Daniel moving into the lion's den of local business, including Corbridge and presumably a few other local business leaders, who would no doubt be seeking a price for their support before the new boy even got started. Tom Corbridge, amiable as he was, always claimed to be acting in the best interests of the town, but more often than not, he was acting in the best interests of Tom Corbridge. She remembered well enough the hoops she had been made to jump through in her efforts to turn the King's Arms into a viable proposition.

An hour before the restaurant opened at seven, she went to see how Austin was. Once again, he had asked to have his friend Mark Sims to a sleepover, and Valerie had agreed readily enough; Mark was no trouble, generally, and she was all too conscious that Austin was an only child and likely to remain so.

Neither of the boys seemed to see or hear her approach; once again, they were engrossed in some scenario connected with Austin's generous collection of Matchbox toys, many of them presents from his father. For a moment, she sat on the lower bunk bed and watched them. There was something vaguely disturbing in how intensely Austin was engaged, as if he was deliberately seeking to blot out of the rest of the world.

In fact, it was Mark who noticed her first.

'Hello, Mrs. Foster,' he said, standing up as he did, and a broad smile broke over his face. He was already a good-looking kid, and no doubt destined to be a heartbreaker. Austin's eyes raised reluctantly, but it was no more than a glance.

'Hi, Mum,' he said. 'Is everything OK?'

'Yes, love, of course,' she said. 'Why wouldn't it be?'

'I don't know,' he said, with an emphasis on the 'I', which seemed to imply he never did understand why anything wasn't. Perhaps not too difficult to understand from a little boy who had, to all intents and purposes, lost his father, for reasons he couldn't possibly understand. But, not for the first time, she consoled herself with the thought that such nuanced thoughts were probably beyond the thinking scope of a six-year-old.

'Nice to see you're both enjoying yourselves,' she said, getting up. They had already returned to their game.

'Wash, pyjamas, teeth, at eight o'clock now,' she said. 'I'll be up shortly after to say good night. And please don't leave everything all over the floor for me to step on.'

Two vague noises of assent returned, followed by another beamer from Mark. Valerie tried to remember the last time Austin had smiled at her.

The Gilard party of four arrived in good time, and her first meeting with Hugo Gilard himself didn't suggest a young rookie come to be fleeced. He was probably in his mid-thirties, sensibly and smartly dressed for the weather in a light blue jacket and open-necked white shirt. Smart casual was her dress code for men; she simply wasn't inflexible enough to insist on ties, especially in the summer.

He was wearing a gentle aftershave, his eyes were blue green, his hand was firm but did not squeeze or press, and while no-one could describe him as classically good-looking, he had an interesting face, one given to animation and expression, which acquired various little laugh lines around the eyes and the mouth when his face broke into a smile. She had never met him before in her life, but he managed to convey an apparently genuine pleasure in meeting her.

'Hugo Gilard, Mrs. Foster. I'm delighted to meet you.'

He used the English pronunciation of his name; good of him to settle that from the start. Tom Corbridge hovered in the background in his usual battered corduroy jacket – she could almost hear him saying to the long-suffering Carol, 'don't need a suit for the Brook, do I? Not so long ago, it was just the local boozer'. Tom already looked slightly disapproving.

'Two further guests to come, both of whom I think you probably know, Mrs. Foster. I am hoping to establish a business here, and I can think of no better way to get started than to meet those who already have. I wondered, in view of the beautiful weather, if we could have a table in your garden?'

'Yes, of course. When days like this come along, we always keep a few prepared. Let me show you to it, and then I'll direct the other gentlemen when they arrive.'

She showed them to the table, gratified to see that the garden was looking well and showing the view to full advantage. Then, just as she was about to take her leave, he spoke to her again, turning fully in his chair to face her.

'I appreciate you have a restaurant to run, Mrs. Foster,' he said. 'But you run a local business yourself, and I believe you have made huge progress since taking it over. Is there any chance you could join us at some point? I really would appreciate your advice.'

Valerie's instincts were to refuse; busy nights could be very demanding. But this was something even her husband, her supposed business partner, had never done, and this was a kind of recognition of her status as an independent entrepreneur – as an equal, in fact.

And if nothing else, the expression of disapproval all over Tom Corbridge's face would have persuaded her.

'In which case, Mr. Gilard, I am happy to offer it. I make my own arrangements for eating in the evening, but when you have reached the coffee, I'll be happy to join you.'

Gilard's other two guests were quick to join him. They were Stan Cooke, representing the biggest estate agent in the town, as scrubbed and supercilious as he always was, and Simon Welham, a painter and decorator, who also had, in the Corbridge way of expressing it, 'pretensions to being a designer'.

It was a hot, sticky evening to work in and she had dressed down as far as she dared, but by the time she sat down with the local businessmen, she was not feeling, or, she suspected, looking at her best. Austin and Mark had complicated bed time by making a fuss about wearing pyjamas – well, Austin had, with Mark's largely mute support. Eventually, she had given in to the extent of no jackets, but she suspected they were back up out of the bunk beds almost as soon as she'd left the room. But going back up after half past eight was difficult, and she relied on them eventually tiring themselves.

The men were well wined and dined, relaxed and vaguely roguish, but it was already clear who was in charge. She accepted Hugo's offer of a brandy, which she felt she could probably do with, and then waited to see if his interest in her opinion was simply part of the charm offensive or a genuine request.

'Thanks for joining us, Mrs. Foster. The gist of it is that I am aiming to open a jewellery shop here, adapting the ex-Denning menswear premises for the purpose. Tom here has given me an idea of what the planning issues might be; Stan has advised on the possible value of the premises when adapted and also what I might have to pay if I decide to live in the area. Simon has ideas on making the shop stand out as well as fit in with the general tone of the town. But the decisive influence on any new jeweller business is the female input, as it tends to be the ladies who buy most of it or specify to their menfolk what they would like bought. You must have quite extensive dealings with the local ladies; could you point me in any interesting directions?'

For ever afterwards, Valerie always saw this moment as one of the great gifts of her life. Such religious feeling as she had, which wasn't much, had been severely dented by the genuine faith and hope she had wrongly invested in Maurice, but if there really was such a thing as a gift sent by God, this was one of the greatest of hers.

Her uncle Ian had been – in fact, at this time, still was – a jeweller, and she loved to visit him and sometimes watch him work. Her own parents, much as she loved them, and she did love them, were solid, reliable and unchangeable, but there was something exciting, daring and wonderfully mysterious about Uncle Ian, his long thin fingers working exquisitely on the tiniest of objects.

For more than twenty minutes, she held forth about her own fascinations with jewellery, and it was a glorious feeling to be talking, as the manager of an independent business, to men on equal terms.

She described how she would watch her uncle bezel setting, a technique of holding a gemstone in place with a narrow band of metal, and mentioned a few people she knew who had rings made in this way. She talked about earring fittings for both the pierced and the unpierced, andralok for the pierced, andraslide for the unpierced, and pointed out that many women she knew or had known were wary of ear piercing.

Real pearls, which were treasured, and faux pearls only worn for show included varieties that most women could distinguish and appreciate; pearl necklaces could still be used by some but lengths varied in six sizes from the twelve to thirteen inch collar to the enormous forty-five inch rope, and what worked very well for some women would be totally inappropriate for others.

She talked of intaglio carved gems engraved into the object, used for signet rings and seals, as opposed to cameo, where the surround is cut away to leave the design; she described chatoyancy, the optical effect of a strip of light reflected in the stone, supposedly resembling the feline eye. She described fineness as being the proportion of silver or gold in a metal alloy, expressed in parts per thousand and contributing to the desirability of objects.

Concerning her own eternity ring, given to her by Maurice on the birth of their son, she kept quiet, but she described how many women appreciate receiving them as tokens of the permanence of their relationships. She could see, at this point, that Hugo Gilard had picked up on this having a personal meaning for her, even if the others hadn't.

Finally, when she could see that the men were becoming restless, she moved to a subject she knew would interest them all: security. Her uncle knew well enough that this was an issue of enormous importance to any serious jeweller and essential also in terms of developing friendly and co-operative relationships between jewellers and other businesses. If a jeweller's shop gained a reputation for being vulnerable, it could result in the shops around it beginning to feel under threat.

Uncle Ian kept his most valuable items in safes at the back of the shop. He had a number of concealed alarm buttons, connected to the local police, dotted around the shop. His business was one of the first to use a concealed camera to watch people entering or leaving his shop. Only one raid on his premises had ever been attempted, and on that occasion, the three men concerned were so intimidated by the alarm sounds that they left without taking anything; two of them were later arrested.

The security talk admitted the men back into the conversation, and by the time the group had been sitting together for forty minutes, Valerie felt she had been accepted into their circle, though it was Hugo Gilard who struck her as clearly the most significant individual in the group. Even after such a relatively short time, she could see the other men deferring to him, especially when he mentioned that this shop was not his first but his fifth.

Valerie then suspected that she had been indulged, but she concluded that the point was, from his point of view, to talk to people in their own area and get the measure of them. And it seemed that she had made a good impression on him. She had to leave their table to attend to other restaurant needs, but later on, when he came to pay his bill, they had a more private conversation.

His bill amounted to quite a lot of money; he had obviously been determined to do the thing properly. However, he was either a very good actor or genuinely quite comfortable with it, and he insisted on including a 'gratuity' for the staff.

'Thank you for this evening, Mrs. Foster,' he said. He seemed quite cool, in spite of the warmth of the evening, and she realised that, however much the others had consumed, he had not himself drunk very much. She was well used to the bedewed foreheads and ruddy complexions of some of her male clients, usually accompanied in the later stages of the evening by some attempts at flirtation. With Hugo, there was none of that, and for once, strangely enough, she found herself wishing there had been, perhaps just a trifle.

'I have to entertain people for business purposes from time to time, and it's reassuring to know there are places I can take them without any fears of being let down. We will meet again, Mrs. Foster.'

With that, he left, patiently fending off Tom Corbridge's attempts to 'carry on a pleasant evening' at some pub he knew, Corbridge already somewhat the worse for wear.

When she checked, the boys were breathing easily; they had left a top window open and most of the toys were at least pushed away to the sides. But, as usual, she felt it wasn't enough, that she should be spending more time with Austin and, as usual again, she felt uneasily that she perhaps didn't give him the full attention he needed because of who his father was and what his father had done, none of which, of course, was any fault of the boy's. Not for the first time, she wondered if she would be able to find him another father in time for it to do him any good.

With the staff gone and the dividing doors between the restaurant downstairs and the living quarters (she refused to think of it as a 'flat') upstairs firmly closed and locked, she relished her independence and solitude. But pictures of Gilard kept returning, and with them a real sense that something very important had just happened. And she couldn't stop herself from wondering whether there was a Mrs. Gilard.

Thursday July 17th 1980

Another year, another summer, and Valerie's star was in the ascendancy. She had dropped the Foster name, reverting to her maiden name of Reynolds, and managed to expand her business from one restaurant to four, using the tactics of borrowing money at reasonable rates of interest and employing people local to each restaurant, thereby establishing enough contacts to get each enterprise started.

She no longer lived 'over the shop', having found a comfortable purpose-built modern apartment not far out of the nearest city centre, Exeter, to her first restaurant. Ten-year-old Austin seemed to have settled well in his new surroundings, and Valerie had decided he would go to an independent fee-paying school when he got to secondary school age. He rarely referred to his father now, and he seemed less withdrawn and more sociable. He had already attained a greater degree of literacy than his father, and while she knew well enough he was no child prodigy, the boy was shaping up to do alright for himself.

Tonight she was to see Hugo Gilard again, but this time it was different; it would be a dinner for two. There had been several more business dinners in the company of Hugo and his guests, and when they attended her restaurant, she once again would join them at some point, though by now she had no further need to prove herself, either to herself or them.

Hugo did give her a few pointers about running a business that now included several outlets, and she knew now that there was a Mrs. Gilard, whose name was Yvonne and who worked as a model, supposedly. But though Hugo never denigrated his wife or criticised her in public, she had the impression that all was not well between them and that their daughter, Amélie, seemed to be increasingly playing the part of a rope in their tug-of-war.

On the only occasion so far when she had met Yvonne, the distance between man and wife was all too obvious, expressing itself most drastically in what was supposedly an academic discussion about girls' education, with Yvonne championing modelling as part of what she called the 'performing arts' and Hugo believing that girls should have at least as thorough a school education as boys before making career choices. On that occasion, the Gilard guests had gradually lapsed into awkward silence as the realisation of the true significance of the encounter became clear.

Valerie had at least established the French connection. The Gilard family were Huguenots, French Protestants, who left Catholic France in the seventeenth century to settle in south-west England. Their original weaving trade gradually changed to the making and marketing of jewellery, as a more lucrative business less likely to be squashed by mass production, as weaving began to be. The lessons they needed to learn to become successful in a new country were learned over time, meaning Hugo's training as an entrepreneur and salesman was built on long traditions of trial-and-error experience.

She regarded Hugo as a business acquaintance and a friend. As yet, he had shown no signs of wanting the relationship to develop beyond that, and Valerie herself remained dubious about another marriage. She knew there was now no chance of a reconciliation with Maurice even if she'd wanted it; such sketchy information as she got from him and her other contacts in Australia suggested that his relaxed and inebriated ideas of how to run a business hadn't changed. His big promises to Austin about long, fun-filled holidays in the Australian sun had failed to materialise, and children's interest fades away rapidly when one broken promise follows another. But Austin's occasional truculence and temperamental outbursts were difficult to handle at times, and she wondered how long it would be before such control as she had would no longer work with him. A new partner might work in that respect, but a new partner might also have, or want, a child or children of his own, and Valerie had concluded that she wouldn't choose to sacrifice her career and business for the sake of children, whether hers or other people's.

In his invitation to her for the evening, Hugo had described it as about discussing their respective business interests, and she could see it as feasible that some organised co-operation between them could come about; three of her restaurants were in places where Hugo had his shops. But she had a feeling, an instinct, that there was something else involved.

Their dinner was to take place in a restaurant in Exeter with a view of the cathedral, and she was to be taxied there and back at his expense. Covering herself was not difficult now; she had competent managers in all her places, chosen by her, and she no longer had to spend whole evenings supervising everything from the kitchen to the bookings.

He was there when she arrived, and though she knew he disliked ties, he was wearing one, as well as a blue made-to-measure suit. She had made the effort herself, with an elegant full-length evening gown, and she was glad the first details of the evening had been successfully sorted out. She had seen often enough the effects of being slapdash in both timing and dress, with some occasions so blown off course from the beginning that they were never able to recover.

'Val, you look marvellous,' he said. 'You really do. What would you like to drink?'

So he hadn't even ordered himself a drink in advance of their meeting. Everything clicked together step by step over the next few hours. Having done the usual exchange of information about 'the kids', the main gist of their meeting became clear as soon as they had both ordered.

'Yvonne and I are separating, Val,' he said. 'I could probably sit here for the next two hours and describe the thing in detail, but what's the point? I found out she was having an affair with one of the photographers she works with, and perhaps I sort of asked for it, with my twenty-four-hour-a-day focus on growing the business into the sizeable concern it is these days, but there's a sense in which we never were compatible. She thinks of herself as an artist, and so she is; she says I'm not truly concerned with anything but making money, though she's happy enough to spend mine when I've earned it. For all her contacts and occasional big spreads, she doesn't make very much herself.'

'You don't need to justify anything to me, Hugo,' Valerie said mildly.

'Well, in a sense I do, because, not to put too fine a point on it, Val, I think I've come to care for you more than I care for her. I know we've always been strictly business, and I know you value your independence in both the business and the personal sense, but all I'm suggesting is that we might see more of each other socially than we do, and perhaps just see how it goes.'

Valerie told herself that she had seen this coming, but her suspicions had always been that it was more about wishful thinking than premonition. She knew enough about Hugo by then to realise that he tended to be at least polite towards everyone, and especially people included in his business dealings; his easy manner and occasionally flattering remarks were not to be taken too seriously. Now he seemed to be asking her directly to take them more seriously, and in spite of her first, disastrous marriage, she felt herself drifting towards Hugo as she had once felt herself drifting towards Maurice. And yet she knew the situations were more different than they were alike. Maurice was the best she thought would be available for her, in the days when she had no immediately clear ways of making a living and she lacked confidence in herself both sexually and vocationally. In that case, the drift was about resignation; this time, it was about aspiration, and the opportunity to find a partner who was not only genuinely her equal but who would be prepared to treat her as his equal.

She realised that she had been silent for some seconds, and the expression on his face was already suggesting that he was misinterpreting her silence.

'I'm not quiet because I'm offended by what you say in any way, Hugo. It's just that you're making happen what I supposed I have wanted to happen for some time, but not necessarily expected. I knew you and Yvonne were two very different people, but I thought it might be a case of opposites attract – I've met Yvonne, remember – and that the tension between you was just part of the dynamics of the relationship.'

He sipped at his drink and his eyes were narrow with thought.

'I suppose there might have been a time when that was true. My family are, in the main, artisans and skilled workers in a variety of fields; few of them, including me, tend to be very demonstrative or extrovert. Yvonne, from the start, was very demonstrative and extrovert, and discovering her was exciting in more ways than one. But there are opposites which attract or complement and there are opposites which simply grate and irritate, and too many of ours were the latter. I'm not looking for some female equivalent of me, if such a thing is possible, and I have no hang-ups about clever and talented women; part of my problems with Yvonne were about the discovery that she isn't, and never has been, as clever and talented as I thought she was. But you would be right to be at least a little suspicious that I might just be on some spectacular rebound, and for all I know, you might have interests elsewhere—'

Valerie smiled.

'I'm a single mum, Hugo, spending some years trying to put together a secure economic base for my son and I; I haven't had much time for interests elsewhere. And I'm still not that far away from a disastrous first marriage, much of it arising from some quite catastrophic and basic miscalculations on my part, reading indolence for charm, a relaxed manner for quiet competence, and ingratiation for sociability. When you've been clumping through a minefield and had one or two go off in your face, you learn to tread carefully. But I think, in that respect, I'm probably preaching to the converted.'

By the end of the meal, they understood each other well enough, and their tentative, exploratory relationship was underway. They had exchanged ideas about where they wanted their respective businesses to go and they had shared parenting experiences with Austin and Hugo's daughter Amélie. The boy, to Valerie's relief, had turned into a normal and apparently quite well-adjusted ten-year-old; the girl, in the full throes of adolescence at fifteen, had both the temperament and the vocabulary to determine where she stood in relation to her parents, and while she would still socialise with and visit her mother, she had made it clear that she would prefer to live with her father.

'Mum's just much too much like hard work on a day-to-day basis,' she'd said to Hugo. 'Terrific for a day out or a visit to one of her shoots; a nightmare to be with all the time, especially mornings and late nights.'

So moving the relationship on from business to personal came with baggage they were both well aware of, including finding themselves as step-parents. And, of course, there was the matter of the physical side of the relationship, and on this front, Valerie was wary. The best thing that could be said for Maurice was that he was considerate and gentle, but certainly not particularly adventurous and tending to connect love-making with alcohol, a dangerous combination. On the night that she had worked out had probably been Austin's conception, they had had a splendid day on a sunny Norfolk coast and a very nice dinner in the hotel's restaurant, and melted and romantic as Maurice was, the act itself was accompanied by beer fumes and heavy breathing and took so long that Valerie reached the point where she was contemplating the use of her hands to reach a conclusion rapidly.

Maurice, dressed up for an occasion, did scrub up well and by anyone's standards could be described as a good-looking man, but she hadn't come to the marriage as a virgin and she knew well enough how deceptive male appearances could be. A close ex-school friend of Valerie's called Denise had married a man who, if not exactly ugly, was far from classically handsome and who was lean to the point of skinniness. However, Denise reported love-making on a grand scale of both energy and inventiveness; perhaps men who did not have such good looks going for them were prepared to work that much harder.

Valerie continued to meet up with Hugo and the relationship gradually developed greater intimacy, but she was adamant that nothing beyond kissing and embracing would happen until his divorce from Yvonne was complete. As Yvonne's affair was common knowledge to both her family and her colleagues, a contested divorce would have been an expensive nonsense. Hugo conceded Yvonne the house, provided she made no future claim on his earnings, and Amélie opted to live with her father, as she had always said she would.

Eventually, in the spring of 1981, with Hugo's divorce completed, he and Valerie carefully arranged the time and date of their first full love-making. It was to happen in a London hotel, just before a long weekend in Paris. They were both aware that giving it too much of a build-up might be setting it up for an inevitable anti-climax, as being simply unable to match up to the long-standing expectations. And while they were still both relatively young – Valerie was thirty-two and Hugo was thirty-eight – they were no longer in the first flush of youth, and epic sessions of repeated orgasms were already overly ambitious.

But they were both determined to do the thing properly, to be fully naked in front of each other without fumbles under sheets or attempts to connect in near-darkness. And it was gratifying to both of them that it all turned out to be quite laid-back and easy. There were no beer fumes or gaspings, since they had decided that alcohol would make more sense afterwards than before, and Hugo proved to be not only gentle and considerate, but also knowledgeable, a man who not only knew what foreplay was, but could put it into practice. Valerie had acquired a few tricks of her own, and while they had generally confused or puzzled Maurice, they entertained Hugo both visibly and audibly.

Love in London was followed by love in Paris, and further discoveries both in and out of the bed. Hugo was fluent in French, which he was probably always going to be in view of his Huguenot background, but seeing it in action in Paris made her all the more impressed by him. Valerie knew most of the cooking methods French chefs tended to use, even if she sometimes struggled to replicate them herself, and her informed conversations with French men or women willing to use their English for someone who knew what she was talking about gave Hugo a pleasant sense of his girlfriend's sophistication.

The long weekend proved to be a resounding success in all departments, but they both retained a wariness about marriage. Both Hugo's relationship with Yvonne and Valerie's with Maurice had begun with a sequence of holidays and dates, meaning they had married without ever having actually lived with their new partners. They consciously and deliberately determined that such a situation would not happen again.

They bought a large, rambling house in Oxfordshire, with plenty of room for the kids to explore and keep pets if they wished, and keep out of each other's way if they preferred to; eleven-year-old boys were no part of Amélie's world, every bit as much as sixteen-year-old girls were no part of Austin's, though he was moving towards the stage where he would quite like them to be. A large inflatable swimming pool, for use in warm weather only, was first worked on a kind of rota system so that Austin and his friends would not use it at the same time as Amélie and hers, but eventually the *détente* between the two, fuelled by Austin's generally outgiving and friendly nature and Amélie relishing the move away from the inward-looking life when tensions between her parents dominated day-to-day living, resulted in them living together as successfully as brothers and sisters ever do.

For the time being, Hugo and Valerie remained unmarried. Everyone around them assumed that they were, and they allowed the assumption to go unchallenged. Valerie overcame her mother's strictures about 'cohabitation' by demonstrating to her the prosperous and successful life she and Hugo were having.

Austin started at a fee-paying school at the age of eleven, but one close enough for him to live at home; Valerie distrusted the boarding school idea and preferred to have her son where she could keep an eye on him. Austin was shaping up quite well; he seemed to have his father's charm and head for figures without his father's natural indolence, but Valerie knew he had yet to be introduced to alcohol, and one more less pleasant hereditary characteristic could still manifest itself.

Amélie started A levels at a local sixth form college and already showed signs of having a specific career in mind, in hospitality. In the days when she would accompany her mother to her shoots, she found herself more interested in the organisation and catering involved in the events than the clothes; much of the clothing her mother modelled she regarded as bizarre or ridiculously expensive. She was inexorably turning from a pretty girl to a beautiful woman, unsurprisingly given her good-looking parents. She allowed her blondish hair to grow long, tying it back whenever the need arose; she used her blue eyes to maximum effect, and kept her figure slim with regular swimming and running. In spite of her natural mother's intrusive curiosity and her stepmother's guarded enquiries, she refused to be drawn on whether or not her virginity was intact. As it happened, it was, but when and how she would lose it would be her decision and hers only, and it certainly wouldn't be in circumstances that might result in a pregnancy.

Into 1982, and the gamble of the new relationship seemed to be working all the way down the line, but it was still a relationship, not a marriage, until Hugo had an idea that was to transform all their lives still further.

Sunday April 25th 1982

Hugo had found his way to one of his favourite spots in what were now the quite extensive gardens of his home, christened Gilrey House as a merger between his surname and Valerie's maiden name Reynolds. It was, when it came down to it, just a bench, but it was so ideally situated to see both the house and the garden to fullest advantage that he found himself using it, not only to admire what he and his family now had, but to give him a place to think.

Hugo didn't consider himself to be a religious man. In spite of, or perhaps because of, the fact that religion had caused the persecution and exile of his French ancestors, he did not consider himself a practising member of any church, though he would refuse, on principle, to enter any Catholic churches or deal with any Catholic priests.

But events sometimes precipitated reflective moods when he did wonder if being bereft of faith was good enough for him to be an effective and honest husband and father.

Yesterday, Saturday 24th, had seen the first English fatality in what he regarded as a largely unnecessary war in the Falklands with the crash of a Sea King helicopter. This was the end of a relatively young life, a man well-trained and equipped to serve his country, and ever since he had heard of it, an uncharacteristic melancholy had settled on him. That guy was someone's son, probably someone's husband, perhaps someone's father. Sacrificed for Britain's need to hold on to what it regarded as its own, a collection of tiny windswept islands in the middle of the Atlantic. Sacrificed to someone giving him orders, which he had a duty to obey.

And, even as he felt pangs of self-contempt to immediately be transferring such thoughts to business, he couldn't help drawing certain lessons from the incident. Ever since Mrs. Thatcher's rise to power, he had begun to admire her determination and ruthlessness, as well as a certain singleness of purpose; Mrs. Thatcher believed the country should be heading in a certain direction and she was going to take it in that direction, kicking and screaming if necessary.

If the war was won, and Hugo had few doubts that it would be – most of the Argentinian troops were young conscripts, inferior to the British troops in both training and equipment – Mrs. Thatcher would undoubtedly win another election, due next year, meaning the country would have Mrs. Thatcher in charge for the foreseeable future. And this would create a climate where the weak would go to the wall; a leader who was quite prepared to see men die for the sake of the Falkland Islands would have no qualms at all about companies that couldn't stand on their own two feet going to the wall. The climate would mean the survival of the fittest; the stronger and more resourced a company was, the better its chances of at least keeping its head above water.

Gilard Limited now had a dozen jeweller's retail shops in the south and Midlands, with a central works providing Gilard brand products to its customers. The company was doing well enough, but in an environment where people were beginning to feel vulnerable and needing to hang on to what wealth they had, one of the first trades to suffer would be jewellery, very much on the luxury and dispensable end of most people's priority lists. If people started losing jobs and smaller companies were forced to close, his own business could find itself in a precarious position.

And so could Val's. Hugo had long since stopped thinking of her as Valerie. Reynolds Limited – Val had reverted to her maiden name for business purposes – now owned eight restaurants, all of them quite upmarket affairs. Eating out was another activity susceptible in economically difficult circumstances. Both he and Val had borrowed from banks to support their acquisitions of new businesses, and if both Gilard and Reynolds were organisations under threat, they would have to look for further support before long to keep their outlets and workforce going. In a difficult retail market, that would inevitably mean more borrowing, and a situation where both businesses finished up being effectively owned by banks. Should they continue to struggle to make their way, the banks would simply shut them down, and both he and Valerie would find themselves in the bankruptcy courts.

A lot to deduce, perhaps, from one death in the Falklands, and his feelings for the serviceman concerned were in no way diminished by the extrapolation of messages for the future from it. Businessman who carried on doing what they were doing regardless of what was happening in the world around them could very quickly and easily find themselves in trouble. The implications for Gilard and Reynolds were clear enough in his mind.

Firstly, they needed to unite; bringing them together would create a much bigger business with therefore greater staying power in tough markets.

Secondly, they needed to diversify. For Gilard, it had to be more than jewellery; it had to be smart stuff obtainable on smaller budgets – dress accessories, small décor items, perhaps even some home furnishing. For Reynolds, take away outlets, tea rooms, town centre cafés, perhaps food deliveries.

And thirdly, they needed to make mutual use of premises, so trouble in one could be countered by the other. Stores should include the new larger range of Gilard goods, as well as convenient places in-store to eat or take food away.

Such talk of unity brought once again to mind the non-business implications of his business mind. He had to stop messing about and marry Val. Once again, his sheer pragmatism gave him some feelings of disgust; did the whole world need to fit into his business model? Not true, he said to himself; the businesses were vital to both of their lives, not to mention the two kids now dependent on them. Their comfortable lifestyle, the kids' good schooling, the future for all of them, everything depended on business survival.

And he was convinced now that he wanted Val as his wife. The staggering contrast between his former life with Yvonne and his present life with Val made the move all too obvious. Even allowing for the demands of running a large and expanding business, he felt more comfortable, more relaxed and more up for the coming challenges than he had felt for years. The time, the circumstances and, above all, the person were right.

He felt in his jacket pocket for the small article which might also contribute to convincing him he wasn't just considering a marriage of convenience and convincing Val that he did have some romance in his soul. In a beautifully-made small dark blue box was a vintage diamond solitaire ring. In its centre was a round brilliant cut diamond weighing 0.40 carat. The diamond was estimated G in colour and SI1 in clarity, and completed with a solid eighteen carat yellow gold shank. The whole ring was worth well over £1,000, and he had deliberately avoided going to his own staff to make it up as economically as possible; he had decided to commission it and pay full market price for it. Valuing and respecting a woman to the extent of wanting to marry her was not enough, he felt; he needed to make some gesture of love that was visible and worthwhile, and he needed to do it without being a cheapskate about it. He knew well enough that he could not 'buy' Val in the material sense, and he knew she was not a woman who was necessarily impressed by glittering baubles of any kind, but there were occasions when he found he could struggle to find words meaningful or appropriate enough, and on such occasions, he needed something to express his feelings if the actual words should fail him.

But, of course, the fact that he had concluded that the time was right for marriage didn't necessarily mean it was going to happen if she didn't feel that way herself. He knew something of her first marriage, and although he'd never met Maurice, he thought he knew the type; men who thought they had enough going for them, the looks, the soothing manner, to not have to work too hard, men who concluded that they just needed someone like Val, presentable, hard-working, a little naïve, and they had a meal ticket for life.

If she regretted divorcing Maurice, she'd shown little sign of it. But it didn't follow that she necessarily wanted to marry again. In their time together, and sometimes during their love- making, establishing the relationship on a more permanent footing had come up and been talked about, of course, but the last two years had hardly left them much time to think things through, and with Val there needed to be a reason for doing something. How exactly he'd shaped up as someone to live with he didn't know. Yvonne was fond of saying he was moody and sometimes withdrawn, but in the circles Yvonne moved in, almost anyone who didn't talk at the top of their voice or throw tantrums or act as if the world was about to end would be considered moody and withdrawn.

But there was only one way of finding out what Val thought, and that was to ask her. Going down on one knee holding a ring up to her, or proposing in some other supposedly romantic or even public way, would cut no ice with Val. He needed to make his case, both as a businessman and a potential husband, and if he was more confident about the first than he was about the second, the first might make a better starting point.

In the house, Val was having a blissful few minutes to herself. Austin was kicking a ball about with a couple of his friends; the boy, like his father, had no problem with making friendships, and Val knew both of the boys concerned, as well as their parents. The house was well endowed with open spaces for the kids, where they could play while remaining on private property. Austin's relationship with Hugo was coming on; the boy was understandably wary, but Hugo did his best to be pleasant without being ingratiating.

Sooner or later, of course, things would have to be put on a more secure footing, but there didn't need to be any rush about it.

Amélie was up in her room, certainly by far and away the biggest bedroom she'd ever had, with finally enough storage to keep all the stuff she seemed to need. She was an avid collector of books and magazines relating to her interests, including subjects connected to hospitality. She already seemed to have some problems distinguishing between work and leisure; for her, much of it amounted to the same thing. Val found her intensity and seriousness of purpose a little worrying, and while she was relieved enough that streams of boys were not endlessly appearing, the suggestion that this was an area that didn't interest Amélie very much at all was as much a source of anxiety as it was relief.

Val was sitting in a bay window looking over the approach to the house, and she noticed Hugo walking, very thoughtfully, across from the west side of the estate, as she liked to call it. She speculated as to what he might have on his mind, as he clearly had something. He wasn't a man who would usually be described as happy-go-lucky, but he wasn't generally much given to misery and introversion either. She'd known him now for seven years, the last two of them very intimately, but there were still times when she struggled to read him. Only just before he entered the house, he saw her, and such a spontaneous smile broke over his face that she suspected good news had arrived, even if it was good news he'd had to have time to think about.

She stood up, they kissed, and then they sat in the window together while he told her what was on his mind. She was to say later that it had started as one of the most carefully reasoned and rational proposals that anyone had ever received, and that it intended to start a corporation as well as a marriage. However, just as she was wondering whether it didn't amount to much more than a business plan, out came the ring. Val had been through the whole classical romantic stuff with Maurice – the knees, the ring, the flowers, the promises, none of them worth a jot when the actual experience of everyday life kicked in – but this, she felt instinctively, was different; she knew this man, she knew his worth, and the romantic part of it was a contributory part, not the whole thing.

He spared her the knees and the flowers. While she was gazing, open-mouthed, at what was in the box he had just given her, he tried for the words and did the best he could.

'You are Diamond Val to me. Precious, beautiful, shiny and unbreakable. I love you and treasure you. Please, please will you marry me?'

For all the magic of the moment, she knew that, for a man to take her down this road again, there needed to be more than hearts and flowers, and that's what Hugo was offering, not just a Maurice-like 'get hitched and hope for the best' line. She wanted security for herself and her son, a man with ideas as well as charm, and a man capable of independent, constructive thought.

'I would suggest that we call it the Gilrey Corporation, taking a bit out of both names, and yes, I know that puts the bit of my name before the bit of your name, but I think it works better than Reygil. And apart from the whole corporation business, Val, I suggest we have a proper wedding with family and friends, and yes, I can hear them all saying "we thought you already were, ha, ha", but I don't much care and I don't suppose, ultimately, they will either. Then, before we get into the whole corporation business, we take ourselves off for a honeymoon – you choose the place, anywhere you like – for at least a fortnight.'

'Yes, that's fine, Hugo. And we'll have a child together.'

Val heard these words come out of her mouth before she realised that she hadn't thought about this before at all, and pleasant as the celebrations would be, there was no need to commit herself in this way. Austin's birth had not been particularly easy and a second child in her thirties could be harder still. Apart from that, it could mean time off that she couldn't easily afford if the corporation was to come about. Nevertheless, she had said it, immediately and enthusiastically, meaning it had come from some inner need, some compulsion that she hadn't even needed to think about, and as such she was going to stick with it. Yes, it was simple; a child each, but both of them were the product of other relationships, and their relationship would be strengthened, as would the family unit as a whole, by a third child entirely of their union. And it would be more difficult for Austin and Amélie to take sides when a third side always had to be taken into consideration.

So the Gilrey Corporation was born and immediately began to grow into a monster. Hugo had called the idea into being, but they both needed to make it work, and make it work they ultimately did, but not before a much more delicate and vulnerable manifestation of their relationship came into the world.

THURSDAY SEPTEMBER 15TH 1983

In the comfortable, expensively appointed waiting room of a private London hospital, Hugo waited quietly, if impatiently, for news. He knew well enough the stereotype of nervous young fathers pacing NHS corridors anxiously seeking news from any passing nurse or doctor, or the more adventurous types actually in the room where their wives or girlfriends were giving birth. He had been in the first situation himself as long ago as 1965, at the tender age of twenty-two. At the time, the idea of husbands being in the birth room was simply not to be contemplated, and he had been the pathetic boy stalking the corridors, anxiously trying to interpret the bizarre collection of noises emerging from the room where his wife lay, and almost leaping on anyone who emerged from it.

At that time, he'd understood entirely why husbands shouldn't be in there. He had only the vaguest ideas of what was actually happening, which tended to be the case with men/boys in 1965, and in the birth room he would simply have been a liability, a nuisance. Now he was forty-one years old, a man of the world and almost middle-aged; he wouldn't concede that forty-one was entirely middle-aged. He knew a great deal more about the business of pregnancy and birth than he had then, and he had been immensely more involved in Val's pregnancy than he'd ever been in Yvonne's; Yvonne had resisted and resented even so much as any questioning about the matter. He could now be present in the birth room without being a liability, though he was still surprised when the choice was made available to him. He chose not to; he knew that male doctors were qualified and entitled to help women give birth, but he also knew that an irrational resentment against them seeing and touching his wife intimately would mean he would probably not contribute anything very useful. And he felt that Val, who he could now read very well, didn't really want him there; being a practical, business-like lady, she wanted the whole business over as quickly and as painlessly as possible.

The private hospital had been his idea. He had no bones to pick with the NHS; rather to the contrary. He believed that if people who could afford private medicine were prepared to use it and did, it relieved the stress and burden placed on the NHS. How much difference there really was between the anxious boy stalking the corridors in 1965 and the forty-something guy sat on comfortable upholstery in 1983 was debatable, but on balance he preferred the latter.

Today was the culmination, and hopefully the ending, of a long discussion between him and Val. It could also be characterised as an argument, but arguments were about coming to an issue from two very different viewpoints, and that wasn't really the case with this one. It was more about ideology and practicality, and strangely, from his point of view, they divided, broadly speaking, into Val championing the ideology and him supporting the practicality. It seemed strange in view of the fact that he was not the one who would have to do the major and most unpleasant part of the business.

His feeling was that, while it would be satisfying to have a child of their own, they did effectively already have two, and both of them being teenagers, eighteen-year-old Amélie and thirteen-year-old Austin, didn't make them any less demanding; if anything, more so in some ways. Amélie fervently wanted to go to university, and was due to start at one within a few weeks; Val's idea that this meant she would pretty much be standing on her own two feet now he regarded with some scepticism. Her parents were going to have to payroll it, and it didn't follow at all that Amélie, still an oddly solitary creature in many ways, would easily take to university.

Austin at thirteen was beginning the early stages of adolescence, the easy-going, friendly boy turning gradually and worryingly into a more taciturn, outspoken creature. He still had plenty of friends, but the kind of activities they now enjoyed were already rather less innocent and uncontroversial than they used to be. It was not too uncommon to detect the smell of beer on the boy. Hugo had also become very aware in recent times that he wasn't actually the boy's father, partly because the boy himself had reminded him of the fact.

In these circumstances, and bearing in mind that neither he nor Val were getting any younger, it made sense to him to stick with the two kids they had. Val, however, was attracted to the idea of a bigger family, and to the notion that having an offspring of their own union, and not just their former relationships, would be a unifying influence for everyone. She also pointed out that the growing power of Gilrey was going to need a substantial family to keep the business going. Hugo had reminded her that when the new addition was still only nineteen, his or her father would be sixty; the business of parenting was going to be continuing for some considerable time.

He was also worried about Val having another child at the age of thirty-five, having had, so he understood, not a particularly easy time of it with her son, born when she was only twenty-two. But he had found himself having to concede to her determination and her vastly superior knowledge about the whole business. His best resolutions about informing himself and taking a more active part in the pregnancy period had largely been blown out of the water by the demands of the Gilrey Corporation, perhaps the most intractable and persistently needy child of all of them.

He was so absorbed in his reflections on the new addition to the Gilard family that he didn't hear a nurse enter the waiting room, though this was partly because the nurses were trained not to make too much of a noise and fuss when going about their business.

'Mr. Gilard?' the nurse said gently.

Hugo looked up into the unblemished, if slightly flushed, face of a uniformed young woman. She was smiling at him, pleasantly if a little uncertainly.

'You have a son.'

Hugo was not quite out of his reverie, and he responded accordingly.

'Yes, I know that well enough; every day I am reminded of it, I assure you—' Then the meaning of the girl's words struck home.

'You mean—'

'I mean your wife has given birth to a baby boy. Congratulations.'

In a split second, his doubts and fears seemed to be swept away, overwhelmed and replaced with a huge sense of well-being and achievement.

'Thank you. Thank you, nurse. Is Val alright? May I see her?'

'Mrs. Gilard is very well. She knew exactly what she was doing from the start, and everything has gone well enough, with an occasional hiccup, but no more than that. She is sitting up in bed with the baby at this minute. Please come with me.'

Val looked a little flushed, and her normal preoccupation with having every hair precisely in place had lapsed a little. Her eyes were bright and moist and Hugo saw, with a pang, that there had been pain involved. He felt a huge surge of love and affection for her, and had to remember to look closely at the baby. It seemed to resemble almost every other baby he had ever seen, but the difference was that this one was his, this was his son, born of the wife he loved.

It seemed that he was allowed to cradle the child in his own arms, and he did just that. For the moment at least, he savoured the great triumph of it, and everything he'd thought he'd been afraid of or worried about seemed to shrink to irrelevance.

'We are going to have to name him, Hugo,' Val said. 'Do you want him to have the name of his father?'

But she who had done all the work – well, most of it – had the rights in that respect, he felt, and his own experience of growing up in an English boys' school with the name of Hugo did not encourage him to cause his son to go through the same thing.

'No, it is best that he has an uncomplicated name, a name which will be suited to his mostly English upbringing. My own idea would be to call him Paul. It's a simple and accepted name, common to a number of languages and difficult to turn into other forms, either babyish or condescending. But if you have another favourite in mind, darling, I will be happy to agree with your choice.'

'Well, Paul was one of the ones I had in mind, and I'm happy to go along with it,' Val said. She took the baby back and kissed him lightly on the forehead.

'Hello, young Paul Gilard. Welcome to the family.'

That, Hugo thought, also completes it. He felt he could persuade Val out of having another baby, because even though her pregnancy with Paul had gone according to plan – though he was to discover later that it hadn't all gone entirely to plan – another might now be pushing her luck. Delighted as he was to have them all, three would do.

At least, that's what he thought at the time.

Friday October 18th 1985

The Gilrey Corporation was going from strength to strength. People were in the mood to spend and socialise, and Gilrey stores allowed them to do both. Val was particularly pleased with the huge popularity of the stores with women, and while she was taking some steps to make the menu family friendly as well, she didn't intend to do anything that would seriously risk losing what appeared to be her main target market.

Val noticed with some surprise and apprehension the general indifference to the burgeoning 'underclass', the people out of work and the people being left behind in the gathering boom and confidence of the decade. But she and Hugo had their family to take care of, and they were determined that the family's welfare and progress would remain their main concern.

Twenty-year-old Amélie was well on her way to an art and design degree at a good university, and the Corporation had already used some of her ideas in relation to the organisation and appearance of Corporation premises. It seemed likely that Hugo's child, rather than Val's, would prove to be the natural heir to the Corporation, but that did not come as too much of a surprise. It's true that Amélie showed flashes from time to time of her mother's sense of melodrama and desire for attention, but her parents calculated that such tendencies would diminish as she gained confidence in her professional abilities.

Austin was most of the things expected of a fifteen-year-old boy – football, both playing and watching, occasional illicit sallies into alcohol, spending most of his time with his friends and not seeming too keen on study – but he had a few points going for him. He was generally acknowledged to be 'good with figures'; his maths results were consistently promising, and he was taking a growing interest in computing developments, insisting to his sceptical parents that this was the way things were going and Gilrey should be getting in on it from the start.

Paul, of course, was still a baby, but clearly a pleasantly good-natured one so far, and generally cherished and fussed over by his two older siblings.

Val had arranged to take this Friday off. Being able to do so now gave her pleasure in itself. All her outlets in the Gilrey stores had competent managers, and she had an able deputy in John Maddox, an unflappable Australian exile who could be outspoken and even ruthless when he had a mind to and who she thought would happily step into her shoes if given the chance to do so. She knew some people in the Gilrey hierarchy did not see this as a healthy situation, and she knew Hugo was a little uneasy about the rapidity of the Maddox rise through the ranks, but she wanted to be sure someone solidly competent was in charge when she wasn't, not someone who would be phoning her every five minutes for advice or reassurance. And she had already decided that being a corporation big shot wasn't necessarily what she wanted to do for the rest of her life.

Being a high-powered businesswoman in an age where they were still few and far between had attracted some media coverage for Val, and she was happy to go along with that and be a figurehead for other career women if such was needed, but part of what emancipation was about, as far as she was concerned, included the freedom to make your own choices, and if she did get to the point where she felt more comfortable running her home and family, including the considerable amount of entertainment, both at home and at work, which she and Hugo needed to undertake, then so be it.

This weekend would involve entertaining, but on a family rather than a business level. A weekend visit was arranged, the visitors being Val's sister Marianne and her husband, Will Forrest. Marianne was Val's only sibling, and they were both aware that their mother had miscarried twice in the three years between their births, meaning Marianne represented the youngest member of the family and always would do. In the early years, even though the family were not particularly well off, the sisters had had a lot of fun; three years was not so huge a gap, and the relationship probably reached its high point when Val was ten and Marianne was seven. Their mother and father ran a corner shop, and the girls concocted elaborate shop games, as well as romping happily through the unusually large garden that came with the shop. They also grew some of their own stuff, a training that served Val well in later years in the restaurant business.

But, of course, adolescence and the process of turning from girls to women brought in competition and aspiration. Marianne eventually rejected the retail and catering area altogether and trained as a teacher, meeting her future husband along the way. Will played rugby and cricket for his college as well as developing effective study procedures and entered teaching with a first-class degree. He became a head of department only four years later, and two years later, so did Marianne.

The sisters had some serious disagreements over Maurice, who, in Marianne's words, 'might fool you, Val, but he doesn't fool me. He's a liability'. During the time when Maurice and Val were struggling with the pub, as Maurice gambled away the profits and spent generously buying rounds for all and sundry, visits from Marianne and Will became more occasional and tense before virtually drying up altogether. Marianne was fond of giving her elder sister advice and acting 'as a shoulder to cry on', as the picture with Maurice showed no signs of improving.

Now, of course, the boot was very much on the other foot. The

Gilrey Corporation was booming, at the same time as Marianne and Will seemed stuck in the same schools undertaking heavy workloads without much promise of advancement. Their first visit to the Gilard home in Oxfordshire left Marianne open-mouthed and speechless. Val wanted her to be pleased that her sister had done so well, and her sister's ultimately lukewarm approval had brought further tensions, not much improved by Will's full-hearted appreciation of his in-laws' progress and man-to-man chats with Hugo, fuelled by very good whisky.

But Marianne then managed a promotion to deputy head, and though it had the consequence of making her work burden even heavier, it seemed to even things up with her sister. Marianne and Will's daughter Jennifer, born in 1977, started to show academic promise even in infant school, and Val and Marianne approached ever closer to a state of sisterly *détente* better than at any time since their childhood.

Val had decided to make a real effort this weekend, not to overawe Marianne and make a big thing of how well Gilrey were doing, but just to try to ensure that she and Marianne got time to talk. Fortunately, Hugo and Will had always got on well, and it didn't look to be too difficult to arrange a weekend of relaxed friendship, meaning Marianne would feel more at home in Val's house and they might see more of each other.

It seemed a shame that Jennifer was not coming; she apparently had a 'long-standing arrangement' with a friend for a sleepover on the friend's birthday. But Val could quite understand why Jennifer might find visits to her aunt's home a bit overpowering; that might be something that could be changed with time, and in any case, the sleepover could be entirely genuine; children seemed to go in for it quite a lot.

Val prepared to meet her sister and her husband in the more intimate places in the house, particularly the smallest of the three living rooms, which the family had come to refer to as the 'snug', and she felt that a visit to the local pub in the evening might create a congenial atmosphere; a taxi could be arranged, so that Hugo and Will could let their hair down to some extent. In any case, Val couldn't remember ever having seen either of them drunk and she saw no reason why they would start now.

A phone call to John Maddox reassured her that everything was in hand on the Rey side of the Corporation. Maddox sounded a little weary, but he habitually curbed his frequent icy sarcasm with Val, and his calm manner was always encouraging. He always gave her the impression that he didn't think anything would be so impertinent as to create any 'issues on my watch', so Val put her anxiety back in its box and determined to concentrate on the family visit.

Marianne and Will had planned to be with her by lunchtime, and she had made plans for a spread, all previously prepared, using mainly local stuff. One o'clock came and went with still no sign of her guests, and Val started feeling pangs of anger.

She was no longer used to being alone, and having experienced a good deal of it in her past, she did not care for it now. Austin was playing football and she knew he would be going to one of his friend's houses for lunch, that house being much nearer to the football ground than his own home was. Amélie had just started her third and hopefully last year at university.

Strictly speaking, of course, she wasn't alone; she never was. Mrs. Ransome the housekeeper was on hand to attend to lunch and subsequently tea, Sam the gardener was somewhere in the grounds, and the whole premises also had a caretaker called Hepton, Mike Hepton, who would be around somewhere doing whatever he needed to do. But Val had reached the stage of not really counting employees as 'people', in that sense, though she would be appalled by such an attitude if anyone pointed it out to her.

As the time ticked on past three-thirty and nearer to what she had planned for tea, she was on the verge of phoning her sister to see if she was still at home, and if so, inquire why, when a large blue and yellow police car turned slowly into the house's drive.

Val froze, apparently mesmerised by the car's stately progress to the front door. A host of previously discounted possibilities crowded into her mind. One of the car doors was already opening when she pulled herself together and stood up to answer the assertive knock.

There were two uniformed people on the doorstep, one woman and one man. The woman spoke first.

'Sorry to disturb you at home. Would you be Mrs. Gilard, may I ask?' Val could do no more than nod.

'I'm afraid there was a nasty accident at about half past eleven this morning, Mrs. Gilard, and we have reason to believe that they were heading for this house. The driver of the car was carrying this address, with today's date and a time for arrival in his jacket pocket.'

The man, huge and pale against the blue of his uniform, spoke for the first time.

'Both the driver and the passenger were taken to hospital, I'm sorry to say. The driver died on the way; the passenger, the lady, is critical and unconscious. We need a definite identification of the gentleman, ma'am.'

'We're sorry to spring such a shock on you, Mrs. Gilard,' his colleague added. 'But if you could accompany us to the hospital, we would be very grateful.'

Val, with an effort, recovered her powers of speech.

'Yes, of course. But I need to phone my husband. Please give me five minutes.'

Val was then some time away from the regular use of a mobile phone, and she felt an urgent need to speak to Hugo before this ordeal broke over her.

The rest of that day remained with her like a wound for many years, but she always acknowledged that the behaviour of her husband did at least dress and soothe the wound. He had a string of meetings and appointments; he simply dropped them all and hastened to the hospital; he was there when she got there. By that time, she had deteriorated into a condition of near hysteria, as the police received the news that Marianne had also died.

Hugo insisted that he could identify the bodies himself, and made sure that Val had a comfortable and quiet hospital waiting room while he did. He returned, pale and visibly shaken, but he did not go into what he had seen other than to confirm that the bodies were those of Marianne and Will, and Val didn't ask.

Eventually, after what seemed like a hospital eternity, they went home. In the morning, Hugo once again passed his work over to his deputy, a Scot called Donald McAdams who had risen rapidly to Assistant Managing Director, and drove to Marianne and Will's home, where Jennifer was being looked after by a policewoman. Hugo gently escorted the puzzled and frightened little girl back to Oxfordshire, where Val had carefully briefed Austin and Amélie about what had happened.

Jennifer had no other relations than her grandmother, Val's mother, who was in no mental or physical shape to bring up a young child. Val spent some time wondering how she could persuade Hugo to adopt Jennifer, remembering how he'd felt about another child after Paul. However, Hugo came through again by suggesting himself that they adopt her.

Austin was so gentle and solicitous with his cousin that Val declared to Hugo that she would never have believed it if she hadn't seen it with her own eyes. Amélie, on her return from university for a weekend, behaved similarly, and Jennifer was to say for years afterwards that the reception she had at her uncle and aunt's house saved her from a depth of despair and misery, young as she was, which could have contorted the rest of her life.

It transpired that the accident had not been in any way the fault of Will, who was driving at the time. He had been in the process of beginning to overtake a large articulated lorry when it suddenly pulled out to overtake the vehicle in front of it, forcing Will to move into the fast lane, directly in the path of a large car driving much too fast, which hit Marianne and Will's car sideways on. Four people died and another five were badly injured.

In addition to a large insurance award made in her favour, Jennifer was the sole inheritor of all her parents' money and assets, and as they lived in the south-east of England and had both been earning respectable incomes for some years, that amounted to a tidy sum. Hugo and Val legally adopted Jennifer, though the girl kept her surname of Forrest. When all the formalities were completed, she was made aware that she had a minor fortune of her own in trust until she reached her majority at twenty-one; she also knew she could challenge the terms if she chose to do so, but she didn't. Hugo and Val were generous in their support of her throughout her schooling and higher education.

And so the Gilrey Corporation and the Gilard family were formed in their entirety, and throughout the heady boom atmosphere of the eighties, they both prospered. Gilrey became an accepted name on the high street, with a reputation for quality and service. After the Big Bang in 1986, the Corporation was listed on the Stock Exchange; Hugo and Val became majority shareholders, making them millionaires many times over, and other members of the family were also allocated shares in trust until their majorities.

Hugo became more comfortable and urbane with each passing year, while Val used Maddox and a few other high-flyers on her side of the business to allow her reasonable amounts of time off. She worried that Hugo didn't seem keen on doing the same, and she felt that, while he increasingly embraced the comfortable life of a rich man rather too thoroughly for her liking, it didn't stop him from working formidably long hours as the years passed and the Corporation grew and grew. She would manage to drag him away on holiday from time to time, but with easier ways of communicating even from country to country, he would spend a fair proportion of his holiday talking to people inside and outside the Corporation wherever in the world they happened to be at the time.

Val felt, as the years went by, that there needed to be something after the Corporation, and as it started running into the more competitive markets of the nineties and the noughties, her mind turned increasingly to plans for retirement, when others could take the strain and she and Hugo could branch out into other interests and pastimes.

What Val didn't fully appreciate was that Messrs. Maddox and McAdams were increasingly working together, and their plans for the Corporation's future didn't entirely fit in with Val's plans for a comfortable retirement. The crunch would come, and in time, it did.

PART TWO

The Battle for the Corporation

Monday September 21ˢᵀ 2015

Val sat alone in the light and airy splendour of the Chairman and Managing Director's Office of the Gilrey Corporation. This had always been Hugo's working palace, suitably set on the top floor overlooking London, while Hugo's courtiers and attendants did his bidding on the floor below.

Hugo had been gone for three months now, his indulgent lifestyle finally catching up with him at the age of seventy-two. One Friday night in June, he had returned home after a thirteen-hour stint in his office and collapsed on the bathroom floor. The only one of the 'children' at home at the time was thirty-two-year-old Paul, on a visit to his father, accompanied by his civil partner Kirk. Being a doctor by profession, Paul knew what to do, and he exercised CPR, cardiopulmonary resuscitation, from the moment he saw Hugo on the floor, while Val frantically called 999. Even a qualified doctor's ministrations were not enough; Hugo's heart had finally and completely given up the ghost, and he died in the ambulance on the way to the hospital.

Val was left cursing herself for not being able to provide more practical assistance to Hugo, who had become obsessed with the efforts of his underlings, in particular Maddox and McAdams, to take control of the Corporation from him. Dismissing them had stopped being an option some time ago. In happier circumstances, he had allowed, in fact encouraged, them to take generous holdings in Gilrey. If he sacked them, apart from the ensuing battle with the squads of lawyers they would have at their back for unfair dismissal, they would sell their substantial holdings of shares and probably start a run on the Corporation's shares, which would devalue and perhaps even wipe out Hugo's holdings.

Val tried, by every persuasive method she knew, to encourage Hugo to make some kind of a deal with Maddox and McAdams, which would allow him to retire, even if it did mean giving up control of the Corporation. But Hugo wouldn't have it; the Corporation, he said, was a Gilard child as much as all the actual Gilard children, and doing some grubby deal with rebellious staff, as he saw them, would be selling out on the birth right of the Gilards.

Whenever Val thought of John Maddox, she felt temper rising within her. If the archetype of the Australian male was a tough, bronzed, monosyllabic, hard-drinking rancher, Maddox was a substantial departure from type; he was tall, yes, but tall and lean, with a very British complexion, short well-groomed dark hair and dark mysterious eyes. His favourite tipples were expensive wines, and he and his English wife saw themselves as collectors and connoisseurs. The impression that he had managed to convey to her in the early years of their association, of a young, earnest character eager to make good and persuade her to put her trust in him, had been replaced by the true picture: an unscrupulous wheeler and dealer quite prepared to make any alliances and strike any deals that would result in his position being improved at the expense of someone else's.

Donald McAdams, universally known, if not to his face, as 'Big Mac', had been with Hugo almost from the very start, when Hugo's business consisted of two or three jewellers. At that time, he had shown no more personal ambition than to do a good job for his boss and be paid accordingly for it. Although he was ten years younger than Hugo, they shared similar backgrounds and McAdams seemed to know what he was talking about in relation both to jewellery and the financial world. McAdams was a misleadingly genial man who appeared to become more avuncular as the years went by, while in fact his ruthlessness and thoroughness in protecting and developing his own interests deepened as he got older.

Always carefully and immaculately dressed, he was apt to sit back in his chair with a warm smile and let whoever he was talking to unburden themselves to him, with occasional nods of understanding and appreciation to help the process along. More often than not, people would realise that they had told him much more than they'd intended to say, but comfort themselves with the thought that he didn't seem to be the kind of man who was likely to retain such information in detail.

Unfortunately, that's exactly what he was. Reluctant to write things down, he compensated for it by a computer-like filing system of a memory. With his handsome flecks of grey hair on a well-groomed head, and dark blue conspiratorial eyes, he was like a favourite old teacher who could suddenly recall a misdemeanour or problem for which he considered proper penance had never been done, or he could issue a reminder of a financial commitment someone might have hoped would have been forgotten long ago.

Some of the staff in Gilrey referred to him as 'Uncle Spider', and the name reverberated through his many dealings inside and outside the Corporation. Hugo, who had at first been largely taken in by McAdams' confidential, understanding manner, seeing it just as the way 'Don' set out to be helpful, realised when McAdams was known to be rapidly building his shareholdings in Gilrey that there was more to the man than he generally let people realise, and when the association with Maddox became more widely known, the penny finally dropped, but by then, the two were too powerful to dispose of.

So Hugo kept going, considering himself still clever and experienced enough to stay one jump ahead of them, but it meant long hours of talks and meetings with all kinds of people, not to mention widespread travelling at times. It also meant, in spite of

Val's repeated attempts, that his eating and drinking habits were random and out of control, including too much alcohol and too many restaurant meals. His system eventually collapsed under the strain, leaving his wife holding the huge and now monstrous Gilrey baby.

The three months since Hugo's death had been crammed with activity, including the arrangements for the funeral, replying to the numerous messages of sympathy and good will that flooded in, and dealing with media demands; Hugo was a prominent and widely known industrialist and his death prompted a glut of biographies and articles. Val had been kept extremely busy, and in some ways she rather relished that than otherwise, since it restricted the time she had to think, reminisce and reflect.

But she knew those with an eye on controlling the Corporation were taking advantage of the situation. Hugo still had a loyal band of supporters and sympathisers, including some powerful figures, but Maddox and McAdams were making hay while their sun shone and Val feared that by the time she was able to fully turn her attention to them, it would already be too late.

Val got up and took a turn around the office, pausing to enjoy the spectacular views over central London. She wondered how many times Hugo had contemplated the same views as he ran the latest developments through his mind and decided where he had to go and what he had to do. At least now she had reached the stage where the rules of the game had become easier to understand.

Donald McAdams and John Maddox were seeking to gain control of the board, and in order to do that, they needed a majority of the shares available. At one time, that would have been impossible for them, because sixty per cent of the shares of Gilrey were held by Hugo and Val. However, the parents had decided, over the years, to spread control around the family.

Hugo felt it would make sense in several ways; it would give all of the family a vested interest in taking care of the Corporation;

it would provide them with a solid income, in terms of annual dividends paid; it would serve as a unifying influence for the now diverse family members and it would help to ensure that future developments could not be operational unless they were supported by the founders of the Corporation and their family.

Each of the four Gilard 'children' had five per cent of the Corporation's shares, and with speculation rising about changes since Hugo's death, five per cent of the shares was currently worth a sum in the region of forty million pounds. For each individual Gilard, this would be enough to see them in comfort for the rest of their lives, though none of them had to date shown any great inclination to work in or for the Corporation, which had been a persistent source of anxiety to Hugo and Val ever since the shares arrangement had been made. The temptation for each of them to make themselves suddenly £40 million richer would by now be considerable, and if any of them hadn't yet realised the wealth that could be theirs, McAdams and Maddox would make sure they did.

If two Gilard children sold out, the shares would be exactly even. If McAdams and Maddox could then induce a third to sell even just part of their holding, they would have control of the Corporation. Val had no illusions that if that happened, she would rapidly be put out to grass and McAdams and Maddox would turn the Corporation into not much more than a discount supermarket. Yes, she would still have her forty per cent, and selling her shares would make her a very rich woman, but she didn't care for the way those two men had behaved towards Hugo and she didn't care for their tactics in trying to break her family apart. She wanted to defeat them and force them out of the Corporation, and only when that happened would she seek people, maybe even one of the Gilard children, who could be relied upon to develop the Corporation in ways that Hugo would have liked, and would she decide to step down and take herself into a comfortable retirement. Much as she loved her Gilrey baby, she was not going to lay down her life for it as poor Hugo had done. Val moved back to her desk. Her decision had been taken. Only with the unity and co-operation of the Gilard family could the Corporation be saved, and she had private e-mail and postal addresses for all of them. Phone calls she didn't trust; she knew the extent of the McAdams and Maddox intelligence operation.

A board meeting was due in eight days. McAdams and Maddox had been working hard, taking advantage of Val's grief, as she saw it, and they had already ensured by various legal shenanigans that 'votes by proxy' would not be allowed for this meeting. The result was that if any shareholders wished to have their say and cast their votes according to their shareholdings, they would have to be physically present at the meeting.

Val needed at least three of the Gilard children to be at the meeting, and she also needed to ensure that they understood the issues and would vote the right way. She also knew that it was by no means out of the question, knowing what she did of McAdams and Maddox methods, that attempts might be made to hold up the children's progress as they returned and/or influence how they cast their vote by whatever means possible.

This gave Val pause for thought. The last thing she wanted was that any of the 'kids' would get hurt. But then she reflected that this wasn't the McAdams/Maddox style, and they would always take very careful steps to avoid any accusations of criminality. They were also well aware that Val had her own networks of intelligence and information. And as she remembered the two men, immaculate in their dark suits and black ties, performing as conscientiously and convincingly as they did at the funeral, she also realised they might be confident enough in their own abilities to think they didn't need to deflect the Gilard children. Having outwitted their father, they would consider themselves well able to do similarly with his children.

For a long moment, Val paused and thought. Forty per cent of the shares, in the region of £320 million, a fortune to provide a fabulous retirement, and no business matters to worry about. But she saw herself sitting alone in her big rambling mansion, staring into mirrors and feeling that, when it came to it, the bad guys had had her for toast. Hugo had fought so hard it had killed him. Maybe it would her. But at least she and her children would have made a fight of it and done honour to Hugo's memory.

She called up Amélie's current address on her computer. 'Darling Amélie,' she started, and smiled to herself. Her eldest was tough, smart and beautiful, and thinking of her always made her smile.

PART THREE

Amélie's Journey

Wednesday September 23ʀᴅ 2015

Madame Amélie Delatour was at home for the afternoon, and about to have a conversation with her husband that she was not particularly anticipating with any great enjoyment. Talking things over with André was normally enjoyable enough, but on this occasion she felt a note of tension would inevitably creep in.

Val had implied that she wanted Amélie to return at once. This was by no means as simple as Val seemed to think it. The Delatours owned four hotels in the Montreal area, all of them designed and furnished by Amélie herself. They were all successful ventures, consistently recording occupancy levels in the seventy to eighty per cent range, and catering for both English- and French-speaking guests.

Amélie had no illusions or false modesty about how important she was to the business. André was essentially a figures man; an accountant by training, he kept the books meticulously and took remedial action whenever they showed an area of the business that wasn't doing very well. Whatever stereotypes anyone might have about accountants, André would be likely to contradict them. Still sexy even at fifty-one, at least as far as Amélie was concerned – she would never have married him otherwise, she wasn't a nun and had no aspirations in that area – he could also be uncompromising if and when the need arose. He also had a very useful antenna for when people were trying to rip him off, which in the hotel business was not uncommon.

She knew he would not see the demands of a mother who wasn't really her mother as sufficient reason to go charging back over the Atlantic, especially as Amélie was the one who ran the design seminars, the hospitality sessions, the exhibitions and invitation events, which kept the Delatour hotels in the public eye and contributed substantially to their profit margins. She knew she would need a very good argument to persuade him and stop a row breaking out, because rowing with André was always difficult, with his remorseless logic and his big, wide 'what's the problem?' Canadian persona. The making up could be a lot of fun too, but Amélie was now forty-eight, and that side of things seemed sometimes these days to be more about effort than enjoyment.

Amélie moved across to the balcony of their house overlooking Mount Royal Park, where the spreading green landscape below never failed to ease her mind and allow her to think logically. Yes, it was true that Val was not her biological mother, but she was her mother in all the senses that mattered; being her father's ultimate choice as a wife and lover had always meant that Val would finish up being Amélie's choice as mother, and she had for some time tended to think of Val as her mother. Her real mother, Yvonne, was a sad figure these days, having married a man who owned a well-known fashion house, only to find that her husband was at least as much attached to male love as he was to female. She also found, too late, that his business was not worth as much as he'd maintained it was, and the struggle had ended in divorce, with Yvonne coming out of it with only barely enough to keep herself; her attempts at becoming a fashion writer had not been entirely successful, and now she was in a retirement home being a daily irritant to her fellow inmates. Comparisons with street-wise, successful businesswoman Val were inevitable.

Amélie knew she was also still in mourning for her father, her real and one and only father, who had given everything for his family. She had returned to England for the funeral, and she knew that a recent trip across the Atlantic was another reason why André probably wouldn't be sympathetic to yet another trip. Val hadn't mentioned the situation with these plotters aiming to wrest the Corporation from Gilard control, but Val was in a devastatingly bad place and could not think very logically about anything, a fact of which these devious bastards were well aware. Returning to England wasn't just about loyalty to Val, it was about loyalty to the memory of Hugo.

She was going to have to fire her big gun, the one she had kept in wraps ever since arriving in Canada with a good degree, five years' design experience and a recommendation from a very well-known supporter. She'd wanted to be her own woman, find her own niche, and Val and Hugo had seemed happy enough with that at the time. She'd known about the five per cent shares, and of course accepted them as a nice parental gesture, but she never suspected that they would grow into the monster they now were.

For André, she had downplayed the family business, because she still wanted to go her own way, and André was part of that. As far as he was concerned, it was something for the future, a nest egg that might help in their retirement, a respectable holding in a quaint old world English company. Now, in order to win him over, she was going to have to tell him she was sitting on forty million quaint old English pounds.

Amélie already knew well enough the loud bray of money talking, and the unpredictable nature of its consequences. André was generally a conscientious and attentive husband, who had not pressurised her regarding children – she had not liked the idea as a young woman and she still didn't like it now, however much her friends would use that wheedling 'who's going to look after you when you get old?' tone. It seemed to be a line particularly favoured by women who had children manifestly unable to look after themselves, let alone their parents. She knew André had had a fling or two and he knew she had had a fling or two, but none of it mattered a great deal; they were too good, and too rich, together to allow anyone else to split it up.

But now, if and when André got to know how much she was really worth, would he resent the hold she would then have over him? André was no submissive male, the type of creature calculated to alienate Amélie, fond as she was of her late father Hugo's quiet control and easy affection. To ensure a peaceful future, she might have to resort to the line that 'my wealth is our wealth, darling; what's mine is yours', but there was a reluctance inside her to create such a hostage to fortune. One more fling might just have him taking his share and swanning off into the sunset with a large dollop of her money, and much as she loved him, in this matter she was her own woman, and very much her mother's daughter as well. She had neglected both her mother and the Gilrey Corporation too much, in her desperation to find a way that was hers and only hers. The past was not so easy to expunge, and why should it be expunged in any case? Her first loyalty had to be to her mother, recently bereaved and seemingly in deep water with the sharks circling around her.

She heard his big car breathe its way easily into the drive, and in a few seconds, André was in the room with her, his eyebrows high and his arms thrown wide.

'Well, here I am, sweetheart, meetings cut off, business postponed, to get back home. What's the big deal? Why couldn't we talk on the phone?'

She told herself to stay very calm, and not be distracted from what she had decided. It was always more difficult when she was confronted with the physical reality of him, a well-built, powerful, good-looking guy, an alpha male if ever there was one, even if his hair was thinning now and his body was not as athletic as it had been.

'I need to go back to England again, André,' she said quietly.

Of course, he was surprised and indignant; she'd just been there, the demands of work were all around them, several big events would have to be called off without her, she had a whole squad of assistants who could go and handle it well enough. He handled arguments like lunging punches, and however much she had thought she might avoid the big revelation by some smart tactic which would occur to her while she was thinking on her feet, she felt punch drunk, on the ropes and needing a breather. Only the big gun, it seemed, would shut him up; with a long inner sigh, she fired.

'Ultimately, it's about who controls the Corporation, and for a variety of very good reasons, it needs to be my mother.'

'OK.' He was on his feet. 'Tell her to tell us what she needs; we'll buy the whole goddam English show and set her up for life. Or you, just as long as you put someone you can trust in charge. What's your share now, your personal share, I mean, not your mother's?'

'Five per cent.'

'Jeez,' he said and whistled to himself. 'Five per cent of the old England store. This is what you want to go scooting across the pond for. What's it worth, babe, your five per cent?'

Light the fuse, stand back immediately. 'As of now, about forty million pounds.'

As if the noise and smoke was still reverberating around his ears, André sat in the nearest chair to him, his eyes almost bulging out of his head.

'I thought—'

'Yes, I know what you thought, André. I've tried many times to stop you thinking it. You have fixed notions in your head about England, all this ye olde theme park crap, and I've seen that even when you're there, you make everything fit the image you've decided to have. You keep on calling it "the family store", and I've tried to tell you it amounts to more than that, it's a corporation with a variety of interests and assets, but you have little old England so fixated in your head that I can't get through to you.'

She moved across to the drinks cabinet to fix him something he would like, and took it to him. He sunk it obediently, like a dose of medicine.

'OK,' he said. 'Maybe I needed telling, but now you have sure as hell told me. So what's the deal with Gilrey Corp?'

'Austin, Paul, Jenny and I have five per cent each. My mother has forty per cent. As long as we act together, we keep control. It just takes two of us to sell out, and she's in danger of losing control. The guys who want to get their hands on it have rigged it so that people have to be there, physically there, to vote.

'Yes, we could do very well; I could put it around that I'm up for doing business, and I might even get it to fifty million by the time I sell. We could be nicely on velvet, André. But I will have sold my good stepmother down the river, betrayed my father's memory, and be condemned to spend the rest of my life as the ultimate rich bitch. I'd never get a good night's sleep again.'

'I can appreciate that, babe. Don't make me out to be some bonehead asshole. I don't know those guys too well, your brothers and your sister. Will any of them sell?'

Typical André, she thought. Straight to the guts of the matter. To her amazement, she realised she hadn't got as far as thinking about that.

'Paul is the youngest, and he's the only one who is actually the child of Dad and Val. He's a doctor now. He was the only one of us there when Dad had his heart attack, and he kept him alive until the ambulance came, but Dad had another attack in the ambulance and it killed him. Paul is probably the most idealistic of us, perhaps least bothered about money, but I can't see him going against the wishes of his mother.

'Jenny was originally Dad's niece, and she's maybe not as close to Val as the rest of us; how bothered she's likely to be about Gilrey I'm not sure, but she has a family and forty million pounds could secure the future of all of them. She just might.

'And as for Austin, Val divorced his father, and he's kept in touch with his father ever since. He's in the same sort of trade as his father was, the pub business, with his father's charm to get the customers in, but unlike his father, he doesn't gamble near to the knuckle every day of his life and he's not an alcoholic. But his wife comes from a long line of tough East Enders, and if they know he's worth forty million pounds, they're maybe not going to bother too much about the Gilrey Corporation. He just might too.'

'Which could leave it fifty-fifty,' André said.

'Which makes it tight. And the guys who are behind this – I could lay odds I know who they are – won't stop there. They'll then be prepared to throw a lot of money at me and Paul; they'd only need two per cent from one of us to clinch it.'

André was on his feet again, with the perpetual restlessness that she knew was typical of him. She was already wondering about why she had tried so hard to keep the truth from him; she recognised that she had not made any real effort to make him understand what Gilrey was about, and already a pang of regret was creeping in. The way he was at the moment, gazing out from the window onto their large and well-appointed garden with his hands folded in front of him, usually signalled an idea was on its way. His talent for thinking on his feet was one of the qualities that had attracted her to him.

'It's not a question to ask an English lady, though maybe I can get away with asking her about her mother. How old is Val now?'

Amélie did a few quick calculations.

'Sixty-seven. So what? You're telling me that she should retire herself, that she's too old for this game?'

André fixed his eyes on her reproachfully.

'People retire and then they die. I don't think Val's going to be too keen on that idea. No, it's just that her age might help if you – what do we call it – counter-attacked?'

Amélie knew now when to hold her silence; it was like waiting for him to lay an egg.

'Your side has sixty per cent together, but you know some of that might be shaky. So who's got the other forty, and where in their ranks is the shakiness? You say you know the guys who are behind this; do they own all forty per cent themselves, or are some of those owned by guys they think they have in their pockets and maybe they don't? Two can play this game, Amélie. We've got guys who can research this stuff. How about it?'

Somewhere inside Amélie, a hard, tight knot of misery was starting to unravel. She had too easily resigned herself to fighting this battle alone, alongside her stepmother like brave lady martyrs for the Gilrey cause. Now, it seemed, she had a few brains and – yes – balls on her side. Her eyes relaxed into André's, and a similar thought occurred to both of them.

As they embraced, André whispered in her ear.

'Yes, I'm up for it too, babe, but let's check the flight times first. You need to be in London soon; I'll keep in touch and feed you everything we can from here. I'll order up a car for the airport, and if we've got time, we'll fill it until he comes. If we haven't, you book yourself a real nice London hotel and I'll be with you in less than a week.'

'One of us has to be here, André,' she whispered back.

'Well, that applies for as long as I haven't fixed it. I'll fix it. We've got some useful guys who can watch the store, at least for a few days while I'm in London.'

As it turned out, there wasn't enough time for both sex and packing, and ever practical as they usually were, the packing won. Amélie had enough for at least a week in London, with a promise of more to be forwarded should she need it.

On the way to the airport, Amélie briefed her partner on all she knew about Maddox and McAdams. André, of course, knew some big time financial journalists who would not only be able to fill him in about the Maddox and McAdams holdings, but also add any further information about their friends. Amélie waved until the plane had risen clear of the ground; people who should be on her side sometimes actually were, she thought. It mattered.

In the Surrey countryside, John Maddox owned a four-year-old purpose-built house with seven en-suite bedrooms and every possible convenience. It included a private suite of bedroom, study and lounge, where he could work, and sometimes even sleep, without being disturbed by other members of the Maddox family. They were under strict instructions to phone through to the paternal quarters before entering them, but there was little danger of either of the two boys, Matthew aged sixteen and Peter aged fourteen, or their sister Monica, aged nineteen, seriously considering trying to enter their father's inner sanctum. John Maddox was the kind of man whose presence made people uncomfortable, people including his children and even his wife, Rosalyn, who had a suite of her own. He was likely to question even casual remarks made in his direction and he tended to regard time spent not working as wasted time. All his children, as far as he was concerned, were heading for university, and the fact that Monica had already started did nothing to ease the pressures on the two boys. Monica, at her father's urging, had chosen law, John considering that having a lawyer in the family whose services would come at reasonable cost could be a huge plus. Matthew, as yet, had chosen rebellion, but his father saw it as largely a 'phase he was going through'.

Rosalyn Maddox took a different view of her children, largely because she knew that her marriage did not have much life left in it, and when the crunch came, at least two of the children would legally be adults, meaning custody would not be an issue and the amount of contact each parent had would be determined by the quality of their relationships with their children. Her husband, she knew, was a serial womaniser, and she knew also the kind of women he womanised with, ambitious girls looking to get on in the world, for whom a rich, powerful man was an essential gatekeeper to the places where they wanted to be. She kept up appearances; with her faintly aristocratic background, largely about cousins on her mother's side, she knew she was still enough of a trophy wife to stop John ditching her without reason, and she had more than enough evidence of her own to stop it when she was good and ready, which was not yet.

So the Maddox household operated as five largely autonomous regions, with Monica's quarters kept just as they were for when she returned from university. Of the three children, Monica was the one who most resembled her father and the only one, as yet, who had admitted any intention of going into the family business, which was about controlling and developing the Maddox portion of the Gilrey Corporation.

John Maddox had a screen in his study that could connect him to whoever in the world he wanted to speak to, and at the moment, the person that was most likely to be would be Donald McAdams, solid old Big Mac, his easy-going manner like the concealed teeth of the piranha fish. John knew that Mac would dispose of him as soon as he thought he could, but it didn't concern him unduly, as he knew he would do exactly the same with Mac as soon as the opportunity arose. The fact that they hunted together did not stop them being tigers.

Mac's bland smiling face was there before him once again, and it evoked the usual strangely energising combination of respect and contempt in John Maddox. They wasted no time in formalities.

'Amélie is on her way to the airport, Mac. That didn't take long.'

'No. Well, it wouldn't, would it?' Mac smiled his habitual beamer, for no good reason that Maddox could see.

'So what do we do? Offer her fifty million pounds on the plane? Get someone from Air Canada to divert the plane to Kabul?'

Mac beamed again.

'Very droll, John. In Amélie's case, there isn't much point in stopping her getting to London. She can speak to her mother anytime in any case. It's what she does when she gets there which matters. And what may have happened back home in Canada in the meantime.'

'And what do we want to happen in Canada in the meantime?'

'Oh, heavens, John. You really should do your homework, you know.' Mac picked up a piece of paper in front of him.

'Delatour Hotels, as in all four of them. Nice places, very lucrative. Seventy per cent controlled by the Delatour family, but they're an odd lot, half French, half English, and one or two with problems which wouldn't make them too difficult to detach from the herd, as it were, if we had to. But I don't think it need come to that.'

'Oh, yes? Sounds promising.'

'They borrowed a fair bit of money, or more specifically André did, to set the business up, and they borrowed most of it from banks, as they would. Amélie would have been trying to avoid getting Gilrey involved, because she wanted this thing to be about her and André. She wanted them to have their own show.'

'Very touching. Very romantic.'

'Well, possibly. Foolhardy might be another word. The Amélie now seeming so concerned to rescue her stepmother wanted at that time to have her own show, and develop it all the way, just like her daddy did.'

'Yes, I see that. So are we going to get to whatever the point is here, Mac?'

Mac sighed.

'John, John. Sometimes I think you have no soul. The point is when the banks start hearing rumours about Delatour possibly floating on thin ice, they may well want to call in loans, and then dear Amélie will have only one way to rescue her own show, which is let the shares go, or at least some of them. And Amélie is the eldest. Where she goes, the others are likely to follow. Domino effect, John. It could be over before the meeting.'

Maddox smiled in his own way, a kind of baring of the lips. 'Which is where I come in, I suppose.'

'Got it in one, John, as you always do, of course. Firstly, get on to all the brokers you know, a nervy lot at the best of times. Start the whisperers whispering. Find something plausible; Delatour over-ambitious development plans, Delatour's occupancy rates diving, maybe even Madame Delatour jetting off to London to fish in big new ponds. The banks will be threatening to pull the plug soon enough.'

'Which will put the question up to Amélie, presumably; who comes first, husband or mother? Her business or Mummy's business?'

'Possibly. It might work, it might not. But there are other options if it doesn't. Amélie is also very indulgent towards all her siblings, perhaps partly because none of them are actually her biological siblings. The one compensates for the other. We are not short of levers, John. But it makes sense to try the most obvious, the most logical, first.'

'OK, Mac. And while I'm blowing up a stink about Delatour, what will you be doing?'

'Well, when we decide to go on the offensive, we must also make sure that our own house is in order. As you know, I was foolish enough to let three per cent of the shares land in the lap of a certain peer of the realm who we needed to go through the right lobby for us. It seems that he belonged to the same club as Hugo Gilard and he was rather shaken by Gilard's death. We can't afford to let even three per cent leak, John.'

'So what have you got, for God's sake, on a peer of the realm?'

'Enough.'

Mac let loose another of his inexplicable beamers, which could be roughly translated as 'that's for me to know and you to guess at'. Maddox wondered once again just how devious a web this spider weaved, and whether he himself was one of the flies already ensnared in it. Not for the first time, John Maddox wondered whether or not he should be doing something about Mac, something which would leave his own leadership absolute and unimpaired. But for the moment, the relationship remained master and pupil, with himself very much the latter.

'OK, Mac. Perhaps we'll talk again when I've done the business re Delatour?'

'Yes, of course, John. Bye till then.'

Mac smiled one last time, but this time the smile disappeared before the image faded away, and Maddox caught a glimpse of the hunter in his natural state, hard-eyed and straight-mouthed.

Those who sup with the devil, he thought, need a very long spoon.

Val was there to meet Amélie when she landed at Heathrow. As usual, Val had everything immaculately arranged, and after a long, lingering embrace, which expressed the anxieties of both women and their delight at being together once again, two beefy suited men took charge of Amélie's cases and packed them into the back of a big corporation Bentley.

On the back seat, the obvious questions came first.

'How's André?' said Val, with the usual underlying resigned inflection of 'same as ever'.

'Not at his best, Mum.'

Amélie had finally settled on Val as 'mum' only some ten years ago, but the very fact of it taking so long contributed to making it irreversible.

'He didn't see why I needed to go back to England when I've already been here just a few weeks ago. For André, me going back to England is like his wife deserting him for her mother. I had to finally make him realise just how big the Corporation is, and I wasn't too subtle about doing it. He's got the message now, but I'm still not sure if that's a good thing or a bad. You should have seen his eyes when I told him what my five per cent is worth.'

'I don't know what you told him. They're already several pounds per share up just on yesterday. And they're showing no sign of slowing down.'

The car stopped at yet another of the interminable traffic lights.

'Mum, jet lag or not, I have to ask you this, because I don't entirely understand it. You know you could sell those shares tomorrow and you would be an extremely wealthy woman, fixed up in comfort for the rest of your life and still able to leave money to all of us if you wanted to. What is so wrong with that prospect? Yes, I know it was a business built up by you and Dad, but ultimately, it managed to kill Dad and that's when there were two of you. It worries me that maybe you're looking to work yourself into an early grave to be with him, and I know that's as much a selfish anxiety as one for you alone. We need you here – me, Austin, Paul and Jenny and the kids too – and we all want to see you relaxed and living in the style you deserve after working all your life.'

Amélie had been gazing forward as she spoke, to concentrate on getting the words right, and now she looked across at her stepmother. Val was in tears. Amélie could see the driver's eyes flicking across towards Val, the expression in them clearly saying, 'you've only just got off the plane and you've got her weeping like a baby. What is the matter with you?' Amélie ventured an arm across to her stepmother's shoulder. Oddly enough, she had never had the same intimate, tactile relationship with Val that she had had with her father.

'Darling,' Val eventually said, very quietly. 'I can't hope to answer that properly without being in Gilrey H.Q., because, yes, it is an emotional issue, but it isn't just that, it's about the practicalities and well-being of other people's lives.'

'I'm sorry, Mum, I didn't mean to upset you.'

'No, I know you didn't, darling. I'm still a bit fragile, I'm afraid. We'll talk soon.' Meaning shut up for the moment, Amélie thought, and she gazed out at the noise and bustle of daytime London, which she had always found both exciting and intimidating simultaneously, perhaps after her predominantly rural upbringing. It occurred to her that the worth of her shares meant that she could live comfortably, even here, and the siren whisper of temptation, which had always lurked in the background ever since she realised the full worth of her shares, sounded again.

In the splendour of the Gilrey M.D.'s office, Amélie felt very young and very out of her depth. She had only ever been in this place a few times, and then it was very much her father's domain. The imposing dimensions of the place, the prevalence of dark polished wood and forbidding iron cabinets, gave the place a heavily masculine feel, and though Val had done her best with vases of flowers and some lightly coloured décor, it still seemed to Amélie to be very much her father's territory.

They moved away from the enormous desk and sat in a more informal armchaired area nearer the imposing views of the London skyline. Val took a thick file from one of the cabinets and laid it on the coffee table in front of her.

'Of course, everything is computerised now, but I'm afraid there are still aspects of the *ancien régime* which I find difficult to abandon. These are some of my personal files on Gilrey employees, and whenever I am feeling old-fashioned and clinging on to power, I have a look at some of these to remind me of the difference between the Corporation in the hands of the Gilard family and the Corporation as it would be if and when these persistent and opportunistic men get their hands on it.

'I'm not going to ask you to wade your way through it, darling; I'll just give you a sample of the kind of people we're talking about. One man in here is a guy who worked for me before Gilrey was ever thought of, in my first restaurant, By the Brook, the place where I met your father. He is rather old and frail now, and he has nothing but the state pension and the pension that he gets from Gilrey. I know that Maddox and McAdams both take the view that Gilrey should be reorganised and refinanced as a totally new company, thereby jettisoning any legal commitment to former Gilrey employees. I know they would be a lot happier to get rid of Gilrey's entire pension liability, regardless of any moral obligations and whoever gets dropped in it as a result.

'There are also a whole bunch of cases in here referring to people who work in departments which Maddox and McAdams have it in mind to "rationalise", which in plain English means throwing large numbers of people out of work. I know many of the people who will come into this category, and again they include some who have worked loyally for your father and I for years, people who have families and mortgages.

'The men who want to take over the board argue that businesses need a certain amount of ruthlessness to make a decent profit. That business leaves no room for sentiment. But Gilrey has always made money *and* treated its people decently; I would argue that the two go together. If you treat people with meanness and contempt, they will return the favour. If they know they can be made redundant at any time, with no comeback, they will not bother about loyalty to the company; they will cheat and pilfer and take short cuts as much as they think they can get away with, and the chances are that they will get away with it, because none of the people who should be motivated to stop them will be bothered to do so.

'It's all too easy for me to decide to take the money and run, but while I'm sunning myself in the south of France or wherever else I finish up, I'm afraid I just won't be able to put out of my head the kind of things Maddox, McAdams and their friends will be doing to people who have rendered this company – my company – good and loyal service. For me, being as rich as Croesus is no use when you know you've sold so many people you esteem down the river. But here we are; you make a kindly inquiry and I burst into tears, and now we are sitting in this awesomely unsettling place while I lecture you like an old schoolmarm. How are you, darling Amélie, really, and how's André?'

'I'm well enough, Mum, and so is he. And I can tell you from the outset that we're on your side absolutely. If that is the kind of vision that Maddox and McAdams have for this organisation, and I can quite believe it – I've met both of them, and Big Mac's funny old uncle act never fooled me for a minute – the family is duty bound to gather together and help out in whatever way we can. Of course, there never has been a time when my siblings could be guaranteed to do anything which I might want them to do, but if we combine forces, I suspect we can bring them all with us.'

'Wonderful, darling, and lovely to have you home. But you must be jetlagged and tired, and I'm forcing all this on you before you've had time to take a breath. I suggest we adjourn immediately to the Gilard country seat, which you will be much more familiar with than you are with this place, and there we can take it easy and talk tactics.'

Sitting on a balcony that evening, with a table between them supporting a good bottle of white wine and two glasses, Val and Amélie looked out over spreading English countryside, only broken, on a good visibility day, by thin road tracks and a few distant high London buildings. Val's first dread, that her stepdaughter might have returned to tell her, with the greatest respects and regrets, no doubt, that her main priority now was Delatour Hotels, had mercifully been laid to rest. She reflected that it had been her near-panic about that which had caused her to take Amélie straight to Gilrey H.Q.; bringing her back to the family country seat might have been a better idea in the first place.

She glanced across at her stepdaughter. Amélie, fortunately, did not resemble her natural mother in most ways, but in profile the resemblance was quite striking. Was it this, Val thought, a suspicion engendered by the knowledge that Amélie was not her natural daughter, which made her so insecure about trusting her fully? The girl had never given her any obvious reason to suspect her loyalty; she had been upfront from the start about her wish to live abroad, at least for a while, and her ideas about going into the hotel business.

She'd had other partners before André, but she had been very careful not to get too involved until she decided who it was going to be, and André, in spite of his mother-in-law's initial suspicions, had so far proved to be at least a reasonable choice.

Val poured the wine and took a generous sip from her own glass.

'You should be meeting up with Austin very soon. He's also promising to come back to London for the meeting.'

'Good. It'll be nice to see him again. Where is he now, anyway?'

'Just at the moment, he's on the Costa del Sol. I don't know whether you remember, but he was always adamant that he could make a better job of running a pub than his father ever did, and that's proved to be the case. I backed him with the leases of a couple of London pubs and he made them pay soon enough. He has most of his father's virtues; he's good at being mine host, he's got a head for figures and he's a very competent organiser. And he doesn't, as yet anyway, show much sign of his father's vices; he doesn't use his head for figures to gamble his money away, and he doesn't drink his own merchandise in large quantities. He's not just a businessman; he's good company with it.'

'That's good to hear. But why the Costa del Sol?'

'He got the idea that if he was going to make a living in the pub business, he might as well do it with decent weather and an outdoor life for him and his family. You know Maureen, his wife, is from the East End?'

'No, I didn't know that. Is it good or bad?'

'Perhaps a bit of both. Her father and brothers are in the pub trade, which is how he met her. She reckoned running a few bars on the Costa was a nicer way of life for their kids than having them running around London getting involved with gangs and God knows what else. Her family had put some money in, and to date, she and Austin have five bars on the Costa. They're doing very nicely for themselves. I've told him that if he ever wanted to buy out Maureen's family, I'll help. They're a bit dodgy, I have to say.'

Amélie looked across, her glass half way to her mouth.

'Great. And do they know he's sitting on forty million pounds' worth of shares?'

'I doubt it. I doubt whether he's even told them he owns five per cent of the company. That's something else he shares with his father; being secretive. But once again, Austin is secretive about things which mean something; his father's secretiveness was about telling me he'd just lost another chunk of the business at the gaming table. I don't think Austin has entirely made up his mind about the Callerton family, even if his wife is one of them.

'He doesn't have any kids as yet, but I think he would much rather have the option of bringing them up himself than letting the Callertons interfere.'

'I had to tell André the story of Gilrey to make it easier for me to come back. What kind of story is Austin going to tell Maureen?'

'Happily, darling,' Val said, 'that's not my business. Or yours. It's Austin's game and he's going to have to play it. But I suspect the story will be that he's coming back to lend his mum moral support, and there are plenty of Callertons around to hold the fort while he does. Selling his shares and breaking with the Callertons doesn't make much sense for him at the moment, because it might mean losing Maureen, who he loves and who's had a lot to do with him making a success of the pub business.'

'It must worry you, Mum.'

Val got up and wandered over to the balcony wall. For a moment, she took in the view and the good country air.

'Yes, it does. Of course it does. I worry about you all, including you, darling, living such a distance away, and in the hotel business, which is never easy. I worry about you never having children, and how that really sits with André…'

'Oh, God, Mum, not all that again. I told you; after the second miscarriage, we decided between us that if it was going to be dangerous and difficult, which is exactly what it was proving to be, we could manage without.'

'Conditions which make pregnancy difficult can be cured. Or you could adopt. It seems such a shame, when you've always been so good with children.'

'Mum. Listen. If Austin has the right to sort his life out the way he wants it, so do I. We've got a lot to do, without bringing up dead issues.'

'Oh, dear. Is that what it is, darling? And when you're my age, who will be sitting where you're sitting now?'

'André, hopefully, Mum. Or maybe a younger friend. In any case, I have no intention of ripping my body apart for further attempts, and I'm already too old to adopt. I'm sorry Austin and Maureen have no children as yet, but I can't do anything about that. Please just accept me as I am. We may have difficult times ahead; we need to unite, not find things to argue about.'

Val kept her peace. She had harboured some hope in the back of her mind that Amélie might see a family crisis as a time to rethink, but the last thing she wanted to do now was to antagonise her daughter, and she knew from past experience just how stubborn Amélie could be when her mind was made up.

Conversation continued on the wider family and comparisons between Canada and the U.K., until Amélie decided a good night's sleep was necessary to prepare for the confrontation ahead.

'We have six days now, darling,' Val said. 'Those two individuals whose fault all this is took advantage of the mourning process, and I think they thought we Gilards would be too weary by the end of it to defy them. I'm looking forward to showing them how wrong they were.'

Even allowing for double glazing and the nearby park land, Montreal was not a quiet environment, and Amélie found the peace of the English countryside soothing, at least for relatively short periods of time. Her idea of having an early night proved better in theory than in practice, however, with various issues revolving in her mind, producing the usual catalogue of unanswerable questions.

By half past eleven, she seemed at last to be sliding away into sleep, and it took her some seconds to place her phone when it sounded its insistent buzz. Amélie didn't believe in lullaby music or tinkling bells for her phone; she wanted to make sure she heard it.

'Hi, babe.' She knew it was André; the voice was familiar enough, but even his two words revealed something in the way of anxiety and tension.

'What is it, André? You never can remember your time zones, can you? It's half past eleven here; I'm in bed.'

'Oh, Jeez. Sorry. I've had such a hell of a day I'm not thinking straight.'

'Why? What's happened?'

'The bank, that's what's happened. Asking a lot of questions about Delatour, what we're doing, occupancy rates, development plans, everything. They want to see our accounts.'

'Well, show them. We have no problems at the moment. How's all this come about?'

'Some fool journalists, picking up on hints that someone is throwing around. Your shares in your big deal Brit corporation may be doing great, but Delatour's shares are not doing too well.

When people start throwing rumours around, there are always plenty of gullible fools ready to believe them.'

'It'll die down, André. This stuff comes and goes. Once the bank are reassured, it will all quieten down.'

Her tone seemed to irritate André.

'Is that right? And what makes you so sure about that? You got some kind of English crystal ball? And how come it's happening just when you are getting ready for your big meeting? If that's a coincidence, it's a hell of a coincidence, and I don't believe in coincidences.

'Someone's leaning on us. Someone wants you to be a good girl and sell them your shares.'

'You're being too suspicious, André. I don't believe they're that clever. Some journalist in Montreal has got hold of the information that I've suddenly flown to England and it might be connected to a big board meeting over here, so they've decided to conclude that I'm planning to leave Delatour and come back to the family firm, because it makes a story for them. Come on, André, you know what they're like. If nothing's happening, they'll make stuff up. If they get a whiff of smoke, they think the world's on fire.'

'You're good at this, babe, aren't you? Maybe you should be a shrink or something.' She laughed, even as her eyes seemed to be closing of their own volition.

'Maybe. But I'm happy enough doing what I'm doing. Let the bank see the books. Put out a statement to the press saying I am visiting my bereaved mother to help her through a difficult period. Ask them to respect the privacy of my family at this time. And let out a few vague threats that legal action might follow if any more unsubstantiated stories start doing the rounds. I'll get a similar statement out here tomorrow. If it is someone trying to influence the meeting, that will give them something to think about. If it isn't, it will shut them up because there was never much there to start with.'

A pause followed at the other end of the line. Amélie began to wonder what was happening, and then André's voice came again, with a very different tone.

'God, you are one hell of a woman. I want to be there in that bed next to you. I could just—'

Amélie giggled. 'I'll bet you could. But I might just fall asleep, babe, I'm afraid. It's been a long day.'

'Yeah, right. Still, I have an imagination, don't I? Talk tomorrow, babe, and you sleep well; you need to feed that gigantic brain of yours.'

A few very frank and intimate remarks followed, and suddenly the blessed silence of the English countryside was resumed. Amélie felt her chances of sleep had just been expunged, but now her mind was full of affectionate memories, and soon after, sleep finally took over.

PART FOUR

Austin's Journey

Thursday September 24th 2015

Austin was, for the moment, taking his ease in the pub/bar he generally regarded as his flagship, the Continental. From a corner of his office, he could see how many customers were eating and/or drinking on the front terrace, and it was currently almost entirely full. He and Maureen were making lots of money, but his in-laws had a habit of hovering about and trying to get in on the act, and if he did what his mother was now asking him to do, he was unsure about what might happen during his absence.

The situation was making him insecure, and he resented it. Ever since the decision had been taken to chance their arm on the Costa del Sol, he had worked hard, and one of the reasons why he had taken it in the first place was to remove himself and his family from the orbit and influence of the Callertons. He hadn't reckoned, at the time, that they would have either the wherewithal to find their way out to Spain or the ability to actually persuade Maureen to let them have even a smell at the business.

He blamed his own weakness. He had seen, clearly enough, his father's decline, apparently driven by personal characteristics that he was unable to control or overcome, notably the gambling addiction. But even as a boy, he could see his father's qualities as well. People liked Maurice, with his relaxed manner, his conscientious attention to being the host, and his fund of jokes and anecdotes. He also kept his accounts in good order, even if time did show him as capable of manipulating them to disguise or enhance what he did or didn't want them to reveal.

He realised at an early age that, whatever else he might have inherited from his father, the gambling urge had missed him altogether; on the contrary, he was very careful with what he had. Maureen had been running a nearby pub when he took over the Essex Arms, which was a pretty rundown traditional boozer at the time. Both Hugo and his mother wanted him to take a job with Gilrey, but he had seen that from the first as more Hugo's business than anything he and his mother should get involved with. He could remember Mum's restaurants, making their way up even as his father's concerns slid away. She had worked very hard to be independent, and while Hugo was a nice enough guy in his own way, Austin thought they could get together, if they must, without Mum's businesses being taken into the new bigger firm.

But it seemed, bewildering as it was to him, that his mother had some sort of hots for Hugo, and he had to admit to himself that all of their lives changed for the better when his mother and Hugo had been married for a few years. He had Amélie to deal with, yes, and that didn't prove too easy at first; she came across to him as a stuck-up snob who regarded him as some horrible imposition on her life that she would much rather not bother with.

But, as time went on and they got to know each other better, they started to talk more and he discovered that she was trying her best to be the way her father wanted her to be, as he was with his mother, and they found a touching point in their mutual anxieties. He also realised that she didn't actually hate him, as he thought she might; she just hadn't had any previous experience of having a brother, as he hadn't of having a sister, so they were both stumbling in the dark to some extent. Then Paul came along, and the whole thing began to feel much more like a family.

Now, of course, Hugo was gone, and his first family loyalty had to be to his mother. But he had a wife as well, and at the very moment when these questions of loyalty went through his head, he saw, down on the terrace, a face turn and he recognised Dan Callerton's unmistakable bulk accompanying it. Dan was Maureen's older brother and he tended to treat the Continental as his second home, not only turning up and eating and drinking 'on the slate' but sometimes having with him some well-known Costa del Sol English runaways and criminals. His companion at the moment was called Mel Downs, a conman and insurance fraudster known to have charges to face in the U.K.

As he watched, Dan clicked his fingers towards Maureen as she and her colleagues were doing their best to serve the increasing numbers of customers.

'Mo!' Dan shouted. 'Two more big ones over here, darling, alright? Bless you.'

One of his father's greatest weaknesses, as Austin remembered, was his apparent terror of confrontation. Apart from some of the guys he played cards with taking him to the cleaners because they were on to all the tricks that Maurice took an age to pick up on himself, there were the drinking hangers-on, pretending to be Maurice's pals in the hope of being invited to one of Maurice's 'lock-ins', when he and his friends would carry on drinking after time – on the house, of course. Maurice let it all happen because he was too easy-going and slapdash to properly deal with people who took advantage.

And now, seeing Dan Callerton, probably the worst of the whole parasitical Callerton mob, ordering his wife about while in the company of known criminals, Austin saw himself already sliding away into the same remorseless downward chute as his father, and he determined that he would not and could not allow it to happen. The widespread maxim that men will always turn into their fathers was something he felt he couldn't afford to believe.

He stamped down into the main bar, his heart accelerating, and called three of his young waiters to him. It had been his policy for a while to appoint fit young men to his serving staff, not because he was sexually inclined in that direction, but because he knew who generally made decisions about where to eat and drink – the women – and an athletic young man showing a fair bit of shoulders, arms and chest tended to be a better come-on to the ladies than nice young girls who their husbands would sit ogling at. The husbands, generally speaking, didn't much care where they ate or drank as long as the beer and the food were decent. Young guys were also better at humping stuff around and more use if and when some punter had had more than was good for him and needed moving along. Almost all of his waiters were Spanish; most of his customers were still Spanish, because much of the menu was designed to cater for them; he needed the Continental to function all year, not just in the summer months. All of his waiters were also bi-lingual, and finding bi-lingual Spaniards was a good deal easier than finding bi-lingual Brits.

Austin also knew that the fact that his establishment was at least as much Spanish as it was British sat well with the local authorities, who knew well enough that some of the English-owned businesses were more accommodating to English criminals than they should be. He was adamant that none of his places, and especially the Continental, were going to become watering holes for Brits on the run or criminals looking to start again in Spain.

With three six-foot-plus Spaniards at his back, Austin walked over to Dan Callerton's table. 'Mr. Downs,' he said quietly. 'I know who and what you are, and you're not welcome in this establishment. Drink up and go.'

'Hang on a minute, Austin, old son,' Dan said, rising slowly to his feet. 'Mel is here as my guest. This is a family business.'

Austin could feel Maureen already hovering uneasily in the background. The moment had come, he felt, for the inevitable confrontation. But he intended to remain in charge.

Shouting and swearing would frighten the clientele; it didn't have to be like that.

'This isn't a family business, Dan, not in the way you mean it. It belongs to my wife and I. If you want to continue eating and drinking here, don't bring known criminals into it. If you do, I'll ban you, Dan. Now I'd be grateful if you'd take yourself somewhere else for a while. We'll see you when we see you.'

Callerton made a move towards him; Austin observed that the other man was not bulky in the muscular sense, he was just fat. The three Spanish boys moved forward in their turn.

Dan Callerton turned towards his sister, standing just five yards away.

'See you later, Mo. Maybe you can calm down your tiger, eh, or he could be getting himself into trouble, know what I mean?'

Austin looked towards his wife, but without much doubt about which way she would turn. Running her own life without being stifled by her family was one of the reasons why she'd married him.

Maureen was holding a tray full of empty glasses; she handed it to one of the boys and approached her brother.

'This is on your own head, Dan. I've told you time and time again that the Continental is not for your dodgy buddies, and we're not having police raids here every other night. Sling it, Dan. We'll talk in a few days, but not here.'

Dan frowned and tutted, but he drank off his beer and left slowly, trundling away like an injured bear.

'Mo, love, we need to talk,' Austin said, as he and his wife walked back into the main bar of the Continental.

'What, about him? No need, Austin. You've marked his card; I'll keep an eye on him. He'll be going home next week.'

'No, not about him. Something much more important than him.'

Austin called across to his bar manager, Diego Alvarez, a tough, middle-aged fixit man from Cadiz, one of his most reliable staff.

'Diego, Señora Foster and I need to be in conference for a while,' Austin said, in the Spanish that his staff always seemed to appreciate. 'Please let me know if Señor Callerton returns to the bar; otherwise, you are in full control.'

Alvarez nodded. Austin and Mo walked into the office, and Austin closed the door. Now he had established in his own mind that he could and would confront when he had to, the time had come to put his cards on the table. He would do what he could not to lose Maureen, but her wider family could no longer be allowed to interfere in anything, and he needed her to see that. Otherwise, he saw himself, in spite of the Corporation money, sliding away into the dead end his father had all too clearly arrived at. And the Corporation money, as he was at last realising, could be much more of an asset and much less of a weight around his neck if he could just start using it properly.

He told Maureen everything, while she sat in the comfortable armchair next to him and her wide-eyed expression stuck fast. He told her what his share of the Corporation was worth and why he had been reluctant to tell her in the past.

'I wanted you to accept me as a businessman in my own right, Mo, not just a son and heir. And I thought that your father and brothers would want even more of the action, meaning we would be forced into argument and I might finish up losing you.'

'So what's changed, Austin? Why tell me now?' Maureen found herself quite surprised that she had recovered her power of speech.

He leaned towards her, his eyes bright.

'Because I want you to understand how free we can be, Mo, if we play our cards right. In another few days, before the big meeting, my shares might reach a value of fifty-five million pounds. Whether my mother sells up or not, she is sixty-seven years old and she will be retiring soon. She just doesn't want to hand her business over to Maddox and McAdams, and with good reason; they're a couple of bandits. I'm sure they think I don't notice what's going on, but I do. If she sells, she'll be worth about £400 million. And I'm one of only four to inherit. We could walk away with fifty million now, or we could stand to inherit £100 million. And I don't want your family to see any of it, Mo. Can you imagine what they would do with that kind of money? Drugs, booze, trafficking, God knows what. You need to break free, Mo. We both do. We need to breathe our own unpolluted air, out of their clutches.'

For a moment, silence fell, as Austin's words remained reverberating around them. To his great distress, tears began to form in Maureen's eyes.

'They made me go on the game, Austin. When I was in my teens and they were trying to keep their bloody pub afloat. "A gorgeous little girl like you, Mo; you don't mind doing a little to help the family kitty, now, do you, girl? Only for a while, darling".'

'Oh, my God.' A great sigh burst from Austin.

'Then I started doing book-keeping, and I told them I'd be more use to them that way than I would be on the streets. I was never very good at that. So they let me do the books; they didn't have a clue about that, and they knew the tax would be after them.'

Austin closed his eyes, and all he could see was fat Dan Callerton, sitting there clicking his fingers. 'Only for a while, darling.' He began to feel sick.

'Then that day you walked in, when you'd started to keep a pub of your own. I never thought you'd take an interest in me.'

Austin breathed in.

'So when you told me you didn't want children—'

'I had to abort one, love. They weren't having it. As of now, it would be very dodgy. But we could look into it, Austin. If that's what you want.'

Austin watched the Mediterranean sun sweep across the terrace of the Continental and listened to the happy buzz of contented customers. What an effort it is, he thought, for all of us to carry on in the teeth of some of the scum around us, working to totally different standards and assumptions. Dan, Tommy and Jack Callerton, one, two, three big hefty boys who did what they wanted with who they wanted, and one little sister trying against the odds to make a decent life for herself.

'It's not what I want, Mo. It's about time you had what you wanted. If you want a kid, we'll do whatever is possible to do. Your bunch of brothers have cheated you of a lot, but they'll cheat you no more.'

He turned away from the window and towards her. It suddenly all seemed very clear. 'Let me tell you what I have in mind, Mo, love. If you like it, that's what we'll do. If you don't, we'll think of something else. We'll go back to England and stay in the countryside with my mother; the Gilard residence is very comfortable and has tight security available if any of your crew should decide to visit, that's if they have any idea where it is, which I doubt. We'll take a bit of time to work out what to do with the family business situation and decide whether we want to keep these Costa del Sol places going. In the meantime, I'll leave Diego in charge of the Continental; he pretty much is anyway, but I'll give him a rise and a kind of boss status. And I'll give him very specific instructions that Dan, Tommy and Jack are not welcome in the Continental either individually or all together; I'll tell him he can take on more boys if he needs to, but I doubt whether he will. What do you say?'

Maureen answered him with a long, tight embrace.

'Forget about the past, Mo, if you can. Let's concentrate on the future.'

After that, it needed only the preparations and formalities, or so they both thought. Austin returned to the Continental for a full briefing with Diego. As he anticipated, his Spanish manager was keen enough on the idea, and had a suggestion of his own to add to it.

'My brother Alejandro is a police inspector only just ten miles away, señor. He left Cadiz at the same time as I did; we were looking for work, and we thought getting nearer to the tourist money would increase our chances. I know part of his work is concentrating on British renegades. I don't often invite him to the Continental, because I didn't know how well you would like the idea. But if he is seen here from time to time, I think we wouldn't see much of Señora Foster's brothers or others like them.'

'That's good thinking, Diego. Please invite him as often as you like. And you have my number; don't hesitate to use it as and when you need to. I have some family business to sort out in the U.K., but that won't stop us talking as and when we need to.'

The flight tickets were bought for the next day. Before leaving the Continental, Austin made a phone call to his mother.

'Mo and I would like to join you in the countryside, Mum, if that's alright, but if it isn't, we'll book a decent hotel somewhere nearby.'

'Oh, heavens, there's no need for that, Austin. I've spent a fair time rattling around this place on my own; I'll enjoy your company. Amélie is here with me.'

'Good; I haven't seen her in a while. André as well?'

'No, André is holding the fort in Montreal. But don't think that makes Maureen any less welcome. It's nice to have the family gathering around me.'

As he put down the phone, something like homesickness came over Austin, and a feeling of weariness with the ups and downs of hospitality businesses. But he knew both emotions were superficial, and his real task over the coming days was to do what he could to rescue the family business. And to come to some kind of terms with what Mo had told him.

Maddox and McAdams were in conference again, but at close quarters this time, in a very nice West End restaurant favoured by Big Mac. John Maddox always thought of his partner as 'old school', and while he personally distrusted what he called 'food fetishism', generally satisfying himself with moderate amounts of 'ordinary food', the place was quiet and private. And the wine, of course, was excellent.

'It seems chick number two is on the point of flying back to the nest,' McAdams said, as he continued the demolition of his substantial steak.

'Meaning Valerie has her fifty per cent, presumably.'

'Probably. But we have a few more options to put into practice yet. Austin is not a million miles from his stepsister in respect of wanting his own show, after all those years under Daddy's big wings, and I think, while obviously not in the anatomical sense, that Amélie has the bigger balls.'

'You admit defeat, then, in your attempt to undermine Delatour Hotels? She has certainly mounted a spirited defence.'

'Yes. She is her father's daughter, and Gilrey could do a lot worse than have her in charge after her mother's retirement.'

'Oh.' Maddox looked puzzled. 'In that case, Mac, what are we about?'

McAdams sighed. John Maddox could be trying; he was an efficient enough operator, but his grasp of affairs could be limited; it seemed constantly to be necessary to spell out implications and consequences to him as if to a novice.

'You don't really believe I'm engaged in all this for the benefit of Gilrey, do you, John? For heaven's sake, man, I don't want to spend the rest of my business career dancing to the Gilrey tune. Hugo was a particularly resilient and intelligent opponent; it took him less time than most to work out what I was at, and I respected him in many ways. But I have never thought I'd ever settle for always being the monkey and never the organ grinder. Having Gilard's daughter in charge might prove to be just as difficult as Gilard himself, and time would then be on the Gilard side rather than mine.

'I want us to run the show, John, and I mean us, because I think you and I would be a match, more than a match, for whichever

Gilard or Gilards remain in charge. Gilrey has been a success, but it could be much, much more, but for the sentimentality and muddled thinking which causes them to drain away invaluable resources on non-productive schemes such as catastrophically expensive pensions. We could take Gilrey, under a new name, of course, to great heights, mega-heights, make a real name for it, with all the clout and yes, wealth, which that entails.'

Maddox smiled. 'OK, Mac, I'm suitably pep-talked. Now what about Mr. Austin Foster and his five per cent?'

McAdams took a long sip of wine and paused for a moment; dramatic effect, Maddox thought, why the hell waste it on me?

'In the case of Mr. Foster, who my Costa del Sol informant tells me has already left the Continental in the charge of a Spanish manager, I do think it would be easier to threaten his little group of five bars. But Austin is actually his mother's son, and whereas Amélie would not be at all happy with the idea of Delatour being subsumed into the Gilrey empire, Austin's little show, Foster Investments, I think it's called, could very easily be taken under Mummy's wing without Austin grousing all that much about it; it will give him ideas that he might be able to take over Gilrey himself, as the oldest son.'

'Mummy might love him dearly, but Mummy isn't that stupid. Neither is Amélie.'

'No, quite, but Austin might not realise that. No, I think in Austin's case, it's about playing the man, not the ball.'

'Oh, God, football analogies. Spell it out, Mac.'

'There are matters which Austin probably doesn't want Mummy to know. The fact that his wife was, for a time, a prostitute, I suspect is certainly one of them. As is the criminal record of two of her brothers, who have both been in prison.'

At moments like this, John Maddox always found himself examining the man in front of him, to see if any sign of the monster within would ever show itself on that bland, urbane face. McAdams continued to smile benignly.

'I won't bother to ask you how you come to know that, knowing how keen you are on protecting your networks. But if you say so with such confidence, I don't doubt that it is true. So what are we talking about, Mac? Blackmail? I'm not particularly keen on acquiring a criminal record myself, or doing time, as they call it.'

'Give me a little credit, John. Nothing so obvious, or not for us, in any case. We will acquaint Austin with the fact that certain journalists have become aware that his wife is an ex-prostitute and a member of a family of habitual criminals. He will be told that there will be no comeback if he removes himself from corporate life by selling at least two per cent of his shares to someone who is not a member of his family. If he doesn't do it by a stated date, articles will begin to appear in national papers.'

Both men paused for thought, also including eating and drinking, while they assimilated the idea along with their dinners.

'We will need to be extremely careful that not even the faintest whiff of it gets back to us,' Maddox said eventually. 'And as we are already widely seen as the beneficiaries of any of the family who sell outside the family, how can a whiff of it not get back to us?'

'It will be a bit whiffy, yes. You can't spread shit without rural aromas. But a whiff isn't enough for anyone to do much about. Journalists have gone to prison rather than reveal their sources, because they know that, if they do, their business is finished. And the fact that someone is fighting very hard to get Gilrey out of the hands of the Gilards will not go unnoticed by all members of the family, especially if any of the rest of them have secrets they don't want anyone to know about.'

Maddox smiled again, with the intention of demonstrating to his partner how much he admired his tactical brain. However, the smile was really about how much material he would have in his data banks about good old Mac when the time finally came to put him out to grass. Ultimately, Maddox didn't believe in power sharing.

As they made their way through Heathrow Airport, Austin and Maureen felt a sense of relief and escape. They had pre-arranged a taxi to take them all the way to the Gilard country seat, and the prospect of a comfortable ride and a quiet, well-equipped refuge at the end of it helped them make their way through the endless airport formalities.

The rude interruption, when it came, therefore, was all the more disturbing. A casually dressed young man suddenly approached them at a fast walk, thrust an envelope into Austin's hand and immediately disappeared into the crowds. They had no real time or opportunity to notice what he looked like or attempt to see any distinguishing characteristics, because there didn't appear to be any.

Austin opened it and took out a single sheet of paper. He glanced through it, and it seemed to Maureen that, tanned as he was, his complexion had paled by the end of his reading.

'What is it, Austin?' she said.

Austin looked about him, as if expecting some other stranger to approach.

'We'll talk about it in the taxi, Mo,' he said. 'The main thing is to get out of these crowds.' Settled on the back seat of the taxi, with the window closed on the driver in front, Austin passed the paper to his wife.

'It's pretty vile stuff, Mo,' he said. 'But there are things we can do about it.' Mo scanned the paper before her; it was unsigned and undated.

> Dear Mr. Foster,
>
> It has come to our notice that your wife Maureen spent some time as a prostitute and two of her brothers have served prison sentences. In view of the size and public exposure of the Gilrey Corporation, it has to be said that this is a public interest matter as well as a family

concern. Many thousands of investors and bankers may be perturbed that such hefty shareholders as yourselves are in such a vulnerable situation, and some will undoubtedly question whether people with criminal pasts and records should be in such positions of wealth and influence.

We feel, therefore, that it is in the public interest to pass the information described above into the hands of the press, unless, of course, you and your wife are prepared to place your Gilrey holdings in other hands and retreat into private life, in which case such details concerning Maureen and her family will be of no interest or business relevance to anyone but the family themselves.

We would emphasise to you that your failure to retire from the Gilrey Corporation into private life will therefore result in the past records of your wife and her family passing into the hands of journalists only too willing to receive such information in the public interest.

Yours regretfully, A Well-wisher.

Maureen put the paper to one side as if it was impregnated with poison.

'Bastards,' she said. 'There's always been some in the East End jealous of the Callertons, but this is ridiculous.'

'Yes,' Austin said, as he watched London fading away into countryside. 'It is ridiculous. It's also vindictive and vicious. And I would put fair odds on it being something to do with the people who are trying to take control of Gilrey. They want to take our shares out of the running; they don't even care who we sell them to, because as soon as we do sell them, they'll buy them back. We need to talk to my mother.'

'Talk to your mother? You mean you want me to tell your mother that I used to be a prostitute? What would that tell her about her daughter-in-law? I don't think I'm her flavour of the month to start with, Austin. This will give her the perfect excuse to get me out of your family; she will pay for the divorce herself.'

Austin turned towards her, and she tried to read his eyes. A man generally amiable and unflappable is not always easy to interpret; had he already come to his own conclusions? But his next remark set them on a different train of thought altogether.

'You said this happened some years ago. How old were you, Mo, when they first sent you out on to the streets?'

'It wasn't for long, Austin; less than two years. And at first I was just seventeen.' Austin suddenly and unexpectedly smiled.

'In that case, Mo, we're not talking about prostitution; we're talking about child abuse.'

'That's what I told them. But they said sixteen was the age of consent for girls.'

'And so it is. But you didn't consent, did you? You were forced into it. If we put a decent law firm up against your family it wouldn't take them long to establish that. That's assuming it ever got as far as a court. No journalist would go near it. Championing child abuse; that's how it will be seen. Well, it will be when the Gilrey lawyers have finished with it.'

Mo felt a sudden surge of tears.

'And what will be left of my family then, Austin? Nothing, not for me or for them.' Austin put one arm around his wife.

'It won't come to that, Mo. Honestly. They won't try to slog it out against the strength of the Corporation. I know that sounds terrible, when you talk about organisations against people, but sometimes you need power behind you and some people deserve to have power behind them. When I first met you, Mo, in the first of those Callerton pubs, it really resounded with me that you were so different from them, and that such success as the Callerton outfit had achieved up to then was mostly down to you. You were too big for them, and what's more, you were too good for them.

But I don't want to destroy them; I just want to get you out of their clutches once and for all. When they understand that's what's happened, you could have the basis of a whole new relationship with them.'

'Yes, perhaps, Austin, though after all that's happened, I'm not sure I want any kind of relationship with them. It's my relationship with your mother and your sister I'm worried about at the moment. I don't want to spend the rest of my life with them looking down their nose at me and making me feel I'm only in their family to be tolerated.'

Austin sighed and glanced out of the window again. The landscape was almost entirely countryside now, and he felt a sense of great relief at being back in his own country with people he knew well. Somehow he had to convince Maureen of what he knew by instinct; yes, his instinct could occasionally be wrong, but he didn't think it would be in this case. Mo was now looking uneasily across at him, as if suspecting that this might be the prelude to a row, even before they had reached the Gilard country home. A wave of cold terror passed over her, in spite of the relaxing scenery, that she might find herself on her own again shortly, with no place left to go but back to her family, with her disgrace now public and her past life exposed to thousands, perhaps millions, of people.

Austin started slowly and rather hesitantly, which sounded to Mo like the beginning of a classic 'we must end it now' speech. She felt frozen to the spot, and only began to relax again when she began to appreciate the full drift of what he was saying.

'Even when you know someone well, it's not easy sometimes to predict what they will do or say, and I know my mother and Amélie better than almost anyone else in my life. I grew up with Amélie, and even though she's not my natural sister and we started off by hardly being able to stand the sight of each other, we kind of grew into the relationship, quite literally, and now we're brother and sister in every way which matters. And I know of her that she doesn't pass judgement on people. Her business is hospitality, and even though hers is rather different from mine in a number of ways, some of the basic rules apply to both. You have to be able to get on with people, not only as customers and clients but also as employees, and if you're the type of person who gets up on your high horse about this, that and the other, all those people are unlikely to place much trust or respect in you; they're more likely to fear and resent you, because we are all vulnerable in one way or another. She's also well aware of what power is about, and its uses and misuses. You only have to look at the near slave labour stuff which some hotel chains use to keep their establishments going to know about power relationships. Amélie is no-one's push over, but she's not a power-crazy tyrant either, and when she sees people oppressed in some way, she will always be on the side of the oppressed, not the oppressor. Unless she's changed a lot in the last few years when I haven't seen so much of her. But I doubt it.'

'Good for her. But what about your mother?'

'Oh, she is the same but even more so. She started at the bottom, trying to run a pub while my father gambled the takings away. I employ scores of people, Amélie employs hundreds, Valerie employs thousands. Mum's feeling for her employees is one of the main reasons why she's fighting to keep the Corporation in her own hands; she knows well enough that the men who want control are unlikely to give a damn about anything or anyone but comfortable profit margins and high share prices.'

Austin, surprised at the emergence of such an unusual rush of words, slowed down and held his wife closer.

'What I'm trying to say, Mo, and taking a long time about it, is that my mother and sister will be on your side when they know what's happened in your life, if they are consistent with all that I know about them. And if, for some reason, they're not, I will sell all the damn shares we have and we'll retire to some place which never gets English newspapers, set up a new business all of our own and make sure nobody ever bothers you about the past again.'

Mo kissed him gently on his cheek. 'Bless you, Austin Foster. Now why don't we just open a window a touch and get a good lung full of country air.'

They spent the rest of the journey in silence, and soon they were approaching the impressive Georgian edifice that represented the Gilard family country home. Mo couldn't help recalling the terror she had felt on her first visit here, a feeling largely alleviated by the way Hugo Gilard made a special effort to make her feel welcome. Austin, too, was remembering his stepfather, who somehow epitomised and personified the whole spirit of the Gilard family. He wondered how his mother could live from day to day with the continuing simultaneous presence and absence of Hugo.

They were warmly welcomed, as ever, and shown to their room, a rather grander affair than the one of Austin's adolescence, which had not been equipped with a large en-suite bathroom and access to a balcony overlooking the countryside. Their villa in the Costa del Sol was far from basic, but there was a grandeur, a permanence, about this house that both relaxed and uplifted all those who knew it belonged to their own family.

Val's approach to catering varied enormously from visitor to visitor. If the person or persons concerned were prospective business associates who needed to be impressed or entertained, she would push the boat out by inviting in caterers. However, family members or family friends needed a different, more intimate approach, and on such occasions, she would either do the cooking herself or work jointly with one of the local chefs she knew.

This particular occasion was as family as it could be, and it amused Austin to see how all of them reverted to their former family roles. Austin had always been a willing helper, even if outside the actual process of producing the food. He had been rather overawed, as a young teenager, when the family had first started living at the place, and he relished the experience of having a full family around him, rather than it just being him and his mother, as it had been for much of his childhood.

He volunteered to set the table, and the feelings of déjà vu became very powerful as he put out the place mats, cutlery, etc. while he listened to the three women in the kitchen working together. Amélie, he knew, was as good a cook as his mother, and Mo, while her range of cuisine might be more limited, was reliable and knowledgeable.

He could tell how amicable or otherwise the women's conversation was without needing to hear the actual words they were saying. The dining room was a sizeable space, as was the kitchen, and when he was working on the table, the noise was mostly a good-natured buzz, with footsteps and occasional peals of laughter punctuating the sound. They were having the same kinds of conversation as had been going on ever since he and Mo arrived: comparisons between their journeys, how London is looking and what still needed doing in relation to its public transport and infrastructure, the improvements they'd been making to their own homes, new fashions they had seen lately.

In this situation, Austin was happy, as he had been as a boy, just to listen or talk to his father or, more recently, to his younger stepbrother Paul or his cousin Jennifer. But now there was no competing noise to the sounds of the kitchen, which made it all the more noticeable when they suddenly changed. While the conversation before had been quite loud and cheerful, it suddenly assumed a different tone; quieter, more hesitant, with pauses and questions.

He knew, almost immediately, that Mo had said something to Amélie and his mother. Mo had jumped the gun, perhaps in her eagerness to know how the information about her past would be received.

'No, not now, girl,' he muttered to himself. He had finished the table by now and was looking out of the dining room window at the courtyard, one of the first sights to be seen on entering the precincts of the house. Here he would sometimes stand, as a boy, waiting for his 'new dad's' car to appear. He and his new dad shared a taste for nice cars, and it made him feel warm inside to see the gleaming Beamer or Jaguar sweep into the courtyard, and the suited figure of his stepfather emerge. Hugo would sometimes wave, and Austin would wave back. It had rarely been the characteristic homecoming of his real father, who would often look hangdog or guilty, as he usually, poor Maurice, did have something or other to feel guilty about.

His memories were disturbed by Valerie and Amélie sweeping into the room, carrying dishes before them.

'Table thoroughly set as ever, Austin,' Val said, in a voice which suggested a kind of forced cheerfulness. 'Well done, darling.'

She turned to go back to the kitchen, but Amélie stepped across to Austin at the window. 'Mo's been telling us something of what's been going on, Austin. We think it might be Maddox and McAdams again.'

'Mo thinks it's people in the East End who have become enemies of her family. You don't muscle in on other people's pubs without making enemies.'

'Maybe. I don't know what the hallmarks of that would look like. But I know what Maddox and McAdams hallmarks look like. André and I have already had a dose of it ourselves, with these mysterious attempts to undermine Delatour.'

'Well, yes, but that's business stuff, isn't it? This thing against Mo is personal, a bit below the belt even for those guys.'

'I wouldn't bet on that. They are nothing if not versatile.' Val came back into the room, bearing more dishes.

'I think I know what you two are talking about, as you're bound to do. But I suggest we sit down and enjoy our dinner first; we don't want Mo to feel awkward about anything. We'll talk it over after dinner, when we can relax with a few drinks.'

It wasn't difficult to avoid a contentious subject during dinner; Austin and Amélie hadn't seen each other for several months, and exchanging information and progress in the very different scenarios of Canada and the Costa del Sol could have covered several dinners.

Absence had drawn the siblings together, and the atmosphere was so literally familiar that Val couldn't help but give rise once again to a theme that often preoccupied her.

'Here we are having a nice family get-together in our lovely British country house, which at the moment we can only do, it seems, once every several months when both of you happen to be in your home country at the same time. Why don't you both just come home and work here, and we can be together as a family pretty much all the time?'

After a brief, thick silence, Amélie was the first to speak.

'Mum, we've been through this before. Many times. If it was just a matter of being a family, then perhaps it would all be easy and pleasant enough, though I would remind you that my husband is Canadian; this isn't his home country. But we're not just a family, are we? We're a corporation. While I'm in Canada, I'm pretty much a private citizen; yes, my business is Delatour, but it's mine and André's. I would think Austin feels the same about Spain. We can be free of the Corporation and the interest of the dear British press.'

'Yes, Mum, Amélie is right. I'm a businessman in Spain, but it's my business. I don't have to watch out for whoever is seeing me going in and out of meetings, or have my time wasted with one of those people who have a foolproof scheme for me to invest all my money. It's lower key than growing up in the royal family, but it's always there.'

Val put down her knife and fork and gazed suspiciously around her.

'So what are we saying here? Is this some kind of roundabout way of telling me you're already thinking of selling your shares?'

'No, Mum, no! There's no need to accuse us of disloyalty; we've never been that. But I think we need to know where we stand – well, Austin will speak for himself, of course, but for me, I am entirely committed to helping you fight off the takeover, and I'm sure we will between us. But what happens then? You can't go on indefinitely, Mum, and after losing Dad so recently, I don't think I could face you going the same way without ever having had the chance of a decent retirement. When we've seen off Maddox and McAdams and you have your own guys in there, what happens then?'

'I don't think there's any of that I could disagree with,' Austin said.

Mo looked from one member of the family to another and increasingly felt out of her depth. She knew that she would shortly have to make her feelings known in this gathering if she was not to be seen as Austin's doormat for the rest of her life, but the group of Gilards seemed to bind themselves in a tight group to keep others out. She waited for her moment, knowing that if it didn't arrive soon, she would have to create it.

'Well,' Val said, hesitantly at first, 'I am rather hoping it will be possible for me to hand it on. Both of you are successful business people, and you generally get on well enough with each other. You've both finished up in a line of work which is not too dissimilar to the Corporation's, and you're both successfully partnered with people who will support you in your private life. Along with Jenny and Paul, the Corporation could remain as a thoroughly successful family affair which would provide generous livings for you and whoever came after you.'

Austin and Amélie exchanged glances, their expressions suggesting something along the lines of 'where do we start?' And into the suddenly deep and lengthening void, Mo felt obliged to make her feelings known.

'I don't want to speak out of turn, and I know I've managed to come here and force on you a problem which we are going to talk about later, but which I think you could have done without. I just have to say that Austin works very hard at his business, which is about running five bars on the Costa del Sol. If running the Corporation means I will get to see him even less than I do now, I'm not sure it's something I'm all that keen on, even if it does mean much more money. And again, if you don't mind me saying so, I think you worry too much if you think you won't stay together as a family if you're working in different places. I'm amazed to come here when you haven't seen each other for months and it's as if you'd never been away from each other. A family so natural doesn't have to worry about working in different places.'

Stopped in their tracks, the family were smiling to themselves and at each other. For a moment, Mo thought she had overstepped the mark, but then Val answered.

'I don't think I've ever been shot down in flames quite so charmingly,' she said. 'Thank you, Mo. We'll have other conversations on the subject of the Corporation, but I take your point; I wouldn't want to see Amélie or Austin work themselves into an early grave either. But now we are together, we can plan on how that can be avoided. Now let's enjoy the rest of this meal, which we have all put together with our own fair hands, and then we can tackle whatever else is on the family agenda.'

They adjourned from the dining room to the living room after the table had been cleared and the dishwasher filled, and the conversation turned back to the blackmail threat against Mo, but only when Val brought the subject up.

'Now I think we need to look at Mo's situation, and I should say to you, Austin, that we ladies have already aired this subject in the kitchen—'

'Yes, I know,' Austin said. The three women looked at him in surprise.

'I couldn't hear your exact words, but I knew from the change in the tone of the conversation that that's what you were talking about.'

For once, Austin found himself the centre of attention, and quite enjoyed it. 'Heavens,' said Val. 'Are we so obvious?'

'Call it male intuition,' Austin said, and grinned, but then he remembered the subject matter, and wiped the grin rapidly.

'Mo had a hell of a time growing up with her three big brothers. I knew they were rough and boisterous and generally lived only just this side of the law, and sometimes not even that. But I never knew they could sink as low as this, however hard times were getting.'

'I can sometimes make a case for them,' said Mo. 'But when they made me do that, I realised that no amount of patience or effort on my part could make them any different. The only thing I can say in their defence is that they were brought up without being taught the proper distinctions between right and wrong. They also knew – all of us did – what real poverty was all about, and it's easier to keep to blameless morals when you're well off, not so easy when you're poor. And it wasn't just me, either. Tommy was the best looking of the lads, and at the same time as they made me go on the game, as they called it, they tried to turn him into a rent boy, to at least lure gay men into being blackmailed or turned over by them. Just like I made myself more useful by taking care of the books, Tommy got increasingly good with computers, but it would be fair to say that Tommy was as much a victim as I was.'

'None of us can come the high and mighty with you, Mo, and none of us would. People think Canada is an affluent country, and it mostly is, but there are sections of the population, sometimes part of the indigenous community who were the original inhabitants of the country, who are far from well off, and the climate of the country takes no prisoners when it comes to those who don't have the resources to properly look after themselves,' said Amélie.

'None of us is without sin, and none of us is throwing any stones,' Val said. 'But whatever the Callertons got up to, I don't believe that they are the people who are behind this. I think it comes from the same source as whoever arranged for Delatour's financial affairs to come under such uncalled-for scrutiny even as Amélie's plane was flying to London. Maddox and McAdams are, once again, at the bottom of this, in my opinion, though this stunt has more of Mac than Maddox about it. Maddox wouldn't have the imagination.'

'Honestly, Mum, do you really think that, or has this takeover business made it difficult for you to see beyond it? Mo thinks it comes from East End jealousies of the Callertons.'

'Well, yes, perhaps, but what do they get out of it? Whereas if it is McAdams or Maddox, they hope to intimidate you, Austin, and Mo into selling your shares and concentrating on your business.'

Austin, who knew both Maddox and McAdams, looked doubtful. 'I know they can be pretty near the knuckle, Mum, but this stuff?' Val took a sip of her brandy.

'In a way, it's quite revealing. I agree, Austin, it's pretty extreme stuff even by their standards, but it does suggest they're getting a little desperate. But we'll come back to them. The immediate issue is about tackling this direct threat to Mo.'

'Hit back hard,' said Amélie. 'They're pushing and prodding to find weak points. We've got to try and make them believe we haven't got any.'

'Yes, you're right, darling,' said Val, who made a mental note that Hugo's daughter might well have inherited something of Hugo's ruthlessness. 'If you must swim with sharks, a harpoon guy is always useful. I suggest, in the first instance, we try a big fat bluff. We'll issue a statement to the effect that the Corporation are aware of this episode in Mo's past and have already launched legal action against the Callertons for sexual abuse of a minor. That will scare the press away, and if we add that it means many details of the case are now sub judice, meaning it would be a contempt of court to publicise them, that will scare them away even more. The last thing most of them want is to appear to be supporting child abusers, and neither are they too keen on being taken to court for contempt.'

'It could work, Mum,' said Austin. 'But the problem with bluffs is that they can be called.'

'Yes, true, Austin. But if it seems as if that will happen, we will stop it being a bluff and instruct lawyers. The share value of the Corporation at the moment is approaching £900 million. We can afford to call our own bluff if we need to.'

For a moment, the others gazed at their mother/stepmother with a mixture of affection and anxiety. They were beginning to wonder whether she would rule out anything in order to keep her grip on the Corporation, and what she said next didn't decrease their anxiety.

'I'm also wondering whether we are still being a little too much on the defensive. Perhaps it's time we launched an attack or two of our own. As they're prodding us around to find the weak points, we could do a little prodding of our own. John Maddox, for example, is extraordinarily – well, I suppose the posh word would be libidinous. The not-so-posh word is womaniser. I don't think we would have to push too hard to find a few wronged ladies.'

'You are perhaps getting his priorities wrong, Mum,' Amélie said. 'I'm not sure Maddox will be all that upset about a few splashes in the paper about what a terrific stud he is. It would certainly never be as important to him as his control of the Corporation, if he thought he was in with a good chance of controlling it.'

'Yes, that's probably true. But I believe he has allowed his daughter Monica the ownership of some of his shares. I know Monica – not well, but I have met her several times – and I would guess John is already regretting making a gift of some shares to her. I think his thinking was to enmesh her in the whole business of the Corporation, but it could have the opposite effect if she knew exactly what kind of man her father is.'

Austin was suddenly on his feet.

'So, Mum, we've now reached the point where you are prepared to destroy a man in the eyes of his daughter to keep control of the Corporation. Where else are you going to go?' Val's face suddenly hardened.

'Perhaps I should point out, Austin, that we are dealing with a man who is quite prepared to ruin the reputation of your wife in front of the whole country.'

'We don't, as yet, have any firm evidence of that. And whatever happened to "when they go low, we go high"? If we are going to defeat the opposition in this, we have to have the neutrals. Maddox and McAdams might think they have all the shares stitched up in the forty per cent of the Corporation we don't own, but when it comes to it, some who don't feel that committed either way might well be influenced by how each side conducts its business. I would also remind you, Mum, that there are now only four days before the board meeting and neither Jen nor Paul are even here yet. What do you think they will make of your tactics? Neither of them have yet shown much inclination to get down and dirty with Corporation affairs, and when they start finding out about the sort of things you are prepared to do to keep control, how keen do you think they're likely to be to get enmeshed in this?'

Now Val was also on her feet.

'I will expect them to show the same loyalty, Austin, as I expect of you. What exactly are you saying? That dirty tricks are OK when your wife is threatened, but not when anyone else's lives are involved? I cannot believe—'

'For heaven's sake! You're doing exactly what they want you to do, can't you see that?'

Amélie didn't bother to rise from her chair, and suddenly Val could hear the voice of Hugo represented by his daughter.

'The whole point of what they're doing, and I'm sorry, Austin, but I think it's a pretty sure fire proposition that they are behind the threat to Mo, is to drive a wedge between us. That's why they are probing the weak points. They start to threaten Delatour, thinking I'm going to run home to Mummy and say, sorry Mum, I'm going to have to sell the shares to rescue my company, thereby precipitating a major family row. They pick on Mo to get to you, Austin, so you will go to your mother to say, I need to protect my wife and I'm going to sell my shares to take us off somewhere obscure where the British press can't get at us, or wouldn't be interested anyway. Thereby precipitating a major family row. And what we should be mostly worried about now is what they're going to do to get at Jen and Paul, because something will be coming their way. They've already driven their wedge into us, can't you see? They're winning. And nothing we can do to get back at them is going to be any good at all if they've already succeeded in driving us apart.'

'I'm just going to say,' said Mo, her tentative voice contrasting oddly with the assertive tones of the previous speakers, 'that it was when my family were divided and tearing each other apart that they finished up doing what they did to me. Tommy was shouting the odds against it, especially when he realised what they had in mind for him. It was the ones with the biggest voices and largest fists who won, and I don't need to tell you who they were.

'There's nothing more dangerous than families falling apart. It's what causes wars.' Now a long silence descended over the family.

'Excuse me for a moment,' Val said. 'I need a bit of air. Don't anyone follow me out, please.

'I have to think, and with due respect to all of you, the person who was always the most adept on helping me to think isn't here any more.'

Val's back garden was a rather artificial construct, since the land on the other side of the fence also belonged to her anyway, but she liked the idea of an enclosed garden as an especially cultivated area. She had a particular chair on a patio towards the rear of the garden, which had become her own special space, imbued with the quiet of the countryside. Hugo, she knew, would be able to call the whole thing to order, but then she immediately reflected that the main reason why Hugo was no longer here was because almost everyone felt like that about him. All well and good to accept that the buck stops here, but taking anything and everything on himself had eventually killed him.

'And, old girl, it's now in the process of killing you,' she murmured aloud.

For a long, long moment, while she looked over her land and contemplated the peace of this spot, she wanted it to be permanent, a place she could come to each day and every day without anything or anybody demanding her time, her patience, her emotions. And yet, at the same time, she knew that without giving herself something to do, it would become like a living death, sitting watching the countryside until her fossilised old body became part of it. She had made herself believe, in spite of her lack of any religious faith, Christian or otherwise, that she would be reunited with Hugo in the afterlife, but whenever she felt his presence or his thoughts calling to her, she couldn't persuade herself that what he was saying was 'come to me now'; it felt more along the lines of 'sort things out, and then come to me'. She knew, from his final words, such as they were, that he thought he'd left the job half done, that he had wanted and needed to purge the Corporation of those whose only interest or concern was with profit and then hand it over to a worthy successor.

And suddenly, almost as if he had stood in front of her and shouted it at her, she knew who he considered the successor ought to be. No, there were no sotto voce heavy breathing ghost voices, no misty manifestations of Hugo in strange supernatural places, just a certainty, as if the notion was a medicine just injected into her system.

Amélie was, had to be, the heiress. Amélie, who even at this moment, was refereeing the family disputes; Amélie, who had, as a result of her determination to run her own show, virtually created and sustained Delatour Hotels single-handedly, because while Val liked André, she had no illusions about who was the driving force behind Delatour. She realised that she did have a certain element of prejudice against Amélie because the girl, as she still thought of her, was not actually her daughter but the daughter of the flighty and ultimately hopeless Yvonne. But, as was so often the case, the final adult turned out to be much more influenced by one parent than the other, and Amélie was, ultimately, her father's daughter. Delatour could easily be absorbed into the Corporation and André was quite capable of running it on his own, with occasional guidance from his wife. But the Corporation, purged of Maddox, McAdams and all their following, would be safe in Amélie's hands, just as long as Amélie could be made to realise it.

Voices were raised inside the house, and Val momentarily dreaded going back in, but the raised voices were followed by a peal of laughter, mainly Austin but with his wife joining in, which could only mean Amélie had said something to make them both laugh. Something, happily, had diffused the atmosphere; with a pang of self-doubt, Val hoped it wasn't some kind of mocking remark directed at her.

The laughter continued as she went back to them, and she looked questioningly at Austin, receiving a broad smile back; she reflected, once again, that Austin the man had retained one of the nicer traits of Austin the boy, in that he didn't dwell on his differences with people; he was a creature of the immediate, probably another characteristic that also, unfortunately, compromised his ability to run a major Corporation, where thinking three steps ahead became more and more necessary.

'My wicked sister has just been speculating on who would

do what to whom if Maddox and McAdams entered into a civil partnership with each other.'

Val laughed. 'God, what a gruesome thought! Amélie, darling, your imagination can be a dark and troublesome land.'

'Yes, I suppose it can,' said Amélie, who could see from the expression on Val's face that something of significance had occurred to her mother. 'But it can sometimes help to understand the enemy if you can put them into various bizarre situations and imagine what they would do. And I think it would be fair to say that all three of us have come to the conclusion that they are the enemy. It's safe to say that we believe you're right to use what tactics you can against them.'

'I'm sorry, Mum, if anything I said led you to think that I'm not committed to the cause,' said Austin. 'The fact that Mo's been hurt by this gambit of theirs should have made me all the more determined to fight them any way we can, but the same thing, Mo getting hurt, also makes me a bit apprehensive about what we're getting into and who's going to get hurt along the way. When the gloves really come off, everyone can get hurt; I just think we all need to remember that.'

'Yes, Austin, you're absolutely right, we do. But we are the microcosm; the Corporation is the macrocosm. It might be necessary for us to be a bit battered about to save the whole Corporation suffering a lot worse. But let's take one thing at a time. We are agreed on what I suggested we do concerning Mo's immediate affairs, our shot across their bows?'

At last, they all signalled their agreement.

'Good. And thank you. Any more tactics regarding the Maddox family can wait for the moment, until we see what their next move will be. Now I will talk to Jennifer this evening about whether she is intending to be at the shareholders' meeting and how she is feeling about the whole business. I'll also contact Paul; it's odd that he is the only one of you who is resident in this country and also the only one from whom I have yet to hear a single word.'

'Paul could be the easiest, but he could just as well be the most difficult,' Amélie said, thereby neatly putting into a few words the thoughts they all shared of the 'kid of the family'. Val thought, once again, how suitable her daughter could be for the top job.

PART FIVE

Jennifer's Journey

Friday September 25th 2015

Madame Jennifer Logier née Forrest was making her way towards the Gare du Nord in a disgruntled frame of mind. She considered that she had been summoned, rather than asked, to attend a supposedly mega-important Gilard board meeting. Suddenly, everything was very urgent, and the woman she still thought of as her aunt was particularly insistent that she needed to be at this meeting.

Madame Logier, now aged thirty-eight, was the co-owner of what was generally regarded as a prestigious international school in Paris, a place where foreign diplomats posted to Paris and allowed to take their families with them sent their children to improve both their French and their English. And not only diplomats; her school had a growing intake of the offspring of show-business people who lived in Paris by accident or design, depending on where they were working and how permanent their jobs were.

Attracting a smattering of rich English émigrés and French parents who wanted their children to grow up with an international background, the *Académie Internationale Logier* had become something of an élite institution, and as far as Jennifer Logier was concerned, it was a good distance away from the whole confusing and overbearing mass of the Gilrey Corporation. She had met and fallen in love with Claude Logier while she was perfecting her French at the Sorbonne. Her late Uncle Hugo, who had so nobly stepped in after the dreadful disaster that had killed her parents, made sure she was provided with plenty of travel and educational opportunities after he realised her interest in languages and the background of the Gilard family.

And throughout all this period, Aunt Val never seemed to have any 'agenda' other than encouraging her niece to go her own way. Now, suddenly, Uncle Hugo had gone and Val wanted Jennifer to involve herself in corporation business, even though she knew very well that Jennifer was not interested in that kind of life or activity.

Her five per cent allocation of shares was not something she had given much thought to. She had accepted it as a courteous gesture from her aunt and uncle some time ago, and entirely consistent with their care for her since the day of that dreadful accident. Now it seemed she was a millionaire many times over. Her senses were reeling, and as if that news wasn't enough to take in, it also seemed that she now had to become embroiled in office politics and turn up at some meeting or other to do as her aunt told her.

Jennifer didn't care very much for any of it. She wanted to oblige her aunt, who had always exhibited care and consideration towards her, but she didn't really understand what it was all about and she didn't particularly want to leave the Académie, especially at such a relatively early stage in the academic year.

The Gare du Nord was in its usual state of subterranean mayhem; the main station was not, of course, underground, but its dimness and dustiness always gave the impression of being so. It was not a place for those whose minds were elsewhere, and certainly not if a particular train and time needed to be located. Jennifer turned her attention to locating and getting on a Eurostar train, and only when she was settled with a meal shortly due to arrive did she resume her contemplation of what might be facing her in England.

Jennifer divided her life very clearly into two parts, which could be summarised as Parents and Post Parents. Her grieving process had taken her a long and painful time to at least partially complete, though she could still slip quite easily into the hollow desolation of the aftermath of the accident.

She had always felt, and she thought she always would feel, enormous affection for the family who had so generously befriended her, and effectively saved her life, because she knew that if someone had not gone out of their way to be kind to her at that time, she might well have given in to total despair and perhaps even suicide, young as she was. She and her parents had been a tight knit, enclosed group of three, and their entire world revolved around education. Her parents talked of it both generally and particularly for most of the time, and they had always been concerned to supplement Jennifer's schooling with some lessons at home. Jennifer, as a child at least, had not found this too irksome. She was an only child, and there seemed to be a certainty with her parents that she would stay as an only child; she knew nothing then of her mother's previous problems and miscarriages. She needed to talk to someone, and as no-one of her own age was available, she talked to her parents whenever the opportunity arose.

At that time, and for many years afterwards, the Gilrey Corporation was no more than an imaginary hill in the distance. She knew her aunt, uncle and cousins were all involved, but she could see clearly enough that neither Amélie nor Austin had any intention of allowing themselves to be swallowed up by it. In due course, she went to the secondary school, a girls' boarding school, which her parents had always had in mind for her. 'Spending the rest of your life at home with your father and I, darling, would be very comfortable and cosy, I'm sure, but there's a big wide world out there that you'll have to know something about before you can start to work in it.'

But by work, of course, her parents meant educational work, and when she discovered, at the age of eighteen, how much she had been left in trust, she realised that, for her, it didn't need to be a matter of starting from the bottom, slogging away as a state teacher for years and hoping for promotions. She had to qualify as a teacher, but she never had a serious moment of doubt that teaching was what she was going to do; she couldn't conceive of doing anything else after the example of her parents.

She qualified as a teacher with a degree at the age of twenty-one in 1998. With the exciting new millennium approaching, it became more exciting still when she met Claude at the Sorbonne as she expanded her teaching qualification into modern languages; her parents had given her a grounding in French and German even before they died.

Claude represented yet more release from the trauma and claustrophobia of her late childhood and adolescence, and they settled on creating an institution that could move beyond the mundane routines of provincial education, educating children with an international background with the varied and challenging curriculum they needed. The Gilrey Corporation became even more of a voice off, a distraction. Claude had money of his own, again from a commercial family enterprise in which he was an unenthusiastic partner. They worked hard on building their different kind of school, which celebrated rather than attempted to standardise the different talents and inclinations of their pupils.

The Logier International School had taken a good deal of time and effort to establish, and Jennifer and Claude believed it genuinely developed and encouraged diversity, with children from many different countries and races. To give such a project up, or even dilute her effort by working some of the time elsewhere, would to Jennifer constitute a kind of betrayal of her parents. The Corporation was, to her, simply a way of making money; money was its be-all and end-all. It had been hinted to her from time to time that her five per cent stake in it might be worth a great deal of money, but if that proved to be the case, such money would be put to a greater purpose than just making more money; her parents' legacy demanded it.

As would her own children, her boys Edouard and Julien, with interchangeable English/American equivalents, both now in their mid-teens and enjoying their time at the International School. They were, Jennifer reflected with some satisfaction, both attractive and personable youths, and in addition to the language skills and international perspectives they were gaining, they would also be making friendships with others, both male and female, who might finish up by being government ministers or even leaders in their future lives, connections that would stand them in good stead for the rest of their lives. And save them from having their lives gobbled up by corporations devoted to simply making money. After finishing her meal, Jennifer dozed a little, and when she woke, she saw that the train was now making its way through southern England. She had treated herself to a nice London hotel for at least one night; she liked visiting London, and living in Paris made such occasional expeditions easy enough. She would then visit the Gilard house in the country, unless whatever it was that Val required of her could be settled by a link from the hotel.

Everything had been carefully planned, as Jennifer preferred when travelling. On arrival in St. Pancras Station, she had a pre-booked taxi to take her on the short journey to her West End hotel, where the booking presented no problems and she had a pleasant room with a view over theatre country. On this occasion, she had decided not to 'take in a show', judging that she had some talking to do to resolve whatever Val wanted of her.

But Val was not the first to contact her. She had no sooner made herself a coffee from the facilities provided when the phone rang, and she knew it must be Claude, as he was the only one who knew which hotel she'd chosen.

'Bonsoir, ma chérie,' he began, and she could see an extra colour to his face – Claude could still blush like a boy on occasion – and hear a tinge of excitement in his voice.

Something had happened; probably good, by the look and sound of him.

'I suppose you would rather I spoke English during the time you're there,' he went on.

'Yes, that's probably for the best, Claude. I am due to have a conversation with Val this evening, and though I know she speaks French at least as well as I do, she is likely to prefer her first language, especially in view of what we are to talk about.'

'Yes, and I think I can give you something you will need to talk about. Someone is offering you seventy million euros for your five per cent of the Gilrey Corporation.'

Jennifer was momentarily struck dumb. Suddenly, out of the mists she had allowed to congregate around anything to do with the Corporation, one very big solid fact had jumped up and demanded her attention. But the point about it that struck her most forcibly to begin with was why did her husband know of this in advance of her?

'Who says, Claude? How do you know this?'

'Our lawyer, the one who handles the legal stuff for Logier International, got in touch with me. I know they are your shares, Jenny, but you know Henri Dupont, he hasn't made it into the twenty-first century yet. He couldn't contact you, but he thought you should know immediately, so he contacted me. He means well.'

'I'm sure he does, but I will see to it in future that he does contact me first.'

'Oh, does it matter, Jenny? In the face of such an awesome sum of money? We could open another school, perhaps there in London, one of the most cosmopolitan cities in the world. We could expand our operations; the possibilities are endless…'

'I have to know more about this. If this is an offer coming from outside the family, I will need to discuss it with Val and the others.'

'Why? These are your shares, Jenny; they're nothing to do with the rest of the family.'

'Val didn't say much when she contacted me; I think she honestly believes someone might be bugging phones. But she did say the matter we needed to discuss, well in advance of the meeting, was to do with who would finish up controlling the Corporation.'

'Why should we care who controls the Corporation? They have no objectives in life apart from making money for themselves…'

'For a man who is going head over heels at the sound of seventy million euros, Claude, you can hardly criticise people who want to make money. Yes, it is a tempting offer, and yes, I can see clearly enough myself what opportunities it might give us, but Aunt Valerie and her children have been extremely kind to me over the years and I am selling nothing until I have talked to her and found out what it is all about.'

'Yes, OK, darling Jen, but don't take too long about it. The offer is on the table, they say, for twenty-four hours.'

'So they say, Claude. I don't profess to be an expert, but that sounds like a pretty crude attempt at arm-twisting to me. If they are so keen to get their hands on the shares, there will be others; they probably know that well enough, which is why they're pressurising.' She could see his face, that bronzed outdoor complexion of his, and his brown eyes alight with confidence and expectation. He was not an easy man to disappoint, and as far as he was concerned, this was a sudden vast sum of money that had descended on them out of a blue sky, and anything less than immediate acceptance was to look a gift horse straight in the face.

'OK, Jen,' he said, and she could hear the disappointment in his voice. 'It's your show; I'm not trying to push you into doing what you don't want to do. But it's my point of view, and I've always believed it to be yours, that the sooner we can cut ourselves free from the Gilrey Corporation and everything it represents, the better, and if it makes us rich in the process, so much the better.'

'There isn't much of that I would disagree with, Claude. But give me a bit of time and space; this is all family stuff, and that's never straightforward.'

After her conversation with Claude, Jennifer lost the urge to go walking around the streets of London, and by now it was getting on for the evening. She ordered a modest room service meal and a half bottle of wine, as if a kind of relaxation workout in preparation for talking to Val. With the best will in the world, and allowing for Val's consistent kindness and support, any dealings with her would always bring back the whole ache of suddenly becoming an orphan, as a little girl whose entire world had just crashed around her ears and left her blundering about, both mentally and physically, in an alien land.

Finally, she was ready, and she called Val Gilard up on the screen in front of her. They exchanged the usual pleasantries with mounting impatience on both sides, Val in relation to time; she wanted the whole family together well in advance of the meeting and didn't understand why Jennifer had chosen to spend time in London before coming to the family home, as she saw it. For her part, Jennifer didn't fully understand why this enormous sum of money was suddenly being offered. She wanted to enjoy a rare visit to London in her own way, and she was, once again, finding herself out of her depth in relation to the monolithic Corporation, looming again over the life she had made for herself.

After a few terse exchanges about how long it would actually take Jennifer to get to Gilard H.Q. in the country, Jennifer let go her bazooka.

'I've already been offered seventy million euros for my holding, Val,' she said. 'I have no roles in the Corporation, either active or passive, and if someone is as keen to have a role as that, I don't see why I should stand in their way, particularly bearing in mind the things that Claude and I and the boys could do with that kind of money.'

'We know the people who are behind that offer, Jenny, and we know what they want to do with the Corporation, our Corporation, created and developed by the Gilard family. I have substantial evidence that they have already tried to influence both Amélie and Austin, but I am not going to go into detail on a link like this because it wouldn't surprise me at all if the people behind the offer to you, or their employees, have not contrived to bug our communications and I am not going to give them the benefit of telling them what we know and how we know it. How long is it since you booked your hotel room?'

'Just a few days ago, Val. This is all sounding a bit like paranoia to me, I have to say. It's one of the reasons why I decided I wanted to steer clear of the business world in general and the Corporation in particular, and also keep my family untouched by it. I will always be grateful to you and Hugo for what you've done for me, but will it really have been worth my steering clear of the Corporation for all this time if I now allow myself to get so thoroughly mixed up in it? I have a family in Paris, Val, and they must always come first.'

Jennifer thought she heard a long sigh, but it may just have been Val gathering her breath. 'So they must, Jenny, and so they will. I only ask that you come here, meet up with the rest of the family and hear what we have to say before you commit yourself to selling the shares.

'How long is it since you met up with everyone?'

Jennifer could not bring herself to exercise her memory.

'I don't know. A long time, I suppose. But I will be with you all tomorrow. Tonight I am going to spend some time in London. I have a few other people to talk to, Val, people in education who have links to Logier International, and yes, a few parents, ex-parents and even potential parents. Logier International School is my world, Val, and that isn't going to change. I will listen carefully to everything that is said to me, but I will not be gobbled up by the Corporation or get involved up to my neck in business politics.'

Val made a few soothing remarks and managed to get a rough arrival time for Jennifer to reach the Gilard country house on the following day, but when her screen went blank, she cursed under her breath and decided she had no other choice but to go on the attack. Undermining Delatour, threatening Austin's Spanish outfit and now, most blatantly and publicly of all, trying to wrest Jennifer's shares away from her by making her an offer she couldn't refuse.

Yes, she could get in touch with Maddox or McAdams and start talking terms. No doubt they would offer her something to make her think, a deluge of money for her shares which would leave her in clover for the rest of her life, enough to help and influence all the members of the family. She would be free to travel to each of them as often as she liked, and when not doing that, she could go to wherever in the world suited her mood or visit one of her many friends all over the globe. Rather than a gradual eclipse, as the burdens of work rose like an incoming tide until she no longer had the strength or guile to keep afloat in them and drowned as poor Hugo had done, she could have an enviable multi-millionaire lifestyle until she eventually passed away at an advanced age, mourned by all.

The other man's grass, the nirvana over the hill, the abdication of responsibility; how seductive are the voices of worlds that might be, worlds always somewhere else, and always just out of reach. How soon would it all bore her, how soon would it be before her children sighed as she once more pushed her nose unasked into their business, and what kind of isolation would be the inevitable consequence of people turning away from her rich woman indulgences?

She could only fight; it seemed as if it had come to be the reason for her continued existence, ever since By the Brook and all the old diehards of the 'traditional' pub were waiting and hoping that she would fall flat on her face. And fighting meant being resourceful, and sometimes even taking the gloves off. McAdams and Maddox had now attempted to intimidate three of her children, and she was not careless enough to dismiss their efforts as amateurish and impotent while she faced a situation where even keeping her family united was no longer to be taken for granted.

In the last resort, fight fire with fire had to be her approach, and keeping control of the Corporation in her family's hands the target. In spite of the reservations of some members of the family, she had decided on an approach to Monica Maddox, and she had also determined that, as long as she continued to be chief executive, these were the kinds of decisions she could still consider herself entitled to take.

Monica Maddox was now twenty and well into her law degree. Val had met Monica on a handful of occasions, and knew some of the details about her, both past and present.

Monica's relationship with her father was increasingly fraught, largely as a result of his infidelities, and she had already shown a tendency to go her own way. In order to prevent her from becoming involved in shared houses with other students, and particularly male students, her father had provided her with a generously sized flat not more than twenty minutes on foot from her university. Val understood that Monica had now chosen to have her current boyfriend, a fellow law student, move in, and told her father about it, while also explaining that if he didn't like it, she would give up the flat and move into a house share.

Val had already worked out her defence, if her children, most particularly Austin, accused her of stooping to low tactics to nobble the opposition. Firstly, she would point out that McAdams and Maddox had already tried to nobble three of her children by varying tactics, which didn't, apparently, include just simply phoning them up and trying to persuade them to sell their shares. Val had no intention of using underhand tactics; she was simply going to phone Monica and try to persuade her to sell her shares, not by threatening anyone she knew or trying to wreck their business, but by straightforward, honest persuasion.

She was prepared to believe that the real mastermind of the opposition was McAdams, with Maddox in a junior role, and she was already researching what could be McAdams' weak spot in the shape of a certain peer of the realm, but Monica would be a good start. If she could be persuaded simply to remain neutral, McAdams and Maddox would then have lost even their forty per cent.

Val looked at her watch. It was the kind of time when twenty-year-olds might be preparing to go out for a night on the town, but what she knew of Monica Maddox suggested that perhaps was one stereotype that didn't work with her. Her father's insistence that she concentrate on corporate law was rumoured by some to have backfired, in that her youthful idealism and natural intelligence had set her against some of the cynical wheeling and dealing that characterised big business.

Val called the number and was pleased when Monica's voice answered; she might have had some work to do, had it been the boyfriend.

'Hello, Monica. It's Val Gilard. Are you busy at the moment or can we talk?'

'Mrs. Gilard. Nice to hear from you, though I think I can make a fair guess at what it's about. I'm working on something I have to send in next week, but if you have something to say, I'm listening.'

Val took a deep breath and plunged in. Something told her this wasn't a girl who wanted to spend time neatly circumventing the main issues.

'Well, to lay it on the line, Monica, your father and his associate Mr. McAdams have so far made three attempts to intimidate my children into selling their shares. In each case, they will deny it if you put it to them, but I have worked with them for some time and I can detect their handiwork. I, on the other hand, am not going to try to intimidate you in any way, but I do think, in the current circumstances and the meeting next week…'

'You want me to sell my shares. Preferably to you, presumably.'

The girl's directness knocked Val slightly out of her stride. But not by much. 'To anyone, to be frank, other than your father or Mr. McAdams.'

'Yes, I think Dad made a tactical error with me. "Here you are, darling, for your eighteenth birthday, something real and tangible as your one and a half per cent of the Corporation." It didn't seem very exciting at the time, a piece of paper for my birthday, gee thanks, Daddy. Then I found out something of what they're worth, and I suppose they're worth rather more now, aren't they?'

'As of today, in the region of twenty million pounds.' A crisp and unladylike expression escaped Monica.

'I'm always amazed Dad spends so much of his time looking at all these stocks and shares prices; what a mega-boring way of passing the time. And then, this. God, what I could do with twenty million quid.'

Going well, thought Val. The iron is hot.

'Yes, absolutely. But all I would ask is that you consider selling them to me. I am fighting to keep control of the Corporation, and I believe in my hands it will continue to operate with a human face—'

'I hope you don't mind me asking you a personal question, Mrs. Gilard. How old are you?' Val's rock of confidence shook suddenly.

'I'm sixty-seven. But fully in control of my faculties, I assure you.'

'I don't doubt it. But anyone thinking of the longer term interests of the Corporation would be looking for someone younger to take over, wouldn't they? I mean, I have no illusions about my father; he has the morality of an alley-cat, and he's already had three affairs which I know about, let alone the ones I don't. But, like Mr. McAdams, he's energetic and ruthless enough to run a Corporation. It's hardly a retirement part-time thing, is it?'

OK, Val thought. Perhaps it's time to set the ball rolling.

'I think, between you and me, Monica, I may well be handing on to Amélie.'

'Really?'

'Yes, and people will say girl power and all that. But I think Amélie is right for it, whatever gender she is. And she will have a formidable operation backing her.'

'I don't doubt it. But when push comes to shove, Mrs. Gilard, it's about keeping it in the control of the Gilard family, isn't it?'

OK, if she wants to fight, let's fight, thought Val.

'Yes, Monica, it is, and it will remain so until someone manages to persuade me that another group of people could do better, while still handling it with a human face. If it's about making money and nothing else, what's the point of it all?'

A short silence followed at the other end of the line. At least, Val thought, she's thinking it over – or at least starting to think about it, now she knows what her one and a half per cent of shares might mean, to others as well as herself.

'Yes, fair enough, Mrs. Gilard, but some of it has to be about making money, doesn't it, if the Corporation is to survive? Whatever I might feel about some stuff my father gets up to, he is a very effective administrator and he knows how to handle money. And with all due respect, Mrs. Gilard, he is where he is largely because you and your husband put him there.' Val took a deep breath.

'We had no reason then, Monica, to see him as anything other than trustworthy, though evidence has emerged since to suggest that his handling of people in his department left a lot to be desired, by any of the normal standards of industrial relations. But part of the activities he and Mr. McAdams are indulging in at the moment are directed at persuading, or perhaps more accurately intimidating, members of my family into selling their shares into the control of Maddox and McAdams. I am not trying to intimidate you into anything. I am not trying to undermine your business, as they are trying to do to two of my grown-up children, or offer a tempting new venture, as they are doing to one other. If those are the tactics they are prepared to use against me, I think I am both morally and practically entitled to simply talk to you.'

She could hear patient sighs on the other end of the line, and hoped the girl wouldn't hear the sound of teeth gritting.

'I'm sure you are, Mrs. Gilard, and you have done. I have to say that I have it in mind to sell my shares; my father would enjoy seeing me getting involved with the Corporation, but I have other plans. However, he is my father, for all his faults, and I'm not perfect myself, if I'm being honest. I want to be independent, but I also want him speaking to me and advising me when I feel it's necessary. Please leave it with me and I promise you I will thoroughly think it over.'

'OK, Monica. I don't think anyone can ask more than that. Thanks for talking to me.'

Clicking her phone off, Val couldn't help thinking things over herself. If one of the qualifications for being a good company M.D. is to be a good plotter, she clearly wasn't in the same league as Maddox and McAdams. And she had also, without actually consulting Amélie about it beforehand, started a story about Amélie succeeding her that could now spread like wildfire, because she didn't doubt Monica would talk to her father about the conversation and Amélie taking over control of the Corporation would now be something else Maddox and McAdams had to work with.

But, as usual, the luxury of taking enough time to think over every step of the way was denied her. A glance at her watch told her that she now only had ten minutes before her pre-arranged call to Paul, and Paul's occupation made it imperative that she went with the time he had named. The truth of what had been said, that Paul could just as easily be the easiest or the hardest, came back to her.

Saturday September 26th 2015

Jennifer felt more rested and relaxed as she settled into the taxi that was to take her to the Gilard country house. At least she fully understood now what the issues were, after a number of occasions in the past when she had felt uncomfortably out of her depth with Corporation business. She knew now that this situation could represent the best chance she had yet been offered to wash her hands of the Corporation once and for all, and she told herself that, however fearful she might be, it did not need to involve washing her hands of the Gilard family as well. Amélie, Austin and Paul all worked independently of the Corporation, and if her shares were worth a lot of money, theirs would be likewise, so the opportunity of independence was on offer to all of them. Jennifer found it difficult to believe that she was the only one who would now be thinking seriously of the possibilities on offer.

Soon enough, the Gilard country seat came in view, and Jennifer gulped once again, as she always had at this point ever since the dreadful occasion of her first arrival here to live rather than visit. With an effort, she stopped the tears rising to her eyes; that was then, this is now, and she was far from a terrified and shattered little girl being delivered into an entirely new and largely alien world. She was a sophisticated and successful businesswoman and her priorities centred on her family and her profession; she would not be steamrollered away from them.

The warmth of her greeting from the family reassured her and slightly unfocussed her at the same time. Some home truths might well be necessarily said, and that is not easy when people are going out of their way to be affectionate and welcoming. She was also, she knew, inclined to be rather awkward and formal at first meetings with people, and she had never met Mo before. That could well be another hark back to the time of her parents' death, when people she scarcely knew or didn't know at all seemed to be appearing with bewildering frequency.

The late September weather, drizzly and windy, precluded any outside socialising, meaning the main gathering of the family on Saturday afternoon had a more formal identity than might have been the case in the summer. The approach, which made perfectly good sense on the surface, was to dispatch the Corporation business during the day and enjoy an informal and more sociable dinner in the evening, though everyone knew well enough that it was more than likely that the business talking would occupy the entire day and probably some of the following one. From what Val knew before the talking started, some people's positions and circumstances could well prove to be irreconcilable with others.

Val began with a summary of where they were, including a report on her conversation with Monica Maddox – greeted with a certain exasperation by Austin in particular – and her thoughts on Donald McAdams' uneasy relationship with a peer of the realm to whom he had sold a two per cent share of the Corporation, 'to get His Lordship's name on the stationery', though at the time the sale was made, Hugo had been M.D. and His Lordship had not been impressed by events since.

Everyone could sense the growing tension in the room as they approached the inevitable moment when Val would ask for their pledges of loyalty, which, with three days left before the meeting, would need to be definitive in one direction or the other. She knew well enough from the stream of communications leaving the house that all her offspring had been talking to their various associates and there wasn't much chance of anyone prevaricating further.

Either because he wanted to postpone the inevitable or because it was a question that he genuinely needed answering, Austin broke into Val's preamble with a question.

'If we're coming to the crunch, Mum, and it sounds very much as though we are, I think we'd all like to know where Paul stands, or at least when he is likely to appear.'

Val looked discomfited and was; she had hoped to deal with this one after the main decisions had been taken, by which time Paul's opinions would no longer be relevant.

'Paul is coming tomorrow. He is not prepared to mess around with his shift pattern or take leave at short notice. But he has said – many times – that he doesn't want to become heavily involved with the workings of the Corporation. My impression is, however, that he is equally unprepared to sell his shares at the moment, because he is in a relationship and children may be involved in the future.'

'What – has he gone straight then?' Jennifer said, before she had stopped to think. Eyes around her raised to the ceiling.

Val was as gentle as she could manage.

'Gay men can and do have families, Jenny, these days. It's by no means unprecedented.' Jenny subsided into silence. Val collected her thoughts and plunged on.

'Assuming, then, that Paul's shares are safely within our holding, we have a safe majority of sixty per cent, against which McAdams and Maddox can do nothing. There is also another one and a half per cent of Monica's shares, which she seems intent on selling, and not to her father, reducing the McAdams maximum possible to thirty-eight and a half per cent, and I suspect the peer's two per cent will also not go to McAdams, meaning they have only thirty-six and a half per cent and, nuisance as they can and no doubt will be, there isn't much they can do to gain control of the Corporation. Their total shareholding doesn't even equal my personal share. But, of course—'

Val sat up in her enormous, throne-like armchair and let her glance take in all of the faces around her.

'I think you already know the rest of that sentence. But before we come to that, there is another development which has a clear bearing on the decisions you take. I want Amélie to succeed me as managing director, with her Delatour business being absorbed into the Corporation and taking over a lot of our provisions for catering and accommodation, its size and wealth increasing the worth of the Corporation and putting an even greater share of it in our hands. If the board appoint her, I will retire, though I reserve the right to establish a little local business of my own, probably a restaurant or hotel.

'Of course, I have approached Amélie with this plan, and she broadly approves it, as does her husband, providing certain arrangements can be made at the board meeting, including appointing André to the board and arranging a friendly takeover of Delatour by the Gilrey Corporation. We would also, Austin, as we've discussed, look to take your business into the Corporation, giving it the full backing of the Corporation's resources and expanding if you so wish it. Similarly, although we haven't yet had the chance to discuss it, we will back your Logier School, Jennifer, with Corporation sponsorship and resources, only if you wish it, of course, thereby expanding the family's influence in the Corporation still further.'

The audible intake of breath from Jennifer at this point did not sound like an approving noise, Val thought, and probably didn't represent an ideal point for her to stop.

'We will also co-opt Mo on to the Board and give her substantial responsibility for expanding the Costa del Sol business. I think the whole plan is a healthy and comprehensive strategy for the future of the Corporation which keeps it firmly in the hands of its founders and prevents it being turned into the personal fiefdom of Donald McAdams and John Maddox. It allows me to retire before I suffer the same fate as Hugo, and it gives me the chance to have somewhere to enjoy my retirement and be hostess to my friends and family. There, I've had my say. The floor is open.'

As if following the dying peals of a thunderclap, silence reverberated around the room, before Val's suspicion that Jennifer's gasp was not one of approval was all too clearly confirmed.

'I really didn't want to be put in this position so early,' Jennifer said, the tension in her evident. 'But I have to be quite clear about this. Logier International School will not, either now or at any time in the future as long as I control it, become some kind of satellite of the Gilrey Corporation. I owe a huge debt of gratitude to this family, and please don't think I'm unaware of that. But that, in a sense, is why. What this family did is put me back on my feet at a time when my life could have plunged into God knows what depths of despair and struggle. But it did put me on my feet, and I liked being there, as I have done ever since. It's where I want to stay, because while my relationship with the Corporation would remain amicable, I hope, the business of the Corporation is very different from the business of the school and it just isn't feasible that I should hand overall control to the Corporation, even if I should want to, which I don't.'

'So what exactly are you saying, Jennifer?' Val spoke into the lengthening silence. 'What are you proposing to do with your shares? Does the fact that you don't want any Corporation involvement with your school mean you don't want to hold Corporation shares either, and if you don't, who would you be prepared to sell them to?'

'I really hadn't got to thinking that far ahead. If you're looking for me to make decisions this weekend, I'm afraid you do need to let me have a little more time, and it seems to me that it's now necessary for Claude to be here, since this is as pertinent to his future as it is to mine. I think we need another day, to allow him to get here and to give everyone time to get their thoughts fully in order. I would also point out that Paul still isn't here, and he has as many shares as we have. If it's the intention of this meeting to steamroller our plans through before Paul has a chance to contribute, then I have to say I fundamentally disagree. In any case, I am not going to make any decision on my shares until I've had a face-to-face meeting with Claude, which means at least tomorrow. If the meeting is on Tuesday, we still have two days after today.'

Val managed to speak again before the silence stretched to embarrassing lengths. Perhaps in the back of her mind, there was a faint suggestion that getting plans in place before Paul's arrival was exactly what she was trying to do. She couldn't help noticing the rather defensive tone her words were starting to adopt.

'That's perfectly true, Jenny, and I respect your wish to consult with Claude on such a matter. And yes, it's true that we do have another two days after today. I know André is scheduled to arrive later today. I am not trying to bounce anyone into anything, but I must point out that the longer this process continues, the more difficult it may be to reach a proper consensus, and the more we concentrate on our differences, the more complicated arriving at that consensus will be. However, riding roughshod over people's views is exactly what this business is about, because if Donald McAdams and John Maddox take control of this Corporation, you can be sure that no other opinions but theirs will have any significance whatsoever, and that includes everyone in this room.

'I suggest we meet again tomorrow, with Paul, André and Claude in attendance, and with the very specific aim of reaching firm decisions about our shareholdings and everyone's part in the future of the Corporation. I do not, I repeat now, want to go into the day before the meeting with us remaining undecided or at odds with each other in any way. Now I bring our formal discussions today to an end, and everyone is at liberty to do as they wish for what remains of the day.'

She looks tired and disillusioned, thought Amélie. She resolved to try to have a few words with Paul and Jennifer herself before the start of Sunday's meeting.

PART SIX

Paul's Journey

Saturday September 26th 2015

Paul woke slowly, with the realisation that he had not just one but three days off causing him to hang on to a certain reluctance about waking up at all. He frequently had complicated dreams that he could only barely remember, but which always featured continuous physical activity with the annoying trait of one task not being finished before the next one demanded attention. He knew his life as a junior doctor was the prompt for such confusion, and it generally caused him to look back over his most recent shift to determine whether the dreams were being reflected in reality. But it was, in some ways, the nature of the job; there were no full stops, no convenient beginnings and endings, and transferring the inevitable anxiety that such work produced to the subconscious was, if not inevitable, then hardly surprising.

For once, however, he was on his own, and that was unfamiliar in itself. His civil partner, Kirk, was on a mercy mission to his home in the Midlands, as it seemed as if his father did not have long to live. In different circumstances, Paul would have gone with him, but their union had never gone down very well with Kirk's parents, and infuriating as Kirk found them at times, they were still his parents. It was an unkind thought that the demise of Kirk's father would probably mean relationships with his mother would improve from that time onwards, but it was probably the reality of it. Kirk was fully aware that Paul spending three precious days of leave in the current atmosphere of Kirk's family was a waste of the leave that Paul urgently needed. And, of course, the whole Corporation business, which Kirk grasped and understood even less than Paul did, was enough to be going on with during the days off. They talked of plans for a 'proper holiday', even if such a prospect could only be vague for the moment.

Taking his time about showering and dressing was a luxury in itself, but it also gave him leisure enough to contemplate his terse conversation with his mother the evening before. Kirk had only recently left, meaning Paul wasn't in the best of moods to start with, and Val's attempts to once again enmesh him in the affairs of the Corporation were bound to meet with a degree of surly resistance. As far as Paul was concerned, the Corporation and the Corporation alone were responsible for the death of his father, and the added humiliation of him being the only member of the family both present and qualified to do something about it at the time of Hugo's fatal heart attack, while failing to avert his father's death, did not make him any more inclined to consider the Corporation as anything but a pernicious monster gobbling up people's lives. He still regretted accepting the allocation of shares his parents had given him, and if an ever-present niggle still remained at the back of his mind telling him he was an ungrateful wretch, his father's death had, for the moment at least, completely swung the argument against involvement with the Corporation.

His agenda with his mother remained too constant to be swept away. As he hardly saw his father from day to day, his dealings with the family were dominated by his mother, and two huge barriers between them had yet to be broken down to the extent of establishing trust on both sides. When he had eventually summoned up the courage to discuss his sexuality with her, at the age of sixteen when he knew without any further reasonable doubt that he was gay, she had refused to credit it and attributed it to a 'phase' he was going through. She then insisted that she blamed herself for sending him to a boys' school; he protested that his feelings had nothing to do with going to a boys' school, and he had understood his nature quite thoroughly before he ever started at the school.

Even now, after his relationship with Kirk had lasted for seven years and they had been civil partnered for four, she still did not seem to have come to terms with the situation and she treated Kirk with detached politeness, as if he was a workmate he'd brought home. He was thirty-two and considering, with Kirk, how well they would like the idea of parenthood or whether the moment had already passed. This, like almost everything else associated with the relationship, Val would not countenance as a serious issue to be discussed.

His choice of career had met with what he saw as an equally negative reaction. His mother seemed to assume that he would work for the Corporation. In the moments when her tactics would largely centre on coercion, she would appeal to what she saw as his 'special status'. 'Paul,' she would say, with a tone of voice and a facial expression that signalled to him clearly enough what was coming down the line, 'you are my only child with your father. Don't you see how important that makes you to me? You are not just his natural heir, you are mine as well. Medicine is an honourable profession, of course it is, but I think everyone does have a duty to look at their natural legacy. Don't your father and I have any claim on your direction? Don't you think being a member of a family as phenomenally successful as ours comes with duties and obligations as well as wealth?'

And the years had entrenched rather than relaxed the divisions between them. For all the psychological tactics he saw her as using on him, she was unable to overbear and intimidate him in his adolescence and she was even less likely to do so now, when he had become a well-established medical professional and established a permanent relationship.

Her approach now indicated clearly enough, from his point of view, that she would stop at nothing to get her way, and here she was blatantly using his father's death to try to bring him in line after all else had failed. Perhaps she saw it as the last and greatest argument, the one to which he would eventually have no response. But he remained unimpressed. She dangled wealth and power in front of him, and all he had to do was let the Corporation monolith swallow him up. He and Kirk would be fabulously rich and parked for ever in the comfortable embrace of the Corporation; perhaps she might even start treating Kirk as her son-in-law, rather than some guy her boy had met along the way.

But their independence, even their integrity, would be gone for ever, whatever she said now; they would be her yes-men, along with all the others, until she herself died or finally decided on something that at least resembled retirement. She would leave him as the heir to the whole ghastly business, and well set up to work himself to death as his father had.

However, as he prepared to set off for the family seat, knowing that a car would be sent to get him, the other side of his relationship with his mother eventually demanded a hearing, as it always did at some stage. She was no saint, but neither was he. She had taken on a challenge in her life, to establish a business that was not only successful but phenomenally so. She was brave, intelligent, resourceful and, after all, since his father died, alone. He had to hear her out and try to respond as constructively as he could, but he would not stop being a doctor and he could not stop being gay. If it had to be a case of an irresistible force meeting an immovable object, they could at least retain a decent amount of respect and affection for each other. She was, after all, sixty-seven, and he could already see an endless succession of regrets and disappointments that he might find himself having to live with after she died.

The car came, and of course it was comfortable and convenient; as ever, he felt vaguely whorish as he surrendered again to the embrace of the Corporation. By the time the car was making its way up the drive of the Gilard family country H.Q., he felt more relaxed and easy- going than he had been for days, though there were always, at any time, a few names in the intensive care ward that never left him, and cases he could not forget about.

Val watched the car every yard of the way. Here he was, the prodigal son, the apple of her eye, the one she wanted to love the most and the one who had never seemed to realise how like his father he was. Hugo did as Hugo decided, and what he created was all his own; here now was his son, with exactly the same determination and single-mindedness, even if it was, as far as she was concerned, misdirected in some ways. Hugo could not be anyone else but Hugo, and Paul could not be anyone else but Paul, whatever the entire rest of creation might think about it. She had worried deeply, as she still did, about the hostility and prejudice that his gay nature would bring down on his head; like many of her generation, she saw the increased tolerance and acceptance of homosexual relationships as still having the potential to be transitory, a fad of fashion, which could bring his star, currently in the ascendancy, crashing disastrously to earth in the future.

She resolved that, to begin with at least, she would set out to be conciliatory.

'How is Kirk?' she said, as he emerged from the car and moved towards her. He saw this as the olive branch it was meant to be, and smiled as he accepted her embrace.

'He's back with his family at the moment. His father's not well; in fact, he's more than not well, he may not have long to live.'

'Oh, dear, Paul. The poor man. We can but hope for the best.'

'Yes,' he said, but he was already nettled. He had told her about where Kirk was going on the previous night, and she was acting as if she'd never heard it. In other words, it hadn't registered with her; she'd forgotten almost immediately after she'd heard it. But, of course, she had a lot on her mind. He would have to keep trying.

'Come into the kitchen with me, and we'll have a coffee.'

'Tea, Mum, for me.' Item 2, he thought; she'd forgotten that he didn't drink coffee.

'Oh, yes, of course. Tea it is.'

In his childhood, their kitchen chats were often cosy and enjoyable to them both. But, of course, he was no longer a child, and that seemed to be taking a very long time to register with her.

He sat up awkwardly on the bar stool next to the central kitchen island, remembering how he would enjoy watching his legs dangling down a good two feet off the floor. She was not very good at making tea, because she rarely drank it; he thought it had a rather proletarian image, as far as she was concerned. But he tried to make it look like he enjoyed it.

'I'm sorry to hijack your time off like this, darling,' she said. 'Three days' leave must be very precious in your line of work…'

'What do you want of me, Mother?' he said, and she saw he was far from conciliated.

'Well, to see you, darling, for a start. Is that so strange? The family are all here, or on their way; André's flying in this afternoon; Claude arrived last night. You'll be able to catch up with all the family news.'

'I'll enjoy seeing them all again. But what you really want to know, Mum, is what am I going to do with all the shares you and Dad so generously gave me.'

She bridled a little.

'Yes, I do, but there is no need to be quite so abrupt about it, Paul. And you're always welcome in this house regardless of what shares you own, you know that. I think I know how you feel about the Corporation and what happened to your father—'

'You mean when he had a heart attack so massive that a trained doctor standing only a few yards away was unable to save him…'

'You don't need to blame yourself, Paul. Hugo was tempting fate, as I said to him on more than one occasion…'

Now, even with the best of intentions, he found himself up on his feet. 'I don't blame myself,' he said, too loudly.

'Yes, I know, you blame me, don't you? As if your father would stop working to please me, or you, or anyone else in the world; you knew him better than that, Paul.'

'I don't blame you,' he said, forcing a control over the volume of his voice. 'I don't blame him, either. I blame the Corporation, which has gobbled up all our lives and is continuing to do so.'

'Oh, here we go again, with your long-standing determination to bite the hand that feeds you. What do you think paid for your very comfortable upbringing, Paul? Not to mention your high-class boys' school, though maybe, looking back, that was a mistake…'

'I am just not going there with that one again. I am and I would have been gay if you'd sent me to the comp down the road. You simply can't, or won't, get that through your head, will you, Mum?'

She sighed. 'You're hardly arrived in the house, and here we are going over the same old ground.'

But he was not to be stopped. 'You will not simply accept me as I am, and you thought, didn't you, that landing all those shares on me would fix me to the Corporation, super-glued there for the rest of my life. How much easier everything would be between us, Mum, without that…'

Once again, something was there in his mind; not a voice, or a vision, but a sense, an understanding of where this needed to go. He hadn't been able to believe that it was Hugo when this had happened to him before, and he found it difficult to do so now, because it was certainly not a piece of advice Hugo, as he was, would have given him. But perhaps Hugo dead had different priorities than Hugo alive.

'Seven million pounds, Mum. How about that, to solve all the differences between us. And maybe even ease your anxiety about me once and for all. I will sell you all my shares, all my ten per cent, or whatever it is, of the Corporation, for seven million pounds. They must be worth at least that by now…'

'They're worth a good deal more than that, Paul; you would be selling yourself short…'

'I don't care. You can re-sell them and make a fat profit if you want. Seven million will give Kirk and I security; it would enable me to do something else, if and when I get too tired or burnt out to carry on as a hospital doctor. And this huge, ugly elephant which is always in the room whenever we talk will be gone for ever. It will make your position even stronger in relation to these characters who are trying to take control of the Corporation away from you. It will grant me my independence, and you will be the one who has given it to me. How about it, Mum?'

Right, Val thought. How about it? How about seeing my only child with Hugo take the money and run, achieving what he calls his independence, probably meaning I'll see him once in a blue moon if at all? Troubled Paul, convinced that the Corporation murdered his father, when it was more a matter of his father murdering himself? Paul who reads my concern for his lifestyle as homophobia, who seems to take personal and lasting offence if I don't leap with enthusiasm at every new step in his journey?

She knew that the offer as it had been made was a sop to her; he could easily obtain seven million pounds by selling part of his shares, probably no more than a quarter. Or did he not realise that? In any case, she could do nothing about it; the shares had been gifted to him, in the probably mistaken notion that spreading them round the family would guarantee Gilard control forever.

But, by now, she was getting to be an expert on doing deals, as Hugo had always been, and here was another one needing to be done.

'OK, Paul, if that's the way you want it, such a transaction is easily done. But I will not buy them before the board meeting on Tuesday.'

He looked puzzled. 'Well, it will take longer than that to complete the deal, won't it?'

'Yes, but that's not the point. It's not when the deal is done that it gets noticed. It gets noticed as soon as it looks like it's going to happen. And if you sell a large clump of shares like that for much less than their current worth, you'll panic the market. They'll assume that, if you're selling a lot of shares at cut price, either you know something is fundamentally wrong with the Corporation's finances or you've lost confidence in the present management. The value of everyone's shares will dive, and you will be, to put it mildly, not liked because of it.'

'Am I liked now?'

She looked at him with genuine surprise.

'Yes, of course you are. Everyone respects who you are and what you'd done. It would probably be fair to say that they see your holier-than-thou attitude to such vulgar activities as trading stuff and making lots of money as a bit misguided; you are, after all, natural heir to the whole shooting match…'

'Me? What about Amélie? What about Austin?'

'Amélie is the daughter of Hugo and Yvonne. Austin is the son of me and Maurice. You are the son of the current chief executive, me, and the previous chief executive, Hugo. I think if it ever finished up in the law courts, which God forbid, you would be accepted as the heir.'

'It's never going to happen, Mum. In any case, you've known me since the day I was born; do you really think I'm cut out for chief executive of a huge corporation?'

'Maybe not, but men who can do twelve-hour shifts on an intensive care ward wouldn't find anything in corporate life beyond them, I don't think. But I'm not trying to change your mind, Paul. I'm just saying, that unless you've got it up your nose so much with the Corporation that you want to leave it with a gaping flesh wound, you'll delay any sale of shares until after the board meeting, when the new management has been determined.'

'OK, Mum, OK. But don't get the idea that the delay will change my mind. It won't.'

Maybe not, son, Val thought. But you've given me a breathing space, and I'm good with breathing spaces. The Gilards wouldn't still be in charge of the show if I wasn't good with breathing spaces. And if McAdams and Maddox do win the day, landing them a gaping fresh wound would be only too gratifying.

So, finally, the scene was set. All the principals were gathered and able to contribute. The Gilards could go into the meeting knowing exactly what they were doing. But there was still a niggle at the back of Val's mind, a hugely momentous memory that, however she tried, she couldn't recall beyond an awareness of how important it was likely to be if she should recall it. Such a combination was so irritating that she'd tried to make herself forget about the whole business, but she still hadn't fully succeeded. She knew it was something to do with Hugo, and she also knew that spending a period of concentrated thought on Hugo could cause a variety of consequences, and few of them were likely to be what she wanted as she was on the eve of a huge meeting for the Corporation's future. It was difficult enough to get herself time to think about anything very much at the moment. But today, this day, her instincts told her that she needed to spend some time to herself thinking very hard indeed.

And because it was about Hugo, she knew she would have to go to all that was left of Hugo, the legacy of his files and paperwork. She had decided soon after his death that she was not going to leave them at Gilrey H.Q. for general access to everyone, and she had had them all moved, hook, line and sinker, to the copious basement of the Gilard country home. The house had been built on an earlier dwelling which had once belonged to a Catholic English family at a time when being Catholic in England was extremely dangerous. The basement had been so cleverly concealed that no-one, unless told, would have realised there was a basement. Now a significant part of it was taken up by wine, and there were also various mementoes, including paintings and photographs, of the house and its former inhabitants. Nevertheless, empty spaces were still available, and in a convenient small dry room, which she subsequently arranged to have locked, she had put all of Hugo's office stuff, most of it still in written form; Hugo had always been suspicious of the internet.

Her expeditions to the basement had been few and far between; being so close to Hugo's files inevitably meant she felt herself once again in proximity to him, which only served to remind her again that he was not here any more. On the two or three occasions she could remember going down to the basement, her good intentions of going through the files had usually ended in a flood of tears.

Now, of all times, there was a need for her to be pragmatic, level-headed and sensible. She knew that, ever since Hugo's death, one question had repeatedly come back to her; did he know what Donald McAdams was up to? Had he any suspicions about the man? Or, for that matter, Maddox? As far as she knew, Hugo had recruited McAdams himself, though Maddox had come through the Reynolds side of the Corporation, and in all her memories of Hugo concerning what and who he was, naïve or gullible would not be words that would easily spring to mind. Did McAdams really sneak past his guard while he persisted in his belief that he was a jolly good fellow, or did he have a plan to deal with both him and Maddox that he couldn't put into action because he ran out of time?

As she made her way past the racks of wine, she was almost tempted to pull a cork and give herself a slug for the sake of Dutch courage. However, the idea of someone finding her down here in a drunken, sobbing mess put her off the idea altogether, and she managed to get to the files without, as yet, any waterworks.

She was sitting down gazing at box after box of the stuff and wondering where on earth she could logically start when the word 'yellow' popped into her head, and then, at last, the cranks of her memory began to turn. Of course, she remembered him referring more than once to the 'yellow security files', but only to her; he never mentioned them to anyone else. After half an hour of inspecting box after box, nothing had appeared, and she was beginning to think tears would be coming soon – this was all that was left of the man she had loved for so long – when a succession of boxes full of yellow files at last appeared.

Her heart was thumping now, and she picked each file up with great eagerness, only to find names she didn't know and a few names she had worked out herself were not good news. Then, at last, it appeared, one of the fattest files in the collection, with the name, Donald McAdams, printed neatly on the front. The cover of the file also had the words 'Confidential; Authorisation required'.

Inside, the first page was a handwritten document; she recognised Hugo's handwriting, which wasn't particularly tidy, but she was familiar enough with it to be able to translate, and the thrill she felt as she read it chased away any thought of tears.

It took me a while to fully understand Donald McAdams. His camouflage is extremely good, and in the early days of his service with the Corporation, he gave every impression of being a very competent administrator who had the gift of being able to get on with many different people in various parts of the Corporation. I didn't recruit him as any kind of potential successor to me, nor did I get the impression that he saw himself as such. He was granted a good deal of flexibility in the early stages, and allowed to run his own department, which at that time was personnel management, by his own rules and principles. The first time I started having any misgivings was when a few long-standing staff in personnel started to leave. McAdams maintained that they were fundamentally outdated in their attitudes and practices, and, though I didn't choose to confront him publicly, I noticed that he had ensured the minimum of publicity for them. I made my own clandestine inquiries; to run a Corporation efficiently, such methods are inevitable. It seemed that he had bought their silence by convincing them that their 'leaving package' would be compromised if they, as he put it, 'embarrassed the Corporation'. As far as I could ascertain, their 'misdemeanours' were largely related to not being prepared to do anything and everything McAdams wanted them to do, and in at least two cases, this could have involved actions which were, at the least, legally dubious.

From then on, McAdams was 'on my radar', as it were, with two important points to be remembered. One was that a major effort, probably involving court action, would be necessary to get rid of him. Secondly, it could not be denied that he was effective; though he sailed close to the wind, he got results.

So I decided on a policy of recording and observation, and the file which bears McAdams' name includes all the relevant papers. Should anything happen to me, I don't doubt that McAdams will do his best to get control of my files, which is why I agreed with my wife some time ago that, in the event of my death, all these records should be removed to the Gilard country home immediately. They are not the property of the Corporation; they are my personal records. Whatever thoughts McAdams might have had about whether I was or wasn't keeping them, he didn't know for sure that I was, and that pause before he tries to take over will be enough to get them to safety.

Detailed examination of my records on McAdams by a good lawyer will reveal that he frequently approached the very edges of legality, both in his personal and business dealings, and on some occasions, he definitely transgressed on to the wrong side of it, sometimes to his own personal profit.

So why, whoever is reading this will probably now wonder, did I not strike against him and see to it that he was removed from the Corporation altogether?

There are three main reasons. Firstly, it would be a hugely expensive enterprise; he is manipulative with lawyers and has a whole collection of them firmly in his pocket, and it would be perfectly possible, even likely, that if he went down, he would take the Corporation with him.

Secondly, the adverse publicity would be immense and the Corporation could well be torn apart in the process of prosecuting him. Taking down McAdams would involve a number of people losing their jobs, not all of them guilty parties, because he is very good at thrashing indiscriminately around him if he is threatened.

Thirdly is the unknown quantity, John Maddox. At the moment, Maddox looks like he is little more than a bagman to McAdams, but I think there is much more to him than that. I suspect McAdams has lodged with him the names of people and organisations which would be forced to take the blame and the responsibility for some of McAdams' more dubious projects, and I also think McAdams has some kind of control over Maddox, who is a notorious womaniser and an occasional big gambler. Maddox, I believe, is both McAdams' front line of defence and his fall guy, and the association between them will only remain a working relationship while McAdams finds him useful. Maddox only holds the shares he does because of McAdams' patronage; I think, at the crucial moment, such as a board meeting to establish who is actually in charge of the Corporation, McAdams will summarily dispense with Maddox, take over his shares and then become the biggest single shareholder in the Corporation apart from Val herself. We will have created our own Frankenstein, a monster who has his own dupe to deflect all blame and accusation from himself. With the consequences described in my first two reasons, except longer and more divisive than ever.

So, for the moment, I am on a watching brief, to see how the McAdams/Maddox relationship develops and to watch for McAdams becoming over-confident, as I think in time he will, and handing me the ultimate 'smoking gun'. Gathering these records together is nevertheless, I think, a necessary move, because if and when the confrontation arrives, I will need all the ammunition I can get, and a good lawyer with extensive connections could already make a substantial case against McAdams on several grounds with this material alone. It is a bazooka which I am determined to keep in Gilard hands, which is why it has been rapidly placed in Gilard H.Q.

Hugo's oddly symmetrical signature followed. Although it could not be said to be a sentimental document, Val was in tears long before the end of it. She could see him talking; she could hear his voice through the document's measured words, and it all had the effect of bringing home to her the tragedy of his death, before he'd had the chance to put the Corporation behind him. It then occurred to her that with so much of this kind of material in the house, the Corporation might never have been behind him; even in retirement, he would be checking through his records to see how he could contribute and authorising legal action as and when he saw fit.

Not for the first time, she found herself wondering whether he loved the Corporation more than he did her, but she suspected that, when it came to it, they were indivisible. Both of their lives had been built around the Corporation; as their marriage had been formed from a union of them as people, so the Corporation was their creation, literally including businesses belonging to each one of them and all the thought and effort that had gone into developing the businesses. For Hugo to give up the Corporation would mean him sacrificing an integral part of himself, something he had created and developed through the entire span of his adult life. Even if he had succeeded in breaking away, the Corporation, like his now grown-up child, would occupy his effort and his interest, even if from a greater distance. It was his legacy to her, yes, but it was also a part of her as much as it had been a part of him, and even if she did criticise him for not letting go until it was too late, she knew she was as yet heading in the same direction and she would have the same kind of difficulty in breaking loose.

Then, just as she was preparing to put the folder back in its place, she caught a comment on a newly revealed earlier page:

'I originally put Donald McAdams' entry into one of the blue "Friends and Assets" folders, when I had no reason to think that he was anything else but a friend and an asset, alongside the likes of Lord Brookland, or Bernard Brookland as he was then.'

Val could not rely on her sixty-seven-year-old memory in the way she once could, but unless she was much mistaken, Lord Brookland was the peer to whom McAdams had sold two per cent of the Corporation shares, presumably in the attempt to get a peer of the realm on his side in the battle for control. As Val remembered, snatches of conversations with Hugo came back to her, in which he talked approvingly of Brookland and predicted that a peerage would come his way in the future. She wondered why, in that case, Brookland seemed to have opted to throw in his lot with McAdams, which inevitably led her to speculate on whether he actually had. The battle for control of the Corporation had been featured in the financial press, but she was not sure whether Brookland's current working or leisure activities would lead him to read the financial press. Then she finally physically placed the man at Hugo's funeral. That day had largely passed in a stricken daze for her, but now she had insisted on her memory doing a bit of work for its keep, she recalled a tall, slightly stooping figure, probably in his mid to late sixties, who had very politely asked her how everything was with her family as everyone was emerging from the church.

Distinguishing individual people on that day had been difficult, and it didn't surprise her that even His Lordship had managed to fade from her memory. But Hugo had specifically identified him as a friend and an asset, and that was enough for Val to go searching among the folders again, this time in the blue pile; even the move from Corporation H.Q. had not been enough to entirely disarrange Hugo's neat classifications.

Bernard Brookland is the kind of man who anyone even remotely inclined to the political left would be likely to dislike or distrust. He inherited a pile of money, originally from the family's textile interests and mills which involved labour which at one time was little short of slave labour. However, that side of the business had died away before he was born, but the family's shrewd investment policies had preserved and increased their fortune. He is a dealer in stocks and shares, and having been involved in such activities since his youth, he is a shrewd businessman who has further enlarged the family's coffers.

However, Bernard is also a philanthropist, with a known tendency to favour organisations working in practical and highly relevant areas, such as Médecins Sans Frontières, the RNLI, Oxfam, Save the Children, etc.; he is less likely to favour small local charities.

I've known Bernard for some time, even before the Corporation was set up, and he made a point of investing in the Corporation in a limited way; he does not like to invest too heavily in specific commercial organisations because it means he will find himself co-opted onto various boards, and he doesn't want that sort of drainage on his time.

Val had read enough. For all she had expected to come away from her visit to Hugo's files heartbroken all over again, his practical and administrative side was what she took away from this visit. Exactly how Lord Brookland might be useful she couldn't say, but a range of possibilities presented themselves. From what Hugo said of him, getting Bernard Brookland to invest heavily in the

Gilrey Corporation might not be easy, but since he already had two per cent, he didn't seem too reluctant to be involved, and his friendship with Hugo might lead him to further involvement if he could see that Hugo's widow wanted that to happen. After a period when everything seemed to be mitigating against her, and even her own children were clearly being intimidated, there was at least the possibility that she could acquire a new and powerful ally for herself.

By the end of the day, she had contact details for Lord Bernard Brookland.

PART SEVEN

Eve of Battle

Sunday September 27th 2015

Phoning people on a Sunday morning about Corporation matters was not something that Val would normally consider polite, but now her time was running so low that her options were limited and shrinking further by the minute.

Initially, she was answered by a smooth-voiced man who was polite but rather distant.

'If this is a business call, Mrs. Gilard, I'm not sure Lord Brookland would regard the timing as entirely appropriate,' said the unruffled voice, with only a hint of indignation. 'Lord Brookland normally tends to reserve Sundays for family matters, and his second son and his family are with us this weekend. Shall I arrange an appointment for next week, when I'm sure he will be delighted to see you?'

'Please understand that I would not be troubling His Lordship unless the matter had a degree of urgency about it. The board of the Gilrey Corporation is to meet on Tuesday, and there are a host of matters to be attended to tomorrow. If Lord Brookland could spare me no more than ten minutes, I feel he would be sure to realise the importance of the matters I would like to discuss.'

'Very well, Mrs. Gilard. I can but try.'

After a wait which seemed interminable to Val, but in fact was only about three minutes, another voice sounded at the end of the phone, saying, simply, the single word 'Brookland'.

'Lord Brookland, it's Valerie Gilard. We spoke at Hugo's funeral, if you remember.'

'Yes, I do indeed, Val, and I remember saying then that if there was anything I could do, please don't hesitate to get in touch. That offer still applies.'

'Thank you, my Lord—'

'Oh, God, Val, no, don't do that. Bernard, please. Hugo was a buddy of mine for years; I tended to see him around the City browsing and sluicing joints mostly, but I think I met you both often enough to be seen as a friend, and I hope you'll regard me as such.'

'Yes, of course, Bernard. And when you were so generous as to say what you did at the funeral, I should have had the sense to remember it and consult you before now.'

'Consult me? Goodness, Val, that sounds a bit ominous.'

As succinctly as she could, Val told him of the impending attempt by McAdams and Maddox to take over the Corporation, as well as their efforts to deprive her children of their shares. It didn't take long for Bernard Brookland to appreciate the gravity of the situation.

'Look, Val,' he said eventually. 'As I said, my son Simon, his wife Ann and their two smashing kids who are rapidly moving on from being kids are with us today, and we have a comfortable lunch planned at a local pub/restaurant we know. I won't be getting sloshed because my days of getting even moderately sloshed are at an end, I'm afraid; doctor's orders and all that. But I appreciate you need to talk about this urgently. Rather than drag you all the way over here, we'll set up the screens they use now for the purpose – why people bother to commute for miles any more I really don't know – and we'll chew it over. Please rest assured that I will do my level best to help. I don't know McAdams at all, though I've heard various things about him, but I do know John Maddox, and in a context which makes me wish I didn't. Shall we make a time this evening when we can comfortably sort it out? I really would like to help if I possibly can.'

The arrangements were made there and then, and Val felt, probably for the first time since her husband had died, that possibly, just possibly, the tide, which had seemed to be so remorselessly flowing against her, might at long last be turning.

The appointed time of seven o'clock in the evening approached, and Val headed for her study for her conference with Lord Brookland. At the same time, another meeting was assembling in the house, a meeting that Val knew about but was not going to attend, partly because of her fixture with Brookland, but also because her daughter, the probable next managing director of the Gilrey Corporation, didn't want her to be there.

Val was, at first, ready to take offence at this proposed arrangement of Amélie's, but then the younger woman, who had clearly been doing a lot of thinking, perhaps as a result of the arrival of her husband, André, sketched out her reasons.

'Firstly, Val, you are the mother, or mother-in-law, of all of them. When parents talk to offspring, they don't, if they've got any sense, start laying down the law; they try to approach subjects diplomatically, and make progress by reason, negotiation, discussion. I am not a parent or a parent-in-law, I am a sister and sister-in-law, and believe me, that makes a lot of difference. I think that certain things to do with loyalty and working together need laying on the line. I grant you, when I first heard from you about this board meeting, I didn't think it was too good an idea, and my initial reaction was to protect my own business before I started charging back across the Atlantic. André and I then had to fight off what turned out to be the first attempts of the opposition to fix the meeting.

'Since then, I've been thinking a lot, and even more so when I knew you were prepared to put your faith in me as the new M.D. I think I have a very good case to make to them about the importance of family above everything, and the debt they owe to the Corporation, whatever they might think of it. And, unlike you, dear Val, I don't have to pull any punches, and what's more, because you're not there, neither do they. I'm going to get at them, on the basis of finding out once and for all if anyone of them have already sold any shares, and if so, to whom. I'm going to make them answer back, so we don't go into the meeting on Tuesday and get some nasty surprises when it's too late for us to do anything about it.

'It could be tough going, Val, but André is there, he knows what I'm going to do, and we make a pretty determined team when we get going. He's already agreed, incidentally, that Delatour should now be an organisation within an organisation, and he's also agreed that he will run it. As part of Gilrey, it will be better protected than ever from stock market predators, and we might well be able to expand it.'

'And is that how you talked him into it, darling, or were there – erm – other means?'

'Yes, a few other means.' Amélie almost blushed, and Val smiled. 'But I can assure you even other means don't necessarily work with André if he's determined not to be convinced. He can also be very naughty at times in pushing me in the direction of other means even when he's already more or less decided that I'm right. As I think you probably know well enough, Val, it doesn't do to underestimate the deviousness of the male. In any case, by one way or another, I have him firmly on my side, and if the sparks are going to fly, he'll be hanging in there with me.

'Your business is Lord Brookland, and if our online researches are even half right, the man is phenomenally rich and resolutely loyal to those who he regards as his friends.'

'And he certainly felt like that about Hugo. I read somewhere that the Brookland family originate on one or the other of their parents' sides from Ireland, so maybe he could see in Hugo's Huguenot background a fellow non-Englishness. They were palling around in London at one time like two raucous public school roustabouts.'

'Well, that's all to the good. We need a big time ally, Val, and if you can get him fully onside this evening, that will be at least as important as anything I'm doing at my meeting. If we can both bring it off, it's curtains for McAdams and Maddox and all systems go for Gilrey as we want Gilrey to be.'

As seven o'clock approached, the family gathered in one of the old house's large basement rooms, not far from where Val, earlier in the day, had been consulting Hugo's files. This room had once been the place that, during the turmoil of seventeenth century politics, had provided the family in residence at the time with a convenient and effective hiding place for family members or friends and associates with prices on their heads. The layout of the house then made it simple enough to disguise the fact that the house had a basement at all. In those days, it had been a dark and dusty place; now, this part of it had been converted into a small, thirty-seat cinema, one of the indulgences Hugo allowed himself in his later years, even though he had precious few opportunities to use it.

Now, the little room was fully lit, and in front of the screen, Amélie was standing watching the rest of the family file in. After a brief discussion, she and André had decided between them that André should sit in the front row and allow Amélie to occupy the space below the big screen on her own, thereby clearly featuring the potential new M.D. as the speaker holding the floor.

Amélie greeted each new entrant cheerfully enough; even if the mood of the meeting was to change, she thought, they could at least start on an amicable footing. However, she didn't want the beginning of the meeting to immediately degenerate into random conversation, and when everyone was in and seated, she went straight for it.

'Thanks to everyone for giving up your Sunday evening time,' she said, 'and I hope you will find it has been worth your while. As you can see, although this is a meeting aimed directly at Corporation interests, Val is not with us. This is because she is in conference with Lord Brookland, who is actually one of our shareholders, though with only two per cent of the shares at the moment. But it's also because I asked her not to be here. I think we have some serious talking to do, and to have the figure most of us see as "Mum" hovering over us might inhibit some of us from speaking as we would want to. And, in that context, I would ask you, please, not to interrupt me until I've finished what I want to say, because each and every one of you will have every chance of speaking your mind, as candidly as you like, when I've finished.

'I've heard it said, by people both inside and outside of this room, that Val would do better to simply retire; she would be well provided for, and she would then not suffer the same fate as Hugo. I have to say that, for anyone who genuinely knows Val, this attitude is naïve.

'Indecently soon after Hugo's death, two unprincipled and disrespectful mavericks have decided they want to take over the Corporation which was Hugo and Val's baby. And, yes, I've heard the stuff about the Corporation being only about money, and if that's what you think, you clearly don't really understand the people or the Corporation. If you really just want to make money, you can play the share market and see how you get on; you can bet on the horses, you can devise some plausible scam which enough members of the gullible public will go for to make you wealthy and comfortable. You don't work your guts out finding a combination of goods and services which people will find meaningful, helpful and maybe even important in their lives. You don't spend long working hours providing thousands of people with worthwhile jobs which will give their lives purpose and reward. You don't graft away at establishing a working environment where people are not randomly used and discarded, where making an occasional mistake doesn't become a capital offence, where forcing people to do as much work for as little pay as you can get away with becomes the chief aim of management.'

Amélie looked directly at Paul, whose eyes were fixedly on her and whose facial expression was difficult to interpret, as it could equally mean furious anger or furious thought.

'The Corporation, as created by Hugo and Val,' she resumed, 'is not an impersonal, monolithic, mindless dictatorship, and for it to become so, as under McAdams and Maddox it almost certainly will, is for Val like seeing one of her precious children turn into a monster. If you have children of your own, you won't find that difficult to understand, and even if you don't, it doesn't need that much imagination to realise how heart-breaking and demoralising such an experience would be. In all honesty, what kind of retirement would it be for Val to watch her life's work being systematically and cynically ripped up and some grotesque Kafkaesque inhuman disaster of an organisation taking its place?'

Amélie saw Jennifer's mouth opening and hurried on; if people were already itching to interrupt, she was working towards the reactions she wanted, but it was too early as yet to go to a general discussion.

'And, if we're going to talk about how Val might feel – well, I am, in any case – it's time we talked about loyalty. All of us, even the orphans amongst us, have parents in their lives.

'Even if the parents are no longer alive, the mother or the father or both would have had a part in the child's life, whether positive or negative. But ultimately, it is for the child to decide who his or her parents should be. I'm a case in point; Val is not my natural mother, but I haven't seen my natural mother now for the best part of fifteen years. Her rather lukewarm involvement in my upbringing seemed to stop when my father married Val. It didn't need to; I was willing to go on seeing her, and for a while I did try, until I realised she was largely indifferent to whether I did or not. So whenever times have been difficult, up to and particularly including the death of my father, it's Val who's done the heavy lifting for me; it's Val, not my mother, who cleared the path for me to become a wealthy, successful and happily married woman. She's not perfect, and she still has bees in her bonnet, one of them being about me having children; with all due respect to anyone and everyone who have got children, I don't want them, and I doubt whether Val and I will ever see eye to eye on that.

'But that doesn't mean I don't owe her loyalty; I do, for all sorts of reasons, and I always will.' (Here goes, girl, Amélie thought, as she took a deep inward breath.) 'As, in my opinion, we all do, even those of you who are only related to Val by marriage. Yes, we've all chosen our own ways, as the offspring of successful parents must, in just about every species you would like to name as well as human beings. We all have to fly the nest, test our mettle, see if we've got what it takes to make it in the big world. And, we would all do well to bear in mind that it's because Val has been the bedrock, the shoulder always there to cry on, the prop always available to keep us standing up, that all of us can now point to a string of successful achievements. We don't just benefit from Val's material help, we also gain advantages from her gentle but insistent guidance, usually calculated to be in the best interests of whoever she's helping.'

Her tone had monopolised the room for some time, but now another voice finally intervened, sounding very harsh and challenging in the subterranean atmosphere of the basement cinema.

'What I've done, I've done in the teeth of her opposition, right from the start,' said Paul. 'Whatever you say, Amélie, she is no saint, and her values sometimes aren't ours.'

'You might have waited until I'd finished, Paul, as I asked you to, and no-one, least of all Val, would belittle what you've achieved. But is it really such a mystery to you that your choice of profession has frightened her? You, who are the only one of us who is actually the offspring of both her and Hugo? Knowing that you would be exposed daily to all sorts of illnesses and all sorts of people? Does it really surprise you that she is so anxious about that? You could well finish up being a father yourself, Paul, as many gay men now do; if your son or your daughter chooses to go into your profession, will you not have a degree of anxiety yourself? And are you not being a touch unfair when you accuse Val of being materialistic and obsessed with profit, when in fact she's just being maternal?'

'I would expect you to be her champion, Amélie, but we all know you can and have been critical of her in the past,' said Paul.

'Yes, and I will again, I don't doubt, Paul.' Amélie's voice rose; her audience stirred in their seats. 'But we're not talking here about disagreements, different interpretations, the clash of motives. We're talking here about loyalty at its most basic, about whether we choose to desert our sixty-seven-year-old mother – because that's what she is to all of us, whatever the variations, and it's certainly what she is to you, Paul – and swan off with the proceeds of the shares she was generous enough to gift us in the first place while the poor woman watches her life work being undone by a couple of crooks and shysters, because that's what they are, those two. Already they've tried to undermine my business, they've tried to do the same to Austin and Maureen's business, including some incredibly low down, dirty tactics aimed at Maureen, and tactics have also been used to get at Jennifer and Paul.

'But even if McAdams and Maddox were as pure as the driven snow, and they are anything but, my first loyalty must and always will be towards Val, and therefore towards the Corporation, because the Corporation as we know it is Val. I suggest the very least we owe Val is to give her full backing up to and throughout Tuesday's meeting; as and when she beats off this takeover attempt, then we will be looking at a different situation where loyalties could be subject to other interpretations, but I am asking for your full backing to put me in as the new M.D. and ensure Val wins this battle, for the sake of all of our futures and, in my opinion, whether it sounds pompous or not, for the sake of the decency and integrity of the whole Gilard family.'

Amélie deliberately moved away from the front of the room and sat in one of the cinema seats, thereby conceding the floor to whoever felt they wanted it. For a moment, the assembled family sat in stunned silence; of all the issues that had been uppermost in their minds over the last few tense days, the simple matter of loyalty had not been as considered as it might have been. After a few seconds, a spontaneous burst of applause broke out, but it was clear that there were varying degrees of enthusiasm amongst the family. Then Austin made his way to the front, with a slightly apologetic smile on his face.

He nodded to the audience, as if confirming what he thought was already in their minds. 'Yes, of course, as you all know well enough, Val *is* my mother, and she's always been happy enough to emphasise it if and when the need arose. She didn't particularly care for me setting up a business in Spain, though she was happy enough to advise and support me when she realised it was what I wanted to do, and even more so when I met Mo. I accept most of what Amélie has said, but I think it's worth pointing out that the loyalty issue perhaps isn't quite as straightforward as she makes it sound. Before she emerged as Val's named heiress to the business, we were faced with a situation where the Corporation had already worked one parent to death and was well on the way to doing the same to the other one. In my book, it seemed like a strange kind of loyalty to watch Val struggling with the power politics inside the Corporation, possibly into her seventies. What Amélie says about her natural mother probably largely applies to my natural father, who didn't spend a lot of time worrying about my welfare when a juicy business opportunity arose in Australia. Hugo was my father, as far as I'm concerned; as Amélie chose Val as her kind of elective mother, so I chose Hugo as my elected father. It's perhaps a salutary warning, looking back on it, that the kind of loyalty which saves people's lives was not more in evidence when Hugo was working himself to death. Loyalty, as I said, is not as simple as it might seem.

'But Amélie being willing to take on the M.D. post changes things quite a lot, for me. It means Val can honourably retire and enjoy the leisure she richly deserves. I got used to the idea of Amélie being my sister at quite an early age, and I think I know her pretty well by now. She and André make a formidable team, and we've already had a dummy run of how she is capable of dealing with McAdams and Maddox when she brushed off their sad attempts to undermine Delatour. She's a smooth operator, like her father always was, but with a human face, like him again.

'I will, here and now, make a solid pledge that I will not sell any of my shares in the Corporation until the new management board is well installed, and Mo and I are happy to work our business under the umbrella of the Corporation. Some other people in this room may be blasé about having a big powerful corporation behind them, but Mo and I have already been on the end of one very painful and personal attempt to rock our boat.

'International business is pretty much a jungle at the best of times, and when a big beast comes for you, having a big beast of your own to call on is not just handy, it's pretty essential for survival.'

Austin got another burst of general applause, but Amélie was not convinced that the day was won yet. Both Jennifer and Paul had applauded, but both of them also looked thoughtful and, in Paul's case particularly, rather troubled.

As all eyes were now turned in their direction, Jennifer got to her feet and held on to the back of the seat in front of her, waving away invitations to come to the front.

'No, I'm not going to make another speech,' she said, a little uncertainly. 'I think we've already had enough speech-making. It would probably be a lot easier if this matter was just all about loyalty to Val, and I know from past experience that when complicated problems arise, there are many people who would love to simplify them and boil them down to their essentials. But this is not as straightforward as it might seem. However, I don't see now as the time when I want to make clear and act upon my longer term intentions. We need to weather the immediate crisis before we can make more lasting decisions. Yes, I will support Amélie for M.D., and I will not sell my shares to anyone until this crucial board meeting is over. But that's as far as I'm prepared to go, and whatever I decide to do is in no way a reflection on how I feel about Val; I love her dearly and I always will, but her working career is just about done and mine still has a long way to go. Disloyalty doesn't enter into it at any point, as I see it; the question is pragmatic and the answer needs to be equally so.'

Paul then got up, almost as soon as Jennifer had finished.

'We've come here,' he said slowly, 'it seems, for the Corporation big beasts to tell us which way we are required to jump. I have given up precious leave from a demanding job to listen to this. If my determination to pursue a medical career is seen as disloyal, then so be it, but we all ultimately have to be true to ourselves, once we're old enough to know what we're all about. My mother would have involved me in a heterosexual marriage, regardless of what she herself knew about my sexuality, and I suppose defying her in that respect is a kind of disloyalty, but I wouldn't then satisfy her ambitions for me by living a lie. The same thing applies to my involvement with the Corporation; it isn't me, it isn't what I am, and no amount of arm-twisting or propaganda speeches about disloyalty is going to make any difference in that respect. I will respect everyone's wishes in the present situation and not sell any shares until after Amélie is installed as M.D., and I do genuinely wish her well in taking on such a job. But after the meeting, when it's been established that control remains in Gilard hands, I am going to sell my shares; I will happily sell them to the new board if they want to increase their holding, but I will sell them, and I will continue practising my chosen profession, whatever anyone else's ideas about loyalty might be. Polonius, in the play *Hamlet*, advises his son, "this above all, to thine own self be true" and that, in my opinion, is the greatest and most valid loyalty of all.'

In the uneasy silence that followed, Amélie once again made her way to the front. She left a decent interval before she began, so as not to give the impression of talking down Paul.

'Thanks to everyone for making their thoughts known. It wasn't in any way my intention to attempt to force a conclusion to our discussions about the future, nor was I seeking to try and cram everyone into the same mindset. It was obvious some time ago that the levels of involvement of different members of the family would vary according to their talents and abilities and their view of the Corporation. Even if uniformity was possible with such a diverse group of people, I wouldn't be attempting to enforce it, and neither would Val. But it seems we are united as regards the immediate future, which is the board meeting on Tuesday. I respect your decisions and thank you for them, and I hope you will not misunderstand my motives if I ask you to take care tomorrow; from what we know of McAdams and Maddox, they will not give up trying to enhance their holding until the very last possible moment, and they may yet have a dirty trick or two up their sleeves. At this very moment, Val is doing her best to bring in a new big beast on our side, and hopefully we will have some good news by the end of the day.

'Val has given me leave to say that everyone is welcome to stay here until the meeting takes place on Tuesday at Gilrey H.Q.; in fact, she particularly asks that you all do, so that we can present a united front before the meeting and make it difficult for McAdams and Maddox to pick anyone off. If you receive any communications by whatever media and you are not sure how to react, please do come and discuss it with me. As usual, breakfast, lunch and dinner will be provided tomorrow for anyone who is staying with us; we won't let standards of Gilard hospitality fall. Thank you.'

It'll do, Amélie thought. But it isn't the end of it, by any means. So far, so more or less good. Now she would need to talk to everyone individually to find out what they have in mind for tomorrow.

She caught sight of André, standing by the door saying goodbye to people as they left. He grinned and winked at her, and she didn't need three guesses to work out what he had in mind for tonight. On this occasion, she felt that she wouldn't need much persuasion.

In her study, Val examined the image of Bernard Brookland on her screen. His face was undoubtedly friendly enough and he was, as ever, immaculately groomed, with even the growing amount of grey hair, especially on the temples and above the ears, brushed and smoothed down. However, there was undoubtedly a quality about him, probably developed after his long years of being 'the boss', that spoke eloquently of a man who would not easily be crossed.

After a few pleasantries concerning his family visit, he got down to business.

'I've been looking into the two characters you were telling me about, Val,' he said. 'Donald McAdams I've only met a handful of times, and always in the company of Hugo. At one time, he used to follow Hugo around like an obedient puppy, though to me there was always something about him which I wouldn't be inclined to trust. I suppose I probably dismissed him as yet another bag man, with little separate personality or talent which wasn't tied up in doing as he was told. It would seem, however, on the basis of what you've told me, that he wasn't always doing as he was told.'

'No,' said Val. 'Perhaps it could be said that he regarded whatever he was told to do as open to interpretation – his interpretation, usually corresponding with his interests. And what about John Maddox?'

She found herself quite startled at the expression that now appeared on Brookland's face. He suddenly turned from an amiable older gentleman to a severe army officer remembering some outrage on the part of one of his subordinates. Val remembered that Bernard Brookland had actually served in the army for a while some years ago.

'When you originally told me the name, a bell rang in this cavernous old memory of mine, and after that, it didn't take too long to pin it down. Maddox, only fairly recently, had an affair with my daughter.'

'Oh, dear, Bernard. I'm sorry to hear that.'

'So was I. The man is a shameless libertine. When I found out about it, and about the fact that he was married, of course, I had every intention of going to him and confronting him about it. But, Hannah being Hannah, she finished with him first, and threatened so convincingly to expose him to his family that he ran a mile. But she was deeply hurt; he had promised her all sorts of stuff to – well, get his way, I suppose you'd call it.'

'How long ago was this?'

'About five years ago now. Hannah was twenty-seven, and on the rebound, I think, from a marriage that really just didn't work for her. Hannah is a great girl with a lot of qualities going for her, but unfortunately her taste in men is not one of them. She was, of course, badly shaken up by the breakdown of the marriage – she had been impressed with the man's apparent sophistication and worldliness, but she discovered too late that he was also, unfortunately, bone idle, especially around the home. "An old-fashioned guy" was how he described himself. "Right," said Hannah, "well, perhaps you should go and find yourself an old-fashioned girl."

'For a while, she was hitting the town and it was in some club or other that she met Maddox, who can charm the birds from the trees if he thinks there's something in it for him. He gave her a lot of stuff about the breakdown of his own marriage, and they started an affair, though it didn't take long for Hannah to suspect things were not as they seemed. She may be impressionable, but she's a long, long way from being stupid.

'Then, on one of the girls' nights out in the City, she happened to run into Maddox's daughter, Monica. It seems that Monica has a rather ambivalent relationship with her father; she loves him as a daughter should, but she has no illusions, if you see what I mean.'

'Yes,' said Val. 'I know Monica, a little vaguely, I suppose, but I think I could readily believe that of her.'

Brookland's frown intensified.

'This time, Hannah wasn't so much cast down and disillusioned as extremely angry, and for a while she kept a dossier on Maddox, in which she put all the information she managed to gather about his affairs. It wasn't particularly difficult; Maddox seems to be incredibly indiscreet for a man in his situation. After a while, Hannah met someone else, the man she is still seeing, as a matter of fact, though I think she will wait for some time before she again commits herself. I have to admit, Val, that it shook me somewhat to discover that this Maddox character is one of the two who are trying to get their hands on the Gilrey Corporation – Gilrey is yours, yours and Hugo's, and I can't imagine, or perhaps I would just rather not imagine, what kind of an organisation those two will turn it into if they get their hands on it. All the same, Val, as that little man in *Blackadder* used to say, "I have a cunning plan", but I only intend to put it into action if you are happy for me to do so. You are the boss of Gilrey.'

'Yes, and I'd love to hear what it is, Bernard.'

'I'm going to make an offer to Maddox that he can't refuse, or rather that it would be unwise for him to refuse if he doesn't want

Hannah's dossier spread across the national front pages. I'm going to buy out his shares. As I understand it, Maddox owns eighteen and a half per cent of the Corporation. It will cost me a hell of a lot of money to do it at market value, and it sticks in my craw a bit to be the means by which Maddox will become a rich man, but the point is that he will be a rich man somewhere else rather than Gilrey. I am filthy rich, Val, as you know well enough, and I have guys of such quality that I'm probably going to go on getting richer. It means your family and your friends, of which I count myself one, will have virtually the entire Corporation bar the twenty per cent McAdams owns. We can heave him off the board if we need to, if he doesn't come to his senses, or alternatively we could buy him out as well. What do you think of my cunning plan, Val?'

Somehow, somewhere in this conversation, Val's eyes had started to water, which she greeted with a mixture of puzzlement and embarrassment; weepiness was not generally a characteristic she ascribed to herself. However, when the circumstances of life keep ratcheting up the tension day after day, it can only be an immense relief, like a glorious liberation, when the tension is suddenly released like the snapping of a rack.

'It's a glorious, wonderful plan, Bernard, though I worry that it may be some years before you get what most people would call a decent return on your investment.'

'Oh, we'll make it work, Val, I'm sure we will. I've already talked it over with Lydia, and we decided that putting such funds into Gilrey is pretty safe, probably as safe as any investment can be, and the fact of me buying in will do the value of the Corporation no harm at all. I never invest substantially in anything without talking it over with Lydia; she keeps herself informed and, as you probably know, she was a successful businesswoman when I met her.' Lydia Castleton Limited, providing a whole series of beauty and health products and treatments, was now largely run by the couple's eldest daughter Hannah, who tended to have a better head for business than she did for men.

'Yes, of course. I am immensely grateful to both of you, Bernard, and I hope you will be able to join us at the board meeting on Tuesday. Presumably your broker will be able to put the deal through tomorrow; I will instruct Corporation H.Q. to do everything they can to get it done in time.'

'I'm sure we can do that, Val, and perhaps you could e-mail the agenda and any other relevant paperwork to me as soon as possible. We both look forward to working with you, Val, and subsequently Amélie. How is she?'

'She is well and prospering, Bernard, and she takes after her father a great deal more than she takes after her mother, I'm glad to say. She might just have inherited her father's tendency to overwork; she certainly has little inclination towards having children and developing her own family life.'

'For the moment, at least, Val, that's probably not a bad idea, from the Corporation point of view. Children are not everyone's cup of tea, in any case. If she is more interested in a career than kids, that's her prerogative.'

'Yes, absolutely.' Val almost physically bit her tongue. After landing such a sensational deal at the last moment, she was not going to rock the boat.

A few minutes later, she clicked her phone off and found herself taking in large gulps of air, as if what had just happened was more than she could easily absorb. She had an overwhelming urge to tell Amélie, who she knew had been valiantly trying to get some last-minute assurances from the rest of the family. As it happened, they could now live with a defection, perhaps even two defections, but Amélie needed to know, as soon as possible, that victory was assured in any case.

Monday September 28th 2015

Donald McAdams was in his Corporation office by 8.30; he had many things to do and many people to talk to before the meeting the next day. He intended to be absolutely certain that all exits had been covered and all foreseeable developments had been foreseen. A screen in his office was dedicated to watching the share price of Gilrey stock and recording any shares bought or sold during the course of the day.

'Whose nerve will give way first, I wonder?' he murmured to himself. He never actually got to the point of putting any money on things he saw as likely to happen, but he carried a kind of scale of odds in his head, and the game of guessing what would come up next was always a mild form of amusement.

Paul. He must be the leading candidate, he thought. Paul who thought the whole Stock Exchange was the devil's work and remained determined to live in his antiseptic medical purity, though perhaps with a few million quid in the bank in case something else came along. Or perhaps Jennifer, pseudo-French snob teacher Jennifer, would ultimately be unable to resist the opportunity to make her posh school even posher. Or maybe Austin would fancy upmarketing from the Costa del Sol to the French Riviera, or some other high-class resort where his clientele wouldn't be so sprinkled with toe-rags on the run from the U.K.

But he knew that his interest was more about vague curiosity than actual expectation. He knew that, by now, Val would have talked a lot about loyalty, probably supported by her formidable eldest stepdaughter, and the pair of them would be likely to have got their troops in line for the coming meeting. He had calculated that catching Val off guard not long after the funeral would not last; her feelings for Hugo would have intensified as a result of the loss of him.

But Donald knew that he could play the long game, and he was quite prepared to do so. He had done just that in his relationship with Hugo Gilard, making himself the obedient servant – and how excruciatingly difficult that had been at times only Donald McAdams knew – on the basis of building up a solid foundation of trust as a springboard to use when the time was right. He could see which way things were going from an early stage; Hugo was a classic workaholic, who made the already complex business of running a Corporation even more difficult by trying to operate it as some kind of democracy, where the opinions and inclinations of the workforce could significantly impact on decision-making and action, usually meaning everything would take twice as long to accomplish, and if and when it was accomplished, it would be a weak, watered down version of what had been intended.

McAdams had worked assiduously on creating his own empire within the Corporation. He eventually got himself appointed as Head of Administration, a fairly nebulous description that could ultimately mean whatever he wanted it to mean, and he used his department as a state within a state, making it clear to all those within it that it would not be a democracy of any kind and those who did not come up to scratch would find themselves out on their ears. He hoped that, in this way, he could create a dynamic section of the Corporation whose example would filter through to the rest of it, allowing his department to gradually gobble up other smaller parts of the firm and sweeping him to power at the top of his pyramid. By the time Hugo worked out what he was doing, as he inevitably would, Donald's power base would be too great for the momentum to be stopped.

But it was Hugo's retirement that Donald was conniving for, not his death. For a day or two afterwards, even the famously laid-back McAdams was genuinely shocked. But it didn't last; he reflected that Gilard's way of operating had made it virtually inevitable. He saw himself as the natural heir and the Corporation's main chance of rescue; a sixty-seven-year-old woman whose only executive job had been to control her minor partnership in the Corporation, a firm of caterers, was not the one to take the whole venture forward if it was to survive in the commercial jungle. Now Val seemed to see it as some kind of glorified family corner shop, with her various children and stepchildren finding comfortable niches for themselves like a kind of nepotistic soap opera.

This time, the Gilards would probably prevail, though Donald knew there were a few alterations and reforms he might get through the board anyway, perhaps, if for no other reason, as a gesture of defiance in the direction of the controlling family. But, as the days turned into weeks and the weeks into months, Paul would be wondering why he has these shares and why the Corporation is still like a millstone around his neck, Jennifer would be looking for ways of boosting her school against the competition, which in a place like Paris will be formidable, Austin will still be seeking to move himself and his vulnerable wife ever further upmarket for the protection of more genteel and respectable circumstances, and perhaps even Amélie might be reflecting that taking care of Delatour had been more fun and less stress than she was now having to endure. Like ripe fruit hanging ever more precariously as it got heavier, they would all start dropping neatly into the McAdams coffers until he was ideally situated to expel the whole wretched family from the Corporation and allow him to run it properly, probably beginning by reducing the size of the workforce by at least a quarter and ending a number of comfortable sinecures developed over the years.

McAdams worked on through the agenda, making sure he had the correct documents to hand for each item, and by the time he felt he had enough resources to see him comfortably through the meeting, he noticed the morning had almost gone. He checked on the share market again; hardly any activity on the Gilrey Corporation at all. He went off to have his usual comfortable lunch and give some thought to the afternoon's confrontation, as confrontation it would surely be.

He had arranged a private dining room for himself when he needed to think as well as eat, which generally turned out to apply to most lunchtimes. Occasionally, he would have 'working lunches' with some other members of the management team, but he disliked even the term itself and too often they seemed to turn into pointless small talk.

The subject of his thoughts today, reluctant as he usually was to devote thinking time to the man, was John Maddox. As his afternoon was going to be spent mostly with Maddox, thinking about the potential end of their relationship, which would almost certainly be the result of the meeting, needed to be done, though he didn't find such thoughts congenial. He had wondered on a number of occasions what really explained his relationship with Maddox. His past experience had suggested that he had a certain fascination with men who were effortlessly successful with women. In his younger days, he sometimes felt afraid that it was a kind of latent homosexuality, in which he diverted his attraction for the men through their female partners, but time and experience had shown that he had no intentions of actively pursuing any kind of homosexual activity. Perhaps it was a kind of envy; Donald himself had no illusions about his sexual magnetism. No sports activity, diets or exercise programmes had ever succeeded in themselves in making him more desirable to the opposite sex. Money and power had achieved his limited successes. He knew well enough that his wife, Susan, liked the idea of their comfortable, affluent life rather more than she liked him, and such attempts at sexual activity as they had spasmodically embarked upon in earlier years had never been enough to actually produce any children, though he suspected Susan would be as blasé about that, had it ever happened, as she was about everything else.

Perhaps John Maddox's totally shameless attitude lent him a certain magnetism for other less amorously successful men. Maddox was widely seen as a dissolute womaniser, even by the women in his own family. McAdams knew, from the careful dossier of evidence he had compiled on Maddox and which he was going to confront him with this afternoon, that Maddox was not above carrying on affairs on Corporation premises, while everyone in the firm knew what he was doing. It was if the man had decided, fairly early on in his life, that women were much more interesting than anything else that he might be doing, and if that was the self-destruct button that fate had decreed to him, he might as well press it with all his might until the magnetism or whatever it was finally started to run out.

But McAdams knew well enough the real answer to his speculation. It was the very reputation of Maddox that was useful to him as a partner in his quest to dominate the Corporation. Men both feared and respected Maddox, a potent combination for anyone seeking to control them, and women were both fascinated and repelled by him at the same time, meaning they found it difficult to resist the challenge of him. Maddox had become Donald's personal guided missile, to be launched at anyone, male or female, who needed to be subdued, implicated or involved.

But that was mostly about the hunt, the tortuous route to the top, which was now all but over. Maddox had outlived his usefulness. If the relationship continued, Donald faced the prospect of sharing his power within the Corporation with him, and that would, in any case, cause the disintegration of any working relationship quite quickly.

Keeping dossiers on people was not unusual for Donald McAdams. There was a pleasing irony in the fact that it was a habit that he had derived largely from Hugo Gilard, who he knew well enough was a careful and conscientious record-keeper. But even before he'd started to write down details, he had trained his memory to retain vast quantities of information; consulting his records was generally a matter of confirmation rather than discovery. He knew the strengths and weaknesses of everyone involved in the management of the Corporation, and a fair few of those further down the pecking order.

He intended to force Maddox to sell him his shares, amounting to eighteen and a half per cent of the total; added to his own eighteen per cent and the two that nominally belonged to Lord Brookland – His Lordship had not evinced any interest in becoming involved at any level, and his broker would act as McAdams wished – the total would amount to thirty-eight and a half per cent of the Corporation. He would become the largest single shareholder apart from Val herself. Val, her children and stepchildren would hold sixty-one and a half per cent of the shares, but large dollops of that holding were obtainable, by one means or another. He had various schemes and ideas for persuading the younger Gilards to put their money elsewhere, and the large chunks of the Corporation that already answered primarily to him would not be slow to pressurise the junior Gilard businesses if they were told to do so. If Amélie was to be in control, as his information was telling him, then whether she would have the authority to hold things together in the way her stepmother could would be a very relevant matter.

As the agreed time for his screen meeting with John Maddox approached, McAdams was conscious of a largely unfamiliar apprehension, which he found difficult to understand; whatever else he may have thought about Maddox, he had never been aware of being afraid of him. It was no more than a suspicion, a rather unsettled feeling in the back of his mind, that he wasn't necessarily as much in control of events as he would like to be.

However, he had no intention of letting any kind of insecurity show itself to Maddox, and when the other man's darkly handsome features appeared on the screen in front of him, McAdams had arranged his features into their usual avuncular detached amusement.

Maddox was smiling, which wasn't a particularly unusual circumstance – Maddox generally had his charm button turned on, whoever he was talking to – but there was something about the way he was smiling that tweaked once again at McAdams' unusual insecurity.

'John,' said McAdams, 'you're looking well, even prosperous, dare I say it.'

'With reason, Donald, I can assure you. But we'll come to that. You, on the other hand, are looking rather serious, by your usual laid-back standards.'

McAdams made himself smile; the ability to smile, or at least manage a creditable imitation of a smile, in every conceivable circumstance was an asset, in his opinion.

'Well, sometimes, John, I'm afraid serious things need to happen, and I rather think we have reached the point in our relationship where it is inevitable. As you know, I've taken an interest in your phenomenal career to date, and I've never before had much in the way of serious doubt about your potential as a high-flyer, a natural leader.'

'Meaning, presumably, that you do now?'

'I'm afraid so. In all honesty, John, you seem to make precious little attempt to tone down what we might call the more colourful side of your life.'

Maddox was silent for a long moment, and when he spoke again, his eyes had narrowed. But he, too, could still keep a kind of smile for all occasions.

'If you're referring to my love life, Donald, as I assume you must be, I would just make two fairly obvious observations. One, my love life is none of your damn business, and two, it never seems to have bothered you before.'

McAdams leaned forward, closer to the screen he was facing.

'No, it wasn't and isn't my business, but it becomes the Corporation's business when you behave as recklessly and indiscreetly as you now constantly do. And I was always optimistic enough, or perhaps a better word would be naïve enough, to believe that the whole thing would moderate itself as you got older. For God's sake, John, you're married; you've got children well on their way to adulthood. Do their feelings not matter?'

The anger rising in Maddox was now very obvious.

'I can hardly believe it's you, McAdams, who are setting yourself up as some kind of moral barometer. You run all those parts of the Corporation you've managed to get your steely claws into like some crazed tyrant, crushing here, blackmailing there, squeezing ever more effort out of your subordinates for as little money as you can get away with. If I'd had twice the women I have, and treated them twice as badly as I have, I would still be a veritable little boy scout compared to the stuff going on every day of your life. There was a time when I admired you, when I was happy to work with you and even do what I was told occasionally, but men like you don't give and take, they just take, and they do nothing useful with what they take, apart from bonfiring it to satisfy their vanity. If ever the blackest of pots was calling the kettle black, McAdams, that's exactly what you're doing here, so take your smug moral outrage and shove it up your arse.'

Donald remained silent for a moment; it would take much worse than this for him to be seriously antagonised by anyone he deemed to be his inferior, meaning almost everyone he knew or had ever known. He expected Maddox to sign off, but Maddox's distrust of McAdams was so deep seated that he wasn't going until he'd found out exactly what the other man wanted.

'Odd that you should mention blackmail, though it often tends to be the case, John, that one man's blackmail is another man's strategic management. I'm looking for you to sell your shares, John, to me, of course, and in that way you will avoid the avalanche of lawsuits that will otherwise be coming your way when the information I have in my dossier finds its way into the hands of several greedy lawyers, of which there is always a generous supply. We simply need to make an appropriate deal, John, something I know you are well able to do, and you will then be suitably anonymous and free to continue your tempestuous affair with the entire female sex, should you choose to do so. You rather misunderstand me if you think I am particularly concerned with the moral high ground; what your adventures might be doing to your immediate family is your concern, not mine. What they are doing to your standing within the Corporation and the public image of the Corporation is rather different, however. Relinquish your shares to me and you can go off into the wild blue yonder doing as you please, just as long as none of it is in any way connected with the Gilrey Corporation.'

McAdams noticed that Maddox had started smiling broadly about half way through this speech. He was not one to let anyone's facial expressions interfere with him saying what he wanted to say, but it was impossible, after a while, to ignore Maddox's expression, since it seemed unsuited to their conversation. For once, even Donald McAdams was slightly riled. 'Perhaps you could let me in on the source of your amusement, John,' he said acidly. 'Or are you losing your mind as well as whatever principles and standards of behaviour you ever possessed?'

'Too late, Uncle Donald, I'm afraid,' Maddox said, and the smile, if anything, broadened.

'I have no shares in the Gilrey Corporation. I sold them, this very morning, to a most generous offer from Lord Brookland, who was seeking to increase his miserly supply, having consulted, I gather, with the good Mrs. Gilard herself.'

Sometimes, if no more than a handful of times in his professional life, even McAdams was stunned into silence, and this news achieved the feat so gratifyingly that Maddox could not resist rubbing it in.

'You see, Donald, that whatever deplorable moral state I may be in, I am not a fool, and if you imagine for one minute that I remained unaware that you would stab me in the back as soon as you felt you had a suitable opportunity, you are perhaps becoming just a little naïve as you stagger towards your dotage. I calculated my own moment of action; it might have been selling out my shares to a grateful Mrs. Gilard within a few hours of the meeting, or it might have been activating a few items in my own dossier. Hugo Gilard had one on you, Donald, as you probably knew, and since I always knew where he kept it, I could dip in and add to my own stock of information from time to time. I don't doubt that it's now in the possession of his widow, which perhaps explains her noticeable lack of panic at any and every little stunt you've tried to pull in the lead-up to the meeting. I don't doubt either that you have squads of witnesses and whole companies of bent lawyers simply waiting in the wings for the chance to dig you out of whatever ordure descends on you, but then there's the expense, Donald, isn't there, which will sit on the shoulders of the Corporation rather more easily than it will on whatever you've managed to accumulate over the years. Don't waste any more time worrying about what's coming my way, Donald; I am now very well looked after, thanks to His Lordship's generosity, and I intend to leave you and the whole miserable pack of Corporation hangers-on to your own devices and live a relaxed life on the continent, enjoying an entertaining mixture of family life and occasional stimulating extra-curricular activities. Bye-bye, you old bandit, and sweet dreams.'

Maddox disappeared and almost as soon as the screen had gone blank, McAdams was checking on his market monitor, which he had been foolish enough not to look at for a few hours. Sure enough, the sale was registered there, meaning Brookland was now a substantial shareholder, and McAdams had little doubt, knowing as he did the long-standing friendship between Brookland and Hugo Gilard, that Brookland was acting in the interests of Gilard's widow.

This battle is over, McAdams reflected. It is a stupid general indeed who does not realise when his forces have been defeated. But battles being won or lost don't necessarily determine the outcome of the war. Control of the Corporation was a war, right enough. As much as any wars fought for land or governments or ideals, battles for big commercial concerns that could make people rich or destitute in the space of a few minutes were wars right enough. Careless and over-confident generals lost battles, usually because of some telling factor or influential individual they had either forgotten about or underestimated, and so it was here. McAdams had not regarded Brookland as important; an ageing peer with a comfortable family life who hadn't shown much inclination to dabble in stocks and shares for years. Now, he knew he should have remembered Brookland's close friendship with Hugo Gilard and got to him before the Gilards did; one fatal mistake ruins the entire strategy.

But, McAdams reflected again, a lost battle doesn't make a lost war. Retrench, reorganise and go again when the troops are refreshed and the weapons reloaded.

He smiled at the empty screen. For all his fine words, John Maddox was the architect of his own downfall, and perhaps it was, in any case, time to move on. Many more fish in the sea, McAdams thought, grinning to himself, and most of them much less slippery than Maddox. He began to review what he knew of Lord Bernard Brookland.

Back in the Gilrey Corporation boardroom, Val was checking on every detail to ensure that the occasion of the board meeting the following day, the first since her husband's death, would not be in any way let down by shoddy preparation. The vast spaces of gleaming wood and metal, positioned next to a generous panorama of the London skyline, were fit for such a day, and good enough to at least dull the many anxieties that still lingered in her mind about the event.

At least two of her children, Jennifer and Paul, had never been in this room, and for their first visit to it to be this confrontation, as it looked as if it would inevitably be, instantly begged the question of how they would react. Jennifer, with her innate reverence for just about everything to do with money and wealth, whatever she might say to the contrary, would be quite likely to be impressed and perhaps even overawed by the occasion. But Paul was built on very different lines. He was, in many ways, very like his father, though he himself wouldn't see the parallels. Neither of them were overawed, either by places or by occasions, and both of them had their own understandings and priorities. Paul was just as committed to what he saw as important in life as Hugo had ever been, even if the focus was almost diametrically opposed. Hugo had seen the Corporation as worthy of being his life work, and an organisation of enormous merit and influence in itself; Paul distrusted almost every institution, even the ones he worked for, and regarded them as having a being and presence concerned only with their own interests, regardless of the welfare of the individuals within them. They both seemed to deal in certainties, and Val envied them that, because so much of her own experience had been with probabilities and possibilities, arguments that needed to be carefully assessed and people whose motives had to be understood. Being sure, really sure, was a luxury rarely afforded to her, and dealing with single-minded people fully dedicated to one cause or another inevitably meant careful negotiation and a lot of time, which she rarely had to spare.

However, the sudden entry of Bernard Brookland into the whole business of the battle for control of the Corporation had considerably boosted her morale, and victory, for the time being at least, seemed to be largely assured. She had also seen enough of Hugo's dossier on Donald McAdams to believe that, if the gloves had to come off now or in the future, she did at least have some power to her elbow. She had also talked to Amélie about the material, and her daughter showed no coyness or reluctance about using what she needed to use as and when it became necessary. Business had hardened Amélie; that had become abundantly obvious, and it was now clear enough to Val that the success of Delatour was not, as she had previously suspected, largely down to André's capacity for ruthlessness.

Now she understood their relationship better, she realised André was actually the more idealistic and easy-going of the two, and much as she rejoiced at her daughter being the battle-hardened boss she needed to be for these Corporation days, a tinge of sadness at the departure of the dreamy girl, with her vaulting ambitions, artistic inclinations and willingness to take people as she found them, still preoccupied her at times.

She glanced at the big chair, almost like a throne, with the Gilrey Corporation's coat of arms embedded into its shining leather, which sat at the head of the table. Hugo's chair, she had always thought it, and sitting in it still felt presumptuous. But she sat in it again now, looking forward to the time when she would be able to hand it over to her daughter.

PART EIGHT

The Board Decides

Tuesday September 29th 2015

Val's first move was to open one of the huge boardroom windows just a touch; the day was pleasant but humid, and whatever confrontations, denunciations or rows might characterise the meeting, a decent supply of fresh air was a necessity, as far as she was concerned.

Immediately, the London noise ratcheted up, a continuous angry mutter from below, punctuated by occasional screaming sirens from near and far. Val found her heart was beating faster than she thought necessary, and she had to acknowledge to herself again the growing awareness in her that she somehow had to change her role in the Corporation very radically. The threatened battle royal facing her on this day would soon be a regular occurrence, perhaps several times a week, if she tried to hold on to her post at the top of the Corporation. It was absolutely vital that Amélie should be appointed as the new managing director as of this meeting, and even though Val knew that she now controlled, with Bernard Brookland's help, an overwhelming number of the shares, her suspicions of McAdams and Maddox had not dissipated yet. What new tricks they might be up to she didn't know yet, but she had little doubt that they would be doing something, or setting up something.

She had emphasised that she wanted to be contacted as soon as Brookland had arrived in the building, and she had specifically asked him to arrive early so that they could talk before the meeting started. At the very moment when her anxieties began to deepen about his arrival, her phone sounded and one of the security men below told her Brookland was on his way up.

By the time he walked in, Val was sitting on her 'throne' at the head of the table, as composed and serene as Hugo had always appeared when he occupied the chair, though she suspected that Hugo was putting on as much of an act as she was.

'Bernard. Wonderful. I thought you on my left and Amélie on my right would probably be the most convenient arrangement. When we appoint Amélie as managing director, she and I will change places. It shouldn't take long, because I'm going to take it as the first item on the agenda – after the minutes, of course.'

Brookland kissed her lightly on the cheek and took his place.

'Very grand in here, Val. Oddly enough, I've never been in this room before. Hugo and I always had a habit of doing our business in restaurants, mainly. Speaking of which, I was hoping you might let me give you dinner tonight; it could perhaps be a first celebration of your new freedom, no longer tied to the coat tails of the Gilrey Corporation.'

'I'd be delighted, Bernard. Do you have a venue in mind?'

'Oh, I thought I'd leave that one up to you, Val, but if it's somewhere we need to book, we'd probably do best to book it before this meeting is over.'

Almost immediately, Val was talking to someone to arrange their table, and Brookland smiled to himself; distractions, especially pleasant distractions, were a good idea for Mrs. Gilard at this moment. Much as he thought of her as Hugo's redoubtable widow, he could see from her pallor when he came in that she was a little on edge, and hardly surprisingly. 'Perhaps we can enjoy together a bit of late good news, Val,' he said. 'I don't know whether you've set a place for John Maddox, but I can tell you now that he won't be coming. As I told you on the phone, I've bagged all his shares, and I do mean all, so he has no further entitlement to be here.'

'I didn't set a place for him, and let me say again how much I appreciate what you've done in that respect, Bernard. Yes, it would have been quite fun to have thrown him out, but generally speaking, I think my nervous system is happier with the knowledge that he won't be here at all. Donald McAdams is quite enough to be going on with.'

Almost on cue, her phone sounded, and a minute later, McAdams walked in, and his easy smile greeted them. He is so good at this, Val thought; I could almost believe he meant it. 'Val, lovely to see you again, and I see your new friend, or perhaps accomplice might be a better word, is with you. Hello, Bernard; will Bernard do, or do I have to spend the entire meeting your lordshipping?'

'Bernard will do, Donald. I don't think I've actually met you since Hugo died, have I? I don't doubt you've been keeping yourself busy.'

McAdams smiled again, ignoring the ghost of a sneer in Brookland's voice.

'Yes, of course. Poor Hugo. I hope we can do due and proper obeisance to his memory today.'

He looked at the expression on Val's face as she managed, with an effort, not to say anything. McAdams' expression remained one of proper gravity.

'And I understand we are to have the delight of every one of the Gilard offspring being with us today, perhaps the very first time the great Gilard holding in the Corporation has been so generously represented. A three-line whip on the family, is it, Val? All hands on deck.'

'One of them is shortly to be the new M.D., Donald, and I don't doubt you will applaud such new blood in the boardroom.'

'Well, we live in hope that blood in the boardroom is something we will manage to avoid, Val. Which we should, of course, if your formidable daughter is all she is renowned to be.'

Val had no wish to continue the conversation, and fortunately she was interrupted at this moment by news of the family's arrival, en masse, in two large taxis booked for the purpose. Within minutes, the Gilards and Lord Brookland were enmeshed in greetings and reunions; even though Val had seen them only a matter of hours ago, she wanted to make a point of meeting and greeting, partly to help them feel at their ease in the palatial surroundings of the boardroom and partly to emphasise McAdams' relative isolation in this company.

The latter aim succeeded only partly, because the arrival of the family was soon followed by various heads of department and legal advisers, most of whom she knew either were in McAdams' pocket or did not have the authority or courage to stand up to him. However, when it came to the vote, it was the shareholders who counted, and in this situation today, McAdams' acolytes would not be able to offer him more than moral support.

As usual, it took a few minutes for everyone to settle in their allocated places, but most of the company were regular meeting-attenders and few had any wish to let the event drag on for too long. Within ten minutes of the last attendees arriving, everyone was seated and Val could begin the meeting, with her eldest stepdaughter on her right-hand side.

'My Lord, ladies and gentlemen,' she began, meaning all eyes momentarily turned to Brookland. 'Printed copies of the minutes of the last meeting, my husband's last as chairman, were sent out over a week ago and I asked then that any matters arising which anyone wants to raise should be notified to me before this meeting. No-one has done so, and therefore, unless there are any objections, I intend to move on to Item 1.'

This was the moment Val had dreaded, when McAdams, simply to establish his authority and willingness to hold proceedings up if he chose to do so, would begin on a list of questions about everything he could dig out of the minutes. However, to her surprise, he sat silently and merely nodded.

As at least a third of the members present had not attended the last meeting, with Hugo in the chair, Val thought it unlikely that anyone but McAdams would want to go over it again, and so it proved, but as she moved on to Item 1, the election of a new M.D., she already had a sense of foreboding, an instinct that McAdams was simply biding his time.

'I don't intend,' she started briskly, 'to make any long summaries of my service to this Corporation. There will be a time and a place for that, I dare say, but it isn't today. We are all aware that the Corporation rules of governance made clear after the death of my husband that I would succeed to the joint position of chairman and managing director, at least until it became possible for a shareholders' election to be held to decide on a permanent successor to Hugo.

'We are now able to do that, and I therefore nominate Madame Amélie Delatour for the position. Her nomination is seconded by Lord Brookland. Any other nominations should have been notified to me before this meeting; I have received none, and consequently, I name Madame Delatour as the new Chairman and Managing Director of the Gilrey Corporation, and I will hand over the chair to her—'

'One moment, Madame Chairman, if I may?'

There it was, the calm, urbane tone she so dreaded, already in action.

'Donald. I don't see there is anything to be said at this stage—'

'Possibly you don't, and of course, none of us here can pretend that this is any kind of democracy. But, while we may be powerless to stop the election of Madame Delatour, we are surely entitled, as members of the board, to ask a few pertinent questions?'

'You can ask, Donald, but I will be the judge of whether or not they are pertinent.'

'Very well. I would simply like to know whether Madame Delatour, or perhaps I can now call her Amélie or we'll be here all day, has any previous experience of managing a corporate enterprise?'

'Amélie has, for some time, been the M.D. of a substantial Canadian hospitality enterprise and can therefore be said to have sound management experience—'

'I see,' said McAdams. 'So Amélie has not only never managed a corporation, she has never managed any commercial enterprise actually in this country. Peter, is there anything of relevance here in the job description—'

'What job description are you talking about, Donald, and what has Peter to do with it?' said Val, an impatience already growing within her.

Peter Kellman was one of the Corporation's main legal advisers, co-opted on to the board by an adroit move by McAdams when Hugo had other things on his mind. Because McAdams had arranged for Kellman to be present at board meetings, he was generally seen to be McAdams' man. Hugo had tried to be rid of him when he realised what had happened, but McAdams had made the contractual position rock-solid for Kellman, meaning legal action would almost certainly be needed to remove him, and Kellman had a whole law firm behind him.

'Mr. Gilard defined the job when he merged the chairmanship with the managing director post, in order to clarify what would be expected of any successor of his,' Peter Kellman said.

Val intervened quickly. 'Those were general notes largely for his own benefit, and to let me know what might be expected if I had to take over. They were not, in any sense, meant to be legally binding.'

'I see. Has that view ever been tested in courts, I wonder, Val?'

Amélie suddenly and decisively made her presence felt. 'These are simply obstructionist tactics and a waste of all our time. My candidacy has been proposed and seconded. I move that we now go straight to a shareholders' vote without any further questions or interruptions.'

'Seconded,' said Brookland.

'All those in favour?' Val said quickly.

The family hands were duly raised, including, after an awkward moment, Paul's; his mind had been wandering, and he felt powerfully that he would rather be just about any place than here.

McAdams raised his arm against the motion, and Val felt almost relieved that he had now declared himself. While Val and Amélie were in the process of swapping chairs, he took his chance.

'I would like it to be minuted, Ms. New Chairman, that your lack of relevant experience to do the job to which you've now been appointed has been commented on by our legal adviser, and the previous chairman's description of the role has been ignored.'

Amélie tried to ride this one out, reflecting later that it had perhaps been her first mistake. 'See to it that it is minuted,' she said to the secretaries on either side of the table.

'Now, my Lord, ladies and gentlemen, this meeting was called with due recognition of proper procedures, but in my opinion and the opinion of most of us around this table, it needed only to do what it has now done. So soon after the death of my stepfather is too soon to be making any substantial changes to policy or structure, and I now intend to adjourn the proceedings until we have all had more time to digest the new situation—' Protests now started up from all around the table, with Amélie momentarily looking perplexed and not in control. She knew well enough that some of the Corporation heads of department were in McAdams' pocket, as well as another two Corporation 'advisers', neither of whom were supposed to be involved in management issues, but they had been briefed to make trouble and they were doing their best to do so.

'So we can see clearly enough where we are with this,' McAdams said, and there were murmurings of assent and supportive words from various parts of the table. Amélie sensed that she had lost the initiative, but McAdams was underway before she could stop him.

'We are looking at a simple coup d'état by the Gilard family. No-one else, apparently, even those of us who have served the Corporation faithfully over many years, has anything to say about it. None of us, I think, really believes that a Corporation can work as a democracy, but if it's a matter of informed legal opinions and long-standing employees simply being ridden over and ignored, we must protest with as much strength as we can muster that this is no way to run a business. I think it should also be pointed out that we have here today a number of members of the Gilard family who, in spite of being substantial shareholders in the Corporation, have never previously graced us with their presence. What expertise or interests are they currently contributing to the welfare of this organisation?'

Incensed and realising she was rapidly losing control, Amélie intervened.

'Mr. McAdams, when you use the phrase "substantial shareholders", you hit the nail on the head. The board members you refer to have the controlling interest in the Corporation, and that means their power includes getting rid of fractious, scheming employees—'

McAdams was now on his feet and, for once, the cool man of business pose was gone.

'So now you are resorting to naked threats, five minutes after being in that chair? And how would it be, Madame Chairman, if I went out now and told the waiting media – there's a squad of them out there, sniffing blood the way they do – that I was putting all of my twenty per cent holdings on the market, the reason being that the Gilard family have bulldozed one of their members into the M.D. role in the teeth of all experience and good sense. How will that go down on the financial markets, I wonder? How much will the rest of your shares be worth then? And how many Gilards will turn up at the next meeting, when like Humpty Dumpty we will all be trying to put the pieces back together?'

Now the familiar voice of the ex-chairman, Valerie Gilard,

broke in, calmer and more measured than McAdams, but determined to make the points she had in mind. A large folder was sitting on the table in front of her.

'Before you do that, Donald, you might wish to talk to me about this. My husband, as you know well enough, was the kind of administrator who liked to keep records, especially pertaining to what certain members of his workforce were up to. He was always willing to give everyone who worked for him every opportunity to do well and achieve remarkable successes, at the same time as keeping an eye on those of them who, perhaps in their over-eagerness to register remarkable achievements, were inclined to bend the rules here and there. Or even break them outright, Donald. At the same time as you're talking to the media about your outrage at your treatment at the hands of the Gilard family, I will be having rather different conversations with them about working practices. Specifically, yours, Donald.'

The boardroom had now fallen very silent. McAdams was staring at Val, who was glowering back at him. Everyone else was hardly daring to breathe.

Val recognised she still had the floor. She went on.

'So what we will then have in prospect, Donald, is a long battle through the courts, and it'll be anyone's guess, won't it, you know this stuff as well as I do, who's going to finish up being awarded costs? Who's going to be king of the castle and who's going to be – well, let's go with the nursery rhyme, the dirty rascal? You, on your own, with your complaisant so-called legal advisers? Or the Gilrey Corporation, and their solid supporters?'

Val glanced at Lord Brookland, who nodded.

'So do you keep your twenty per cent of the Corporation, and your peace, Donald, and carry on in the interests of us all, or are we both to be shortly enmeshed with the pack of media sharks out there? Which would you rather, Mr. McAdams, because I'm on for both if I need to be?'

Once again, an electric silence had taken over the room. McAdams was now smiling, very slightly, as if trying very hard to do so.

'One thing I will always remember is the name Hugo consistently used for you. He called you Diamond Val. "Precious, beautiful, shiny and unbreakable", I think was one quote which registered with me. But you knew that, of course?'

Val vowed not to let anything like a tear appear; she stared steadily back.

'Yes, Donald, of course I did. It was a name he chose for me and it has always been precious to me. But in relation to what we are currently talking about, what of it?'

'I have no desire to spend years wrangling with you in the courts, Diamond Val, if you are so adamant that your daughter should be the successor to your husband. Blood is thicker than water, as they say, but I don't think it's too outrageous of me to make the point, on behalf of all of us involved with this Corporation who are not Gilards, that whatever virtues Amélie may possess, and I don't doubt there are many, she has yet to have any substantial experience of managing a sizeable business in this country. We are risking the whole future of the Corporation on an untested young woman, mainly, and it has to be said, because of our fondness and respect for our recently deceased managing director.'

'So what exactly are you saying, McAdams? That the new M.D. should be you? And how much experience do you have of managing a corporation, may I ask?' Brookland said, while other members of the board contemplated how and when to stop the meeting.

'My Lord, I'm sure we are all grateful that you have so graciously come among us, albeit somewhat late in the day. I will make the obvious point that, unlike the entire Gilard contingent suddenly gathered around this table, I have been working for this

Corporation almost from the moment of its conception. I know it inside out and upside down. Unlike many of us here present, Amélie included. I see Austin is with us; the last I heard, Austin and his wife were running several pubs in the Costa del Sol; suddenly, he's a Corporation man. Jennifer there, is running an international school in Paris, I understand, and she has never previously, as far as I know, taken an interest in Corporation affairs. And we also have young Paul with us for the first time, a young man who has done well in medical circles and has perhaps done greater good for mankind in his relatively short life than the rest of us combined. All three Gilards just mentioned were, I believe, considering selling their entire Gilrey Corporation interest only a matter of days ago, so seriously do they take their commitment to the Corporation…'

Val whispered to Amélie by her side, both of them realising that allowing McAdams to go on for much longer could create a permanent split in the Corporation management structure. Amélie nodded, and got to her feet to emphasise her intentions.

'Mr. McAdams, you are out of order. I have already made clear that the business of this meeting, which was to elect a new chairman and managing director, has been accomplished, and no further discussion on the subject is needed or wanted. The vote of the board has been very clear. The meeting is closed.'

Amélie nodded to Val and pointedly began collecting together her paperwork; the other Gilards took their cue from her, and within less than two minutes, people were starting to drift out of the boardroom. McAdams remained sitting quietly where he was, and only when most of the board had drifted away did he turn again to Peter Kellman. As Val followed her daughter, she looked back to see McAdams and Kellman engaged in a quiet but very animated conversation. She knew that the family were intending to hold a celebration of her retirement in the main Gilrey hospitality suite, normally reserved for impressing foreign visitors or government ministers; she had made clear her views on 'surprise' parties, but this was an event she had been properly warned about. Somehow, the sight of McAdams obviously still conspiring seemed to dampen her satisfaction at finally leaving the hot seat.

McAdams' long conversation with Kellman expanded to include several other McAdams allies within the Corporation, and by the time their deliberations finally finished, McAdams was left in the boardroom on his own. For a while, he sat and stared at the head chair, Gilard's throne, as he had often called it. After the death of Hugo Gilard, Donald had felt sure that, correctly handled, he could be the successor to the big job. He still felt that his long service to the Corporation entitled him to rescue it from the general amateurish chaos of Gilard domination. There had been a time when his respect for Hugo Gilard had been immense, when he had looked up to his chief as a model to emulate, but over the years, Gilard increasingly became alienated from him; Gilard was too idealistic, too fussily concerned with propriety, and too indulgent towards employees who, for one reason or another, were simply not up to scratch. And then, of course, there was the Gilard brood, the whole gang of them, not one of them a serious or worthwhile member of a company board, operating the whole Corporation like a personal family fiefdom.

But, while they had won this round, there was a longer battle already underway. He could remember the expression on Jennifer's face, a mixture of guilt and embarrassment, as she wondered what she was doing here and why. And, of course, young Paul, whose reluctance to even be there was all too obvious and who had clearly only been able to stop himself from yawning with an effort. When he mentioned Paul's name, it was a few seconds before it registered with the boy, who clearly had not been listening to what was happening. And these were supposed to be the professional members of the Corporation board, their presence in the room only secured because Mummy and Daddy gave them a bit of their big juicy Corporation like a Christmas stocking.

The McAdams matriarch, Donald's late lamented mother, returned to his thoughts. An unmoved, uncompromising, taciturn Scottish lady, quite happy to be in the next room to where one or other of her sons was being soundly beaten, either by Donald's hapless father or by some mountainous manservant appointed for the purpose. McAdams could remember one occasion in particular when he was paraded in front of her – he must have been about twelve, and simple enough to believe that he had become too old for this sort of thing – while she barked at her towering jack of all trades, McAskill, 'Very well; fetch the strap, Mr. McAskill.'

'Smoking on the family premises, Donald, is strictly forbidden and this has been made clear to you on several occasions. What have you to say for yourself?'

'Ryan was doing it,' Donald managed to get out, though even to his own ears it sounded like a sad bleat in the distance.

'Ryan is a village boy who runs around with every urchin and farmer's boy from miles away.

'You are not; you are a McAdams, and your father's heir. You must work and play to different standards, Donald, or you will never' – her voice slowed and rose – 'amount to anything at all. McAskill will now teach you the price to be paid for allowing such standards to fall.'

Being carried away, quite literally, by McAskill, Donald looked back to see his mother sipping nonchalantly at her tea. He was only in the adjoining room while he was suffering McAskill's ministrations with the strap, and all his best efforts could not stop him yelping like a whipped dog, but he felt quite sure that she remained coolly enjoying her tea throughout his ordeal, and his distaste for her slowly warped into hatred.

And, of course, there was Uncle James, whose disciplinary methods were similar, except he did not allow any proxies to do it for him; he did it himself, and while one hand was using the strap, the other was engaged in activities that Donald only fully understood years later and represented, by anyone's definition, straightforward sexual abuse.

They were both dead now, his mother and Uncle James, though the old man himself, now the McAdams patriarch, hung on doggedly, and Donald knew there would be precious little to inherit when he finally did.

He had seen to it that both his mother and Uncle James were fully appraised of his opinions of their behaviour in later years, and he made a point of being especially rude and ribald at James's funeral. He also determined, even before his boyhood had fully ended, that no-one and nothing would ever denigrate or humiliate him again, without paying a full and suitable price for having done so.

And even though, in the recent exchanges with the assembled Gilards, he had given as good as he got, in his opinion, it was not enough. He intended to be sitting on Hugo Gilard's throne at the top of this table; it might take a long time, it might take until Diamond Val was in her grave and he had one foot firmly in it, but he, the professional administrator, the true Corporation man, would amount to something alright, something much more than evil old Maggie McAdams née Stewart and her bent brother James, something meaning he was in charge of the entire Gilrey outfit and had seen off the entire brood of Gilard whelps.

He finally gathered together his papers and headed for the door, but as he passed the 'Hugo throne', he patted it softly and said, 'OK, little Amélie's nice little bum will keep you warm for me, but the day will come when mine will be in permanent residence, and then things will be done properly around here.'

As he moved away from the exalted heights of the management suite on top of the building, he could hear Val's do warming up. It might be fun, he thought, to just turn up and see what happened. But then he rejected the idea.

'I can bide my time. Then it will be so much more satisfying,' he said aloud, as he closed the door on the Gilrey boardroom.

Val had a particular affection for the hospitality suite, not least because she had been so heavily involved in its design. Hugo was the model of hospitality at the personal level; he retained everyone's names and those of their nearest and dearest, and he always saw to it that they were properly looked after. But working out the actual layout of the suite was not his strong suit, and Val had been the main mover in designing and equipping the suite. She knew that most of the people who came here would be middle-aged, and the emphasis was much more on comfortable furniture and mixed catering than on wide open spaces and well-stocked bars.

She was well-practised at not drinking very much while not causing offence to people by refusing drinks. She never had been a big drinker, and while the demands of hospitality had increased considerably over the years as the Corporation grew, she was too wary to allow herself to fall into the trap that so many of the people involved seem to do, particularly the men, which is drink casually while in conversation and lose track of how much they'd actually consumed.

She also had what she tended to think of as an escape hatch, and it gave her particular satisfaction when she remembered that it had been her own idea, deliberately included in the design from the start. The suite would, of course, need a store room; bottles, cans, glasses, etc., could not be simply left randomly spread around, and in putting the store room into the design, she had thought suddenly of the advisability of giving it a small additional area at the back, with no more than a few comfortable chairs, equipment for making hot drinks and some first aid provisions.

The quiet room, as she'd christened it, had come in handy on several occasions, including the later stages of Hugo's life, and Val had, on more than one occasion, sneaked away to it to recharge her batteries and gather her thoughts, most particularly when someone was using a social occasion to pressure her on a matter of policy or filling Corporation vacancies.

About an hour and a quarter of the retirement do had passed pleasantly enough when she retired to the quiet room for a ten-minute break. Only a few staff and family members knew of the place's existence, so she felt fairly confident that she would have a moment to herself, and she made a mug of coffee to work against her growing fatigue.

She had dreaded McAdams turning up; as such a senior member of the Corporation, it would have been difficult and embarrassing to refuse him, and his presence would be bound to sour the proceedings to some extent. Thankfully, he hadn't but, of course, her two youngest children, Jennifer and Paul, both had, though neither of them had brought their partners with them. As she saw them dealing with the do as best they could, which in Paul's case meant taking a drink out on to the patio surrounding the suite and sitting there watching the view, she came to a few sombre realisations about the future.

Sitting in the quiet room with her coffee, she reflected on beginnings and endings, and how artificial they seemed to be. In theory, this was the end of the story as far as her stint as boss of the Corporation was concerned, but then again, how could it be? Unless Amélie could achieve a miracle and manage to keep everyone happy at the same time, there would be attempts to undermine her, plots against her, and circumstances that might force her to seek alliances with people she didn't fully trust or work against people she did. And, even if she didn't choose to involve Val by asking for her advice or support, Val would still be placed in ambiguous positions, of either helping out while not appearing to be helping out or intervening directly and risking Amélie's irritation or worse.

How naïve it had been for her to imagine there could just be an ending, with one era concluding itself and a brand new one starting. Almost as soon as Amélie had walked into the hospitality suite, with André gamely by her side aiming to protect her as much as he could, she had been surrounded by people wanting her attention. Val knew some of them were simply on the make, trying to ingratiate themselves with the new M.D. for a number of their own reasons; some of them were quite genuine and sincere in what they were trying to do; some were inherently treacherous and already working on how they could be difficult and obstructive; and some were, whatever their official designations might be, politically minded people looking to improve their power base.

It seemed in some ways like throwing her daughter to the wolves to watch her gamely coping with the multitude of demands on her, no doubt outdistancing by some measure the daily routine she would experience at Delatour. Val watched the men who wanted to flirt, bully or impress, and the women who wanted to make a powerful friend or get the measure of a potential enemy, and she felt as if she should be like a little bird sitting on Amélie's shoulder, pouring gems of advice into her ear as each new face appeared.

Stories didn't end; stories never ended, they just changed scenery, personnel or circumstance and carried on. The Gilrey story would go on, whether she was there with them or not; the stories of each of her children had their span to run and they would, with Val's contribution and influence in their lives diminishing as time went on. When Val was long gone, the story would still be continuing, past her own children to their children, long after Gilrey was just a vague memory in a long lost family past.

So, when all was said and done, she thought, what was wrong with her detaching herself from it and having a bit of a jamboree to finish it all in her last years? She had changed the story as much as she could; she had succeeded in keeping Gilrey out of the hands of McAdams and Maddox and even managed to drop one of them out of her life altogether.

The story wasn't all her story; it never had been. Diamond Val; how she'd treasured the good man's love that had created the name for her, and maybe the unbreakable bit was right after all, much as she had wondered about it in the past. Her part of the story could at least have the ending that she decided to put on it; her retirement had freed her, she could see, but only if she allowed herself to be freed. The future still had a big question mark lingering over it, but at least it was now a recognisable future, not a perpetually repeating rehash of the past.

PART NINE

Aftermath

Tuesday September 27ᵀᴴ 2016, Gran Canaria

The decision to mark the first anniversary of Amélie's appointment as managing director of Gilrey with a holiday abroad was initially Val's. That tense, hectic month, full of apprehension and negotiation while she was still raw after the death of Hugo, was not a period she looked back on with any great affection, but she felt there was cause enough for celebration in the simple matter of having come through it successfully.

Whether Amélie herself would consider that she had time and leisure enough for a holiday, even a short holiday, became the next question, but it didn't take Val long to establish that her daughter believed herself entitled to holidays on a regular basis. Although Val initially contacted Gilrey headquarters during the day, it was well into the evening by the time the two women were able to talk, but Amélie seemed willing enough to talk once the opportunity to do so had finally been settled.

'That's a very good idea just at the moment, to tell you the truth, Val. Much of my life has become a kind of chess game with McAdams; he tries to see my moves some time in advance and I find myself arranging my defences like I'm planning a battlefield. But I'm learning quickly. He likes to find men, in the main – women instinctively don't trust him, most of the time – who like someone telling them what to do, especially if that someone promises them they will come out of it quite well financially. Or in terms of the power they can hold in their hands and wield if they want to. Where he puts his guys, I put mine, specially selected to deal with his. Quite a few of my guys are women, because the kind of men McAdams tends to recruit don't like having to deal with women, especially the kind of women I like to employ.'

'I always had the feeling that you were the one of us best equipped to tackle dear Donald,' said Val.

'Yes, well I'd like to think you were right, but it's hard work much of the time. André still spends most of his time keeping Delatour ticking over, and we don't get enough time together. He'd be on for a break as well, I don't doubt. Where had you in mind, Val, and please don't make it in Britain. Or Canada, for that matter. We spend most of our lives being sitting ducks for the media in both places; anyone would think we were royals or something, the way they follow us about. I've got a hunch dear Donald has his pals out and about looking for something, anything, he can make capital of.'

'Well, you remember I told you that Austin and Mo were thinking about going into the business of self-catering stuff – villas, apartments and the like. Good money and not such hard work as running the pubs, so they think.'

'Yes, I remember you saying that. I wondered how they were doing.'

'They're doing very well, partly because they decided to expand from the Costa del Sol and start up an operation in the Canary Islands. Austin still has his pubs – five, I think, at the last count – but he's got quite a number of villas and apartments now as well, and a few of the villas are really fabulous. Media-proof, too; after the security issues they've had in Spain keeping Mo's relatives and other Brit exiles on the run out of their establishments, providing proper arrangements for their upmarket villas is no problem for them. Austin and Mo are on for a bit of a break, too, and we could find a villa big enough for the five of us, I don't doubt. For at least four or five days. What do you think, darling?'

'Five days is about right, Val. I've got a working deputy here, a lady called Annie Shields, northerner and tough as old boots while quite clever with it. She's about ready to be given a bit of time in charge; it will do her good and irritate the hell out of McAdams. And we will enjoy seeing Austin and Mo again. You set it up your end, Val, and we'll be there.'

The villa selected by Austin and Mo for the occasion was a fantastic place, with spectacular sea views from the balconies at the front and equally glorious island views from balconies at the back. It was equipped with its own pool, catering and cleaning establishment, and easily secured on all sides; Val was delighted with the pictures of it and even more delighted when she saw the actual place, which showed that, for once, the pictures had not lied.

She had the usual passing pangs of guilt when she realised that she had already ruled out Jennifer, Paul and their respective partners joining them, but the pangs were brief; they had both chosen their own way, and the few days she had in mind were aimed at being an uncomplicated family get-together, not another business confrontation.

The one secret she still maintained to herself, even after the villa had been booked, was the most difficult to judge. She had met a guy, and whether or not he was to be introduced to the family was still an 'if' rather than a 'when'.

Chester Mulholland was in his early seventies, but would easily pass, and sometimes did, for his mid-fifties. He had made a lot of money from adventure and travel holidays, mostly in the wide open spaces of Canada, and could lay claim to a few intrepid adventures himself, being an experienced climber, kayaker and swimmer. Val had met him during a visit to one of the Delatour hotels in Canada. He hadn't impressed her because he was a loud, robust, pushy sort of character; rather the reverse, in fact. In spite of being an obviously successful and wealthy man, he tended to keep himself to himself. He was in the hotel largely to negotiate with Delatour about links between his holidays and their hotels.

According to André, they found the Mulholland company reliable and well-organised partners, and it was not surprising that a friendship had been formed between Chester and André, since André was quite an active outdoor man himself.

Val noticed him because Chester was a difficult man not to notice; he was a good six and a half feet tall, and he had a presence whenever he walked into a room, but Val could see a certain underlying sadness in him. It didn't surprise her very much when she discovered that he had lost his wife of nearly forty years, Eileen, only two years ago.

Sitting one morning on a splendid hotel terrace looking across a stunning view of forests and mountains, Val and Chester got talking, and Val was impressed again with the lack of front about the man, who talked most of the time about other subjects apart from himself and had a genuine curiosity about Val's connections to André and the Delatour family.

It didn't take the two of them long to discover that they were both fairly recently bereaved, and Chester, like Val, had yet to reach the point where the pain of the bereavement might significantly ease.

Since that first meeting, the two of them had corresponded and talked on the phone enough for Val to acknowledge to herself that there was now another man in her life, and when the get-together in Gran Canaria was suggested, Val eventually, after some hesitation, decided that it might be a good idea to invite Chester to the gathering, though strictly on a separate-room basis. But she didn't hold back from talking to him about the possible obstacles to a relationship developing between them.

'I suppose I'd have to say that I am still Hugo's girl, pretty much, Chester, and from what I know of you so far, I would say you're still Eileen's man. But there's nothing to say that we can't be friends, and if that's what we're going to be, I'm not going to go in for any kind of clandestine relationship where we hide away from people as though we're ashamed of something. And if it was being honest, I'd have to say that it's allies I need as well as friends, not because I want to start fighting the Corporation battles all over again, but to help me put a life together outside the Corporation.'

Chester did what Chester seemed to typically do; he spent some time mulling it over, and delivered a response that showed clearly enough that he had devoted some thought to the subject.

'You're right when you reckon I'm not ready for another relationship, in the full sense of the term, after Eileen, and I can't guarantee to you or anyone else that I ever will be. But it's got clearer to me, especially over recent months, that I need friendships, and I mean meaningful friendships. I know plenty of people, but in the main they don't get too close because I don't want them to get too close; there's a security in a long relationship that leaves you very vulnerable when it suddenly ends, as you know well enough, Val. At my age, I don't know how long I've got left, but I do know I'm past the stage where I can change anything very much about myself, even if I wanted to. One thing I want to tell you, Val, because as soon as we start seeing each other regularly, even as good friends, we both know the sort of things people will say, is that at the last count a few months ago I was worth in the region of 250 million Canadian dollars, which is about a 170 million British pounds, and that's a hell of a useful statistic for you to have in your locker if and when your friends and family start talking about this Canadian gold digger who's trying to set up with rich Val and get his hands on her fortune.'

So Chester Mulholland came to the Gran Canaria party, staying in a separate room from Val and strictly on the ticket of being her friend, and Val didn't hesitate to hit Amélie with the money statistic when Amélie at first looked rather doubtful about the idea. Amélie smiled and looked just a little bit ashamed.

'Yes, I know that bit, Val; I've already checked him out. Sorry, but it isn't just the Corporation I think I need to be looking after these days. But you do need to bear in mind that the family, in this case in the shape of Austin and Mo, are almost certain to read it as someone sitting in the chair where Hugo used to be, whether you talk about just good friends or not.'

'Sure, Amélie, and what you need to remember is that Hugo was not Austin's father, and that, along with the boy's easy sociability, suggests to me that he will take him as he finds him, and in any case, Chester isn't going to pretend to be anything he's not.'

So the Gran Canaria house party was established, and as the villa chosen had six good-sized bedrooms, there was room for anyone else in the family who cared to join it, meaning accusations of shutting them out could be avoided. The behaviour of Jennifer and Paul since the board meeting had not encouraged the idea that they would wish to join the party, but if they did choose to be excluded, they should realise that it was a choice and not an imposition. Amélie made sure that she personally invited both of them and their partners, and she received what she largely expected to receive, vague statements that they would attend if their other commitments allowed them to do so. By the time the week arrived, it seemed clear enough that the other commitments didn't. In the last few days, Amélie debated with herself whether or not to remind them, but decided against it. The idea of a relaxed get-together was the main aim, and that would be difficult to bring about if anyone felt that their arms were being twisted, and Amélie knew that, for Paul in particular, his time off was like gold dust and his priority was always to spend it with his partner.

By the evening of the first day, Tuesday, everyone seemed relaxed with each other. The party had wandered into the nearby small Canarian coastal town at lunchtime and enjoyed the pleasant weather and the unhurried, easy-going atmosphere of the place. Chester's abstinence at lunch was noticed – 'middle of the day drinking, no, sir' – and Val felt encouraged that his daredevil reputation was not accompanied by hard drinking, as she had seen it in other men of the outdoor type.

The afternoon largely left everyone to their own devices, and for most of them, that inevitably involved the pool. Val had never been a particularly good swimmer, and at sixty- eight, she found herself indifferent to that part of the proceedings, but she found herself approving of Chester's willingness to do a few lengths of the pool, even though he was her senior. He had an astonishing powerful and well-built body for a man of his age, and the younger men of the party, Austin and André, seemed to warm to him as the day went on. Val also noticed that Austin's earlier tendency to start acquiring midriff flab had obviously been attended to, probably because of Mo's ministrations, though the impulse was just as likely to be Austin's distaste for being seen to resemble his father, whose flabby build was evident from his early thirties.

André, of course, remained the bronzed and fit outdoor man he had always been, and he took easily enough to his countryman Chester. The only woman to spend part of the afternoon in the pool was Amélie, and Val noticed that her trim, well-maintained body attracted glances from all the men at one time or another. She seemed to have energy to spare, but Val knew her very well, of course, and she sensed an underlying anxiety that never entirely left her daughter, even when she was apparently relaxing. It gave Val pause for thought, because she could not avoid a reluctant awareness that she had perhaps laid down her burden only to load it on to the back of her daughter.

However, by the evening, everyone was laid-back and easy with each other. Some Spanish caterers had been booked for the evening meal, to avoid any members of the party having to work on their holiday, and they were asked to use as much as possible of the local Canarian produce. They didn't disappoint, and when the party relaxed with coffee and drinks, full of the best of local meat and fish, the atmosphere was warm in most senses of the term.

There had been various attempts at banter, especially amongst the men, since the start of the day, and it seemed that Austin was taking advantage of that when he adopted a tone of mock formality and turned to Chester on his right.

'And so, Mr. Mulholland, are your intentions towards my mother honourable?'

'For heaven's sake, Austin,' Val said, considering that the question was impertinent even when presented as bantering, but Chester seemed to be willing to take it seriously.

'Yes, I know you're kind of half-joking, Austin, but although I never met Hugo Gilard, I've known people who have, and he was obviously a great man in many ways. He was Val's partner and husband; I'm just Val's friend. Val is an extraordinary lady and I'm pleased enough that she's prepared to accept me as her friend. I don't know whether the rest of you are aware of this, but I lost my wife, Eileen, not long before Val lost Hugo, and life can get lonely quite quickly when you've been used to having someone special, and Eileen was very special, around for so long. I know your question wasn't meant to be taken that seriously, Austin, and it shows that we can already be easy with each other, but the answer is really that I haven't got any intentions, other to enjoy again the company of a remarkable lady.'

Amélie smiled. 'Delatour had dealings with your company, Chester; we still do. And I can remember going to a few leisure conferences when Eileen, and sometimes you, were there.

'Canada's a huge country, but when you're in the same business, you do meet up with people again from time to time. I don't remember having had a conversation with Eileen, but I do remember how well she was thought of by everyone.'

'Thank you, Amélie. It's nice to know that. I wasn't too sure about coming to your family gathering here; I'm not one to gatecrash the party. But it seems we're not entirely strangers to each other. I'm starting to feel like I may not be so far from home.'

'You're very welcome among us, Chester,' said Austin, and Val, who knew her son very well, could see that he was telling the truth.

As the easy-going, friendly chat continued, Val finally decided that she had made the right choice in inviting Chester, in spite of her misgivings over recent days, and it was almost exactly at this moment of gratified realisation that the chest pain once again made an appearance. For a moment, she thought she was going to gasp out loud, but she controlled herself with an effort.

'Excuse me for a moment,' she managed to say, but as she moved back into the main house, the pain came again. This wasn't the first time, but it had a level of intensity that she had not known before. She reached the nearest bathroom, one on the ground floor, and locked the door.

For a while, she simply sat and tried to breathe as smoothly and regularly as she could. At first, the pain did not relent, and it briefly even intensified; Val found herself momentarily on the edge of a blind panic. She could remember only too well an occasion about three months from Hugo's death, when he seemed to be encountering something very similar, even as he sat in his managing director's chair at Gilrey H.Q. She urged him then to immediately call in a doctor.

'Chest pain is not something to ignore, Hugo; let me get some help now.'

But in a few minutes, the pain had eased, and Hugo was his philosophical self once again. 'It happens from time to time, Val. It's not an easy job I do here. But if I call doctors in every time, I'd be struggling to get anything done. We'll talk about it later.'

And Val remembered trying to talk about it later, but by then other matters had usurped his agenda, and he didn't want to 'make a fuss'. Was this some sort of payback for her negligence then?

But, even as these reflections ebbed away, she realised that the pain had eased. Now, once again, calling in a doctor would probably be 'making a fuss' and he or she would find there was nothing wrong with her. Perhaps it was an overwrought reaction to the flight, though she had made many longer flights in her time. Perhaps it was caused by the unaccustomed heat of the day after leaving a damp and overcast Britain.

She moved out of the bathroom, and as she made her way back towards her companions, she saw them all, laughing and joking with each other in the cool, aromatic Canarian evening. No need to spoil the party for a bit of old-woman angst, she thought.

But she decided she would see a doctor, just as soon as she conveniently could.

Wednesday September 28th 2016

It surprised Donald McAdams that he hadn't noticed before how generous a space John Maddox had enjoyed when he worked for the Corporation. Not quite the palatial surroundings of the top floor, where Hugo Gilard had so recently held court, but much bigger than one man's office needed to be, and bigger, he noted ruefully, than his own. Maddox was like that; it was one of the reasons why he had once thought that the man could be useful to him, when he saw the Maddox genius at getting what he wanted here, there and everywhere.

The last he had heard of Maddox, he had become right-hand man to one of his more lucrative conquests, an extraordinary American lady who had developed her cosmetics enterprise into a multi-million-dollar business and had reputedly hired Maddox for his experience of British and European economies, though McAdams suspected that she had more basic motivations. Maddox, he thought, would finish up where perhaps he had always wanted to be, as a kind of international gigolo.

It seemed appropriate on a number of levels to commandeer Maddox's ex-office to become a kind of rival boardroom to the main one currently monopolised by the Gilard family. The administration department, which McAdams ruled as his own personal empire, and which had once included Maddox, was the engine room of the Corporation, at least as far as those who worked for it were concerned, and it was staffed by McAdams' people.

Anyone he didn't like or trust would be transferred to other departments within the Corporation or urged, unsubtly, to move on. He knew the other departments had some colourful names for admin – 'the anthill' was one of the repeatable ones – because of its reputation for being a place where the work ethic was so strong that work would be created if enough wasn't already available. Whatever anyone else thought, McAdams considered it the place where the Corporation functioned at its most basic, and the place that could bring the whole operation grinding to a halt if it was seriously mucked about.

He had even started talking about the 'Admin Board', and it was this gathering, known officially as the Department of Administration Committee, that he was about to address on another overcast English morning when, he knew, most of the Gilard dynasty were gathering in the Canary Islands. Such an opportunity was too good to miss.

'Ladies and gentlemen,' he began, 'at this moment, and for the next few days, the notion that we are the beating heart of this Corporation becomes a reality in fact as well as in the informed opinion of most of us. It is an excellent time for us to once again attempt to improve the overall efficiency and effectiveness of this organisation without anyone with some obscure grievance against us to go bellyaching to the nearest Gilard.'

A ripple of subdued sniggering greeted this remark, which McAdams would normally consider unacceptable at such a meeting, but on this occasion he let it go, seeing it as indicating that everyone present had more or less the right idea.

'However, in the interests of efficiency and success, it's imperative that we box clever. We must seek to make our help available to other departments as freely as possible, because if we bring that about, they will come to understand that they need us at least as much as, if not more than, we need them.

'Take the production department, for example, still turning out various trinkets to fill the Gilrey stores as well as the equipment constantly needed to keep the stores functioning.

'None of their stuff can leave here without the proper paperwork, as you all know well enough, and if they don't want their production lines to get snarled up, they must know the correct procedures and put them properly into place. Likewise, look at the personnel department; they might be experts on employment rules and regulations, but how good are they at maintaining the flow of paperwork which enacts them? They must understand that if they don't work with us and use the procedures we've established, there are likely to be unhappy consequences in various directions, which could see them facing tribunals and political questions. We know we are necessary to the working of this organisation, and we must make other departments understand that. But always remember; if you have to use an iron fist, a velvet glove is an excellent disguise. Admin, like it or not, is about diplomacy as well as efficiency.'

At the back of the room, a young man was correctly making notes as his department head outlined how things should be done. He was not, actually, as young as he looked; he could easily have passed for being in his mid-twenties, but in fact he was thirty-three. He was now in his fifth year with the Corporation, and already holding down an important job in keeping up with news and legislation regarding sales at home and abroad, so that the sales department could be made aware of the latest information on what was selling well and where, and also understand what they could and couldn't do in various countries. His name was Ian Bradley, and he was generally regarded as one of the bright young prospects of the Corporation. He was also a childhood friend of Paul Gilard, who he had known since they were both in infant school.

When he had first applied for the post within the Corporation, he had not made the connection between it and his friend Paul, perhaps because Paul rarely, if ever, referred to the Corporation. But when he was sharing a holiday with Paul and a few other friends, including the man who became Paul's partner, they realised the link between them, and Paul, indifferent as he was to Corporation matters most of the time, realised that this was an opportunity that could prove to be useful.

'So you're working in the department of my mother's arch-enemy Donald McAdams, Ian?' Paul said, as the two of them were reclining on a Florida beach.

'Is he? Well, it doesn't surprise me. The guy gives me the creeps a lot of the time.'

'Well, why don't you sort of keep me briefed, if that's not going against your working code of ethics or something? I'm determined I'm not going to spend the rest of my life enmeshed in the bloody Corporation, and the more I know about how Mum's bogeyman works, the more power to my elbow, if and when it comes to looking after my interests.'

'OK, a favour for a friend is no problem. And it doesn't surprise me that your mother is wary of him; my impression so far is that he's one of these guys who makes up the rules as he goes along, and if anyone doesn't like it, tough.'

The arrangement had continued, and the weekend following the McAdams meeting saw the two friends meeting up again at one of their favourite clubs.

'I've got no problem with reporting this stuff to you, Paul,' Ian said. 'I just wonder if it's going to turn out to be any use to you. If you'll forgive me for saying so, your level of interest in the Corporation is usually pretty lukewarm, which is probably putting it mildly.' Ian was an old friend, and Paul had trusted him with confidences in the past, which Ian had never betrayed. When Paul was going through the teenage agonies of not only coming to terms with being gay, but also deciding when, where and how he would come out, he had confided in Ian, and that trust had been honoured, because it became evident some time later when Paul did come out that no-one had known about it beforehand.

Now a scheme was slowly forming in his mind, which could give rise to a course of action in aid of his mother and perhaps contradict the impression that he suspected she had that he was totally indifferent to her problems. He explained as much to Ian, though he still didn't go into his shareholding and its probable current worth.

'So,' he concluded, 'even though my mother has now retired, in theory at least, she still cares that McAdams might one day work himself into a dominant position in the Corporation and then take it in directions where she really doesn't want it to go, partly because of McAdams' attitudes to his employees and how the Corporation should be run.

'The more we know about what McAdams is doing and why, the more likely it will be that my mother and my stepsister might be able to stop him.'

'Well, I'll tell you this much, Paul, even though as yet it is more conjecture than fact. He is getting a substantial private income from somewhere. Yes, he's a top executive, and he would be on a pretty good salary to begin with, but he lives beyond that; he and his wife take regular and very expensive holidays, he drives very expensive cars, and one or two of the people closest to him, who are sometimes not as discreet as they ought to be, make estimates of his personal wealth which are way in excess of what even someone in his position would have.'

'Finding out more about that would be a great help too, if you think you can do it without putting your own career in danger.'

'I doubt whether that would happen,' Ian said. 'I've noticed one of his characteristic actions when he wants to get rid of people is to give them shining references, probably so that he not only gets rid of them, but they don't give him any problems when they've gone. If he gets the impression I'm a bit nosey, he'll move me on, and I'll probably get a promotion out of it. Working for Gilrey is alright, but I'm not one of these people who wants to spend a lifetime working for the same outfit. I'll keep you posted, Paul.'

Conversation drifted away into other areas, but Paul, who was already becoming used to arriving at detailed diagnoses on the basis of evidence, thought that gathering more evidence on McAdams from the inside might usefully contribute to a diagnosis that mattered to him, concerning his mother's anxieties and wishes for the future.

That same evening, he confided in Kirk, as they enjoyed the rare pleasure of both having some time off at the same time and decided to divide a bottle of wine between them.

'You look very thoughtful about something, buddy,' Kirk said.

Paul lifted his eyes from the mesmerising shiny red liquid of his glass.

'Yes. I think I might actually have found a way of being useful to my mother, without necessarily getting myself dragged any further into Corporation affairs.'

'That's all to the good. But don't tell me now; we'll talk about it later. Right now, I have a few other ideas in mind, you know what I mean?'

'Yes,' said Paul faintly, realising, ridiculous as it was, that he was blushing. 'Yes, I know what you mean.'

Even as they drifted into energetic distractions, Paul remained aware of a new sense of himself as a conspirator, and rather liked the idea.

Thursday September 29th 2016, Latin Quarter, Paris

Jennifer was enjoying one of the rare treats she allowed herself, spending the afternoon drifting aimlessly through the Latin

Quarter, a part of Paris she had always loved. Of course, it was besieged by tourists as ever, but she had developed the ability, during her bemused and sometimes tempestuous adolescence, of keeping herself to herself even in the most crowded of places. Occasionally getting away from the school made her appreciate it all the more when she returned to it, and today was a particularly appropriate time to remind herself of the beauty of the country she had chosen for her exile.

Her French citizenship had been approved, and she now officially had dual French and British nationality. Whatever peculiarities the recent Brexit foolishness might have injected into her life were largely negatived by her French citizenship; it would make matters easier both personally and professionally.

She had enjoyed a simple enough lunch of a croque monsieur and a glass of Chablis, which had put her into a relaxed enough mood to imitate the tourist trail herself, even though she now saw Paris as her home city. In the café where Jean-Paul Sartre, Albert Camus and their intellectual friends once passed the time of day, she had a coffee and watched the world go by, marvelling at the extraordinary mixture of age, gender, clothing and race that drifted past her.

She was still only half way through her coffee when a moment of decision, final and irrevocable, struck her almost like a blow. Yes, she had to face it; even allowing for her duty to Hugo and Val Gilard and her gratitude to them for giving her a new life when her old one was so brutally shattered, it was that old life that now, increasingly, called her back. The educational world, which had involved both of her parents, the academic world of the mind, of language, literature and study, that was her home territory. The world of business, the endless intrigues and demands of the Corporation, was a puzzling and ultimately unsatisfying country, which she had visited and investigated, but now was the time for the final return to where both her heart and mind lived, and essentially always had done.

She had done what Val had asked of her, enduring the unpleasant and bewildering atmosphere of the meeting's confrontation, and Val had won; the Corporation was still firmly in Gilard hands. Her shares, she understood, were now worth even more, as the market had generally approved of the new Gilrey arrangements, and especially the substantial new investment of Lord Brookland. The money they would generate would not only secure the future of the School; it would allow for a significant expansion, which would mean the investment would pay for itself and in time improve the profit situation. Impatient as she was with financial considerations and calculations, putting the School on an even firmer footing would give her less reason to have to think about them.

She was going to sell her shares, and finally cut the knot that still connected her to the Gilard business world. No doubt they would accuse her of disloyalty, but they had to realise that because her situation had caused her to temporarily take up residence in their world, without her having much choice in it at the time, she did not have to remain there for ever afterwards, especially after her involvement had become obsolete and unnecessary.

She knew there was no need to consult Claude about her decision, as he had been urging her to sell her shares ever since he realised the worth of her Corporation holdings. The knowledge seemed to have fed some of Claude's insecurities; like Jennifer, he had had a troubled childhood with the untimely death of his father and his mother's subsequent difficulties with drugs. He had been brought up from the age of twelve by ageing grandparents, and while neither of them had known the details of each other's family years when they first came together, the similarities between them had subsequently struck them as extraordinary and confirmed their impression that they were, in some way, destined for each other. Claude needed her to commit to the Logier school and their life together, without some gigantic distraction constantly lurking in the wings. It was not only a matter of duty; it was a matter of honesty and trust.

During her stay in England, she had obtained a contact phone number for Donald McAdams, even in spite of her shame at allowing herself to do such a thing. Now the decision was taken, she needed to act on it and stop it hanging around like some ominous lurking shadow on the periphery of her life.

She clicked in the number, still with mixed emotions, but, as her educational experience had taught her, there was no such thing as a decision that didn't have both pluses and minuses.

McAdams was closeted in his private office with Kellman, on a regular session that concentrated on looking at his various existing investments and considering any which might have promise for the future. Kellman did not question where the funds were coming from; he suspected that McAdams was not as scrupulous in separating the Corporation's money from his own as he really ought to be, but Kellman did not make a comfortable living out of being too scrupulous himself.

His P.A.'s interruption was, at first, not well received.

'Who is it, Elaine? For goodness' sake, I left specific instructions…'

'Jennifer Logier, sir. Née Gilard.'

'Oh, really? Yes, put her through, with my blessing.' He held the phone away and turned to his companion.

'Sorry, Kellman, but this might just be of interest to both of us.'

Ten minutes later, he put the phone down on the desk in front of him and smiled widely at Kellman, who responded with raised eyebrows. Smiles were not an over-used currency in investment meetings.

'Well, Mr. Kellman, rejoice with me. My holdings in Gilrey have just gone up to nearly twenty-five per cent. I am the largest single shareholder in Gilrey after the great Gilard matriarch herself, and I strongly suspect she doesn't know about it. Yet. She shortly will, though. I might even tell her myself.'

Another smile, almost a giggle, and Kellman looked again at the papers in front of him. Such jollity did not suit the matters in hand, in his opinion.

At the same moment, Val was coming to the end of a conversation with one of her oldest associates, a doctor called Jocelyn Howden. Calling it a friendship would probably not accurately describe the nature of the relationship, given the circumstances in which they tended to talk. However, Val appreciated the situation of not having to speak in euphemisms or diplomatic niceties; in matters of health, there were occasions when a spade needed to be called a spade.

'If there is any serious danger of heart failure, I'd be happier if we could establish some kind of emergency procedure. I have to admit it, Jocelyn; I'm an old lady, and dropping dead suddenly is not what I had in mind for my declining years.'

'We can work out a system of back-up if it's needed, Val, I don't doubt. From what you tell me, it sounds very much like angina, but I am going to have to take a look at you before we come to any final diagnosis. Can you come to me, Val, or shall I come to you?'

'I think me coming to you would be easier. I don't want to start worrying any of the family with my problem until I know that I have a problem. I occasionally go to London for various purposes, and I could perhaps arrange to call on you then, Jocelyn, without raising any alarms with anyone.'

Before the call ended, a date and time had been arranged within the forthcoming week. 'It isn't the kind of can you should just kick down the road, Val,' Jocelyn said. 'It needs sorting as soon as possible.'

As Val clicked off her phone, she caught sight of one of her favourite photos of Hugo, taken in Tuscany on a holiday some years ago. He looked tanned, fit and happy.

'I'd love to see you again soon, Hugo,' she whispered to herself. 'But maybe not too soon.' As she walked back into the main living room, she saw a dove land on the bird table that she kept within easy sight of the doors leading out into the garden. For a moment, it seemed to be examining her intently, its whole body still. Then, suddenly, it flew away.